THE GLASS PUZZLE

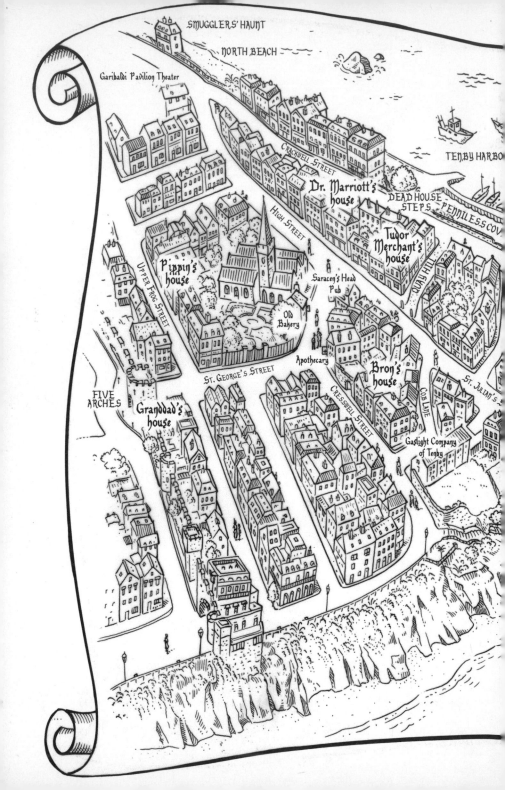

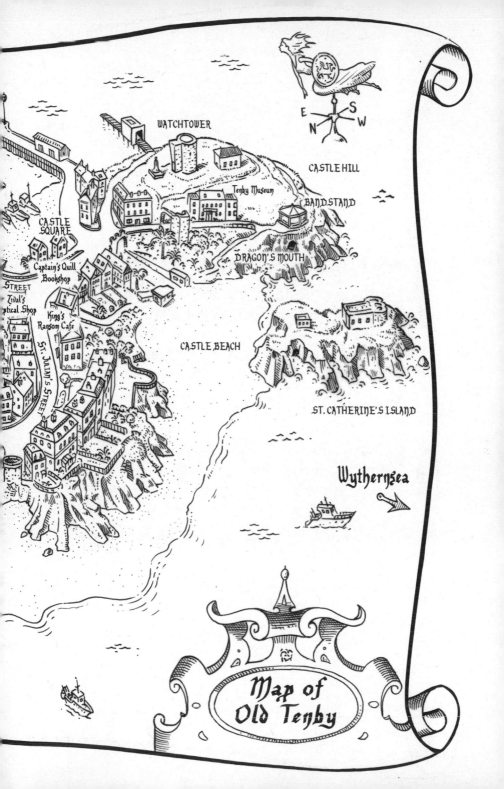

ALSO BY CHRISTINE BRODIEN-JONES

THE OWL KEEPER

THE SCORPIONS OF ZAHIR

THE GLASS PUZZLE

CHRISTINE BRODIEN-JONES

DELACORTE PRESS

· Text copyright © 2013 by Christine L. Jones
Jacket art copyright © 2013 by Fernando Juarez
Interior illustrations copyright © 2013 by Charles Santoso
Map copyright © 2013 by Fred van Deelen

Visit us on the Web! randomhouse.com/kids

Educators and librarians, for a variety of teaching tools,
visit us at RHTeachersLibrarians.com

Library of Congress Cataloging-in-Publication Data
Brodien-Jones, Chris.
The glass puzzle / Christine Brodien-Jones. — 1st ed.
p. cm.
Summary: While spending the summer in Tenby, Wales,
with their grandfather, American cousins Zoé and Ian assemble
an old glass puzzle, inadvertently unleashing ancient forces that threaten
the island and allowing them to travel into the past.
ISBN 978-0-385-74297-9 (hc) — ISBN 978-0-375-99087-8 (glb) —
ISBN 978-0-307-97993-3 (ebook) — ISBN 978-0-385-74298-6 (tr. pbk.)
[1. Supernatural—Fiction. 2. Adventure and adventurers—Fiction. 3. Cousins—
Fiction. 4. Time travel—Fiction. 5. Tenby (Wales)—Fiction. 6. Wales—Fiction.
7. Wales—History—1063–1284—Fiction.] I. Title.
PZ7.B786114Gl 2013
[Fic]—dc23
2012015999

The text of this book is set in 13-point Adobe Jenson.
Book design by Jinna Shin

Printed in the United States of America
10 9 8 7 6 5 4 3 2 1
First Edition

In memory of my father, Cecil "Cec" Brodien,
who as a boy inscribed his own box of treasures
with the words Hero, Inventor, Mastermind

Contents

IN 1349, THE YEAR THE PLAGUE REACHED WALES, THE ISLAND OF WYTHERNSEA—NEAR CALDEY ISLAND, OFF THE COAST OF TENBY—WAS SUBMERGED FOLLOWING A VIOLENT WINTER STORM. IT IS SAID THAT AT LOW TIDE THE TOWERS OF WYTHERNSEA'S ANCIENT CASTLE CAN BE SEEN, AND THE BELLS OF ITS CHURCH CAN BE HEARD RINGING IN THE FOG.

—BROTHER RHYS EVANS,
ORDER OF REFORMED CISTERCIANS
CALDEY ABBEY, CALDEY ISLAND, WALES
23 SEPTEMBER 1932

CHAPTER ONE
DROWNED ISLANDS
AND TUNNELS TO THE SEA

On a foggy June morning in Wales, Zoé Badger wandered the crooked streets of Tenby, dreaming of pirates and tunnels to the sea. The wind tore at her hair, while gulls shrieked overhead and boats rocked in the harbor below. Beneath the town ran tunnels used by smugglers centuries ago. Her granddad said they'd come from France and beyond, landing on North Beach and hauling their loot by hand through the tunnels into Tenby to sell at contraband prices.

She sniffed the salty air and, popping a Welsh toffee into her mouth, imagined pirates scaling the cliffs with knives between their teeth. When they opened their sacks of gold, they'd find her inside. Cursing, they'd dump her on the rocks and she'd stand bravely while they made her turn her pockets inside out. After stealing her toffees, they'd threaten to throw her into the sea. Pirates never showed any mercy, everyone knew that.

Pulling out her journal, she wrote, "Zoé Badger was eleven, with raven-black hair cut straight across Cleopatra-style. Everything about her was sharp and angular—her hair, her nose, her bony knees—and her eyes were green like the sea beyond the cliffs of Carmarthen Bay. Quick as a wink, Zoé outwitted the pirates, corkscrewing into the air, dazzling them with Tai Chi moves. Then she vanished into a tunnel—she had escaped!—and they never saw her again."

Every year Zoé and her cousin Ian Blackwood flew to Britain from America to spend summers with their grand-dad. Tenby was the one place where Zoé felt totally at home, since her parents were divorced and her mom's career as a freelance travel writer meant frequent moves from one town to the next.

At each new school Zoé told the kids that Wales was her true home. She'd lived in other places—too many to count—but they all blurred together in her memory. She always bragged that she was descended from a ship's captain, saying the waters of the Irish Sea flowed through her veins.

Only in Tenby did she feel bold and adventurous, infused with the spirits of long-dead pirates. In this corner of Wales, she knew there were secrets to be found and mysteries to be solved, and when she was away she felt an ache in her heart.

Granddad called it *hiraeth,* a Welsh word meaning a kind of nostalgia—a yearning for home.

Her cousin Ian had gone off to Maisie's Sweet Shop to buy lemon swirls and Zanzibar crunches. Zoé was taking a roundabout route to their meeting place, the King's Ransom Café on St. Julian's Street, a winding lane overlooking the sea. Tenby was a small and safe little town, where everyone seemed to know one another, so Granddad never worried about Zoé and Ian wandering on their own. He asked only that they stay inside the Old Town walls.

Zoé always felt a sense of timelessness when here, with streets running at angles to the harbor and pastel-colored houses looking out to sea, and she wanted it to stay that way forever. Walking along, she studied the medieval buildings and the crumbling wall that encircled the Old Town, checking to see whether anything had changed in her absence. She always worried that something drastic might happen, like the gargoyles on the church roof coming to life and attacking people, or Caldey Island disappearing in a storm the way Wythernsea did in 1349.

But everything looked exactly the same as last year, except for a new shop at the bottom of St. Julian's Street across from the Captain's Quill Bookshop. *Keep an eye out for Zival's Optical,* read a hand-carved sign—the O was shaded in like an eye—*Opening soon!* The sign was quaint, like everything in Tenby, and Zoé was charmed by it.

Suddenly a thick fog enveloped her, swirling around Zival's sign, erasing the words and cloaking the buildings on all sides. She couldn't see the overhead sign for the bookshop—it seemed to have vanished, too. But it was there: she could hear its hinges creaking with each gust of wind.

Still focused on the fog ahead, Zoé wasn't aware of the door to the bookshop banging wide open and a set of boots thumping down the steps. A stack of books was drifting in her direction, and seconds later that same pile collided into her. With an "Oomph!" she fell to the ground.

Catching her breath, Zoé sat up and looked at a girl sprawled next to her, wispy brown hair flying in all directions. The girl wore a pink jacket, ragged at the cuffs, and scuffed pointy-toed boots. A black beret had slipped to one side of her head. Books, pens and papers lay scattered around her on the cobblestones.

Zoé rubbed her arm, blinking back tears. She wasn't hurt, except for a bruised elbow. "It wasn't my fault," she said, retrieving her journal. To her dismay, the sparkly yellow cover was all wet. "You should pay attention to where you're going. You knocked me down!"

Ignoring her, the girl continued picking up the books. Her hands were rough and chapped, and her jacket was much too small. A gray pleated skirt drooped at her knees—a school uniform, Zoé guessed, since British students were in school this time of year. It was June now, and their summer vacation didn't start until mid-July.

"Foreigners," muttered the girl, jamming papers into a canvas satchel.

"I'm not a *foreigner*," protested Zoé. "My mom grew up

in Tenby and my granddad's John Lloyd Blackwood and he speaks Welsh—*ancient* Welsh," she added importantly, rescuing a pencil box.

"And what other kind of Welsh is there, I'd like to know?" snapped the girl, grabbing the box away.

What kind of kid uses a pencil box? wondered Zoé. *Those are so last century.*

"And you look like a foreigner to me. Anyone can tell by your clothes—and that accent of yours is a dead giveaway." The girl wrinkled her freckled nose and sniffed, piling the remaining books on top of her satchel. "We've heaps of tourists from America. No end of money to burn, the Americans. S'pose it's all right: Auntie says in summer it's foreigners that keep our shops ticking over."

"I have dual citizenship!" Zoé shouted angrily. "That means I'm as Welsh as you are!"

"Not blooming likely," said the girl, stamping off into the fog.

CHAPTER TWO
THE KING'S RANSOM CAFÉ

Rain spattered the windows of the King's Ransom Café as the smell of smoked bacon wafted through the air. Sitting at a vinyl-covered table, Zoé pulled out her liquid gel ink pens, preparing to write in her journal. The cover was soggy but the pages inside were dry.

The café's wall fixtures threw off a dim light, giving the place a grainy, out-of-focus appearance. It reminded her of the black-and-white films she watched when she was on the road with her mom and they stayed in motels with basic cable. The low-ceilinged room, papered with daffodils, was crowded with tables and chairs—all empty except for hers—and a chalkboard advertising *Special today~pork pie & chips*, followed by *Fresh strawberries & clotted cream.*

In the margins of her journal were symbols that resembled crushed insects, remnants of a code Ian had invented last summer for their secret agent game. (Unfortunately, she'd lost the symbol key and had no idea what they meant.) On the back pages she'd listed famous pirates that Granddad had told her stories about, like Anne Bonny and Calico Jack, and the names of ancient Welsh sites she'd discovered in an old book at Granddad's cottage. Her favorite was the castle Dolwyddelan, birthplace of Llywelyn—*Llywelyn's Dolwyddelan*—tricky to pronounce, but it had a mysterious ring.

With her favorite purple pen, she wrote: "Unsheathing her cutlass, Charlotte Badger crept through the tunnel, dragging a sack filled with doubloons and pieces of eight." Pieces of eight and doubloons were famous pirate treasure, according to Granddad, and Charlotte Badger had been a real pirate. Zoé often fantasized that she was distantly related to Charlotte, since they shared the same last name.

She was always inspired to write about the tunnels of Tenby, a maze of passageways that Granddad said had never been mapped. Built by smugglers, they ran directly beneath the streets of the Old Town, and it was rumored that a secret tunnel beneath the harbor went all the way from the mainland to Caldey Island.

A bell tinkled as Ian stomped through the door, water dripping from his windbreaker. "Hey, Zoé," he said, slinging his messenger bag over the chair. "After I left the sweet shop, I took some amazing pictures of the Tudor Merchant's House on Quay Hill."

"Cool," said Zoé, wishing she had a messenger bag like his, with Velcro snaps and pockets for organizing pens and notebooks.

Ian's wiry blond hair, ruddy cheeks and brown eyes reminded her of a comic book kid, as if a kindergartner had colored him in with crayons. Zoé always felt as if her adventurous side clicked into place when she was with her cousin, especially when they were exploring the back streets of Tenby or making up games involving pirates, monsters and spies.

"What's with the sparkles in your hair?" he said, offering her a paper bag filled with licorice allsorts, jelly babies, peppermint creams and gobstoppers.

"Flitter. That's short for fairy-sparkle glitter." She flashed a toothy grin. "You just sprinkle it in your hair. My mom gave it to me."

Zoé was attracted to verve and splash, what her granddad called panache, and what her mom called bling: fake fingernails, tiaras, clashing colors, neon-shiny fabrics, and jewelry fashioned from odds and ends. Unlike Ian's mother, who bought his clothes from expensive online stores, her mom favored unconventional styles and shopped at places like the Salvation Army and the A-Number-One Thrift Shop, which was why most of her clothes never fit quite right. Today she wore lime-green Capri pants, plaid sneakers and a tangerine sweatshirt with DINBYCH-Y-PYSGOD (the Welsh name for Tenby), LITTLE TOWN OF THE FISHES silk-screened on the front.

"Where did you say your mom went this summer?" asked

Ian. His parents always spent their summers going on package tours to Europe.

"Paradise, Arizona," said Zoé. "She's investigating nouveau styling techniques with some hairdressers who invented a radical haircut where you use a razor."

"Sounds lethal."

"Yeah, it is, sort of," she said, showing him the scab on her earlobe where her mom nicked it while experimenting with the Cleopatra cut.

"No sweets allowed on the premises, dearie," said a dry, papery voice behind her.

Zoé jumped, startled to see Iris Tintern blinking through round yellow plastic-rimmed glasses with tinted lenses that seemed to cover half her face. Iris owned the café and lived in the flat upstairs.

Frowning, Zoé handed the bag of candy to Ian.

"Right then, what will it be today?" Iris waved her pencil stub. "I've just had a brand-new Electro Freeze soft-serve machine installed. You can be the first to try my Mister Whippy–style ice cream."

Zoé made mental notes to write in her journal: "Swimming behind thick lenses, the café owner's eyes looked like smooth black pebbles at the bottom of the sea." Aside from her new glasses, Iris looked the same: nylon apron tied over a wrinkled dress, oatmeal-colored sweater buttoned up to her chin, hairnet stretched over blue rinsed curls. As usual, her clothes smelled damp, as if she'd pulled them from the bottom of a clothes hamper.

"I'll have the soft-serve ice cream, Ms. Tintern," said Ian. "Chocolate, please." Ian always used a formal tone with Iris Tintern.

"Same for me, please," said Zoé.

Stopping by the King's Ransom Café was a summer ritual for the two cousins. Zoé didn't care if the restaurant was gloomy and run-down, because she found it captivating: going there took her back to a distant era, making her feel as if she were living in Tenby centuries ago. And that was what gave the café its mystique. Something about the King's Ransom spoke to her passion for adventure and intrigue.

"Ms. Tintern, do you mind if I take your picture for my history project?" Ian pulled his camera from the messenger bag. "I'm documenting local landmarks and the old historic district and it'd be great to have a photo of you for my collection. For future generations."

"I don't think so," said Iris, shaking her head. "No, I never—"

"It's okay, Ms. Tintern, I'm his fact-checker," said Zoé, who had agreed to help Ian with his project, even though she suspected checking facts was boring. "We'd like to include you and your café." She suddenly wondered how old Iris Tintern *really* was. "Those new glasses are real nice," she added, trying to soften Iris up a bit. "I like the blue lenses."

Iris gave a stiff nod, clearly ignoring Zoé's compliment. "Very well. If you must."

Iris's lips peeled back in a wide grimace, revealing a set of uneven yellow teeth, though Zoé noticed she avoided looking directly at the camera. *Wow, Iris looks totally ancient*, she thought.

Yet something about Iris struck her as being a little *off*, as Granddad would say, as if she wasn't quite connected to her surroundings. Maybe it was the blackness of Iris's eyes behind the tinted lenses or the way she kept glancing to one side. Zoé remembered Iris as an in-your-face sort of person, always staring right at you when she took your order.

"I'm running a special on Count Dracula fangs," said Iris when Ian was finished. "Cut-rate prices, today only. Any takers?"

"Awesome," said Ian. "I'd like some fangs."

"The vampire teeth I saw were kind of melted," said Zoé, remembering how Iris always tried to cheat her customers. "Could you give us a deal?"

"They are *all* melted, dearie, which is why I've marked them down," snapped Iris. "If I charged any less, I'd be giving them away."

"Okay, okay," said Zoé. "Er, could we have two of the least-melted vampire teeth? Please?" she added sweetly.

With a scornful frown, Iris shuffled off in her crepe-soled shoes. You could always count on Iris to be crabby and rude.

"Hey, Ian," Zoé whispered, "doesn't Iris seem different to you? I can't put my finger on it, but there's something strange about her today. She wouldn't even look at us."

Ian gave her a confused glance, as if he had no idea what she was talking about. "Iris is Iris," he said, "always with a sour expression, like she just ate a ground-glass sandwich.

You know what Granddad says: Iris was born old and cantankerous—she hasn't changed in sixty years and neither has her café."

"I know, I know. That's why my mom loathes Tenby so much: nothing ever changes." Zoé enjoyed using words that sounded last-century, like *loathe* and *maudlin* and *languish*. "She used to get panic attacks because Tenby was so backward and out of date. That's why she eloped with my dad to America." She was fascinated by the idea of two people madly in love running off together—those kinds of things happened in the old days—but it made her sad to think how her parents' marriage had fizzled.

Ian threw her a sympathetic glance, which she appreciated, since she'd told him several different versions of this story, and she knew he felt sorry for her not having a dad. But it only bothered her a little bit, since she had no memories of her father at all.

"I want to move to Tenby and live here forever," she went on, "but my mom says don't get any ideas because she's not coming back to Wales. She wants to be on the road with an exciting career."

On the road about summed up her life. Her father had *jumped ship* (her mom's expression) when Zoé was six months old. Now that she was eleven, Zoé wanted to go to school in Tenby, where she was sure there were kids like her: kids whose desks were hopelessly cluttered and who were terrible at long division, free-thinking types who invented secret codes and drew astrological signs on their fingers. Tenby was different from the other towns and cities: it was the only place she seemed to fit in.

Two sets of pale white vampire fangs clattered onto the table.

"There you go," Iris said, and walked off.

The wax teeth were majorly melted, but Zoé didn't complain. Although she'd never admit it, not even to Ian, she found Iris somewhat intimidating.

Predictably, Ian reached for the more crumpled set of teeth. That was the chivalrous side of his nature, which in Zoé's opinion balanced out his serious, nerdy side. Although he didn't know it, Ian often appeared as the hero in the stories she wrote.

Iris's odd behavior made Zoé think of something. "Hey, did you ever see *Invasion of the Body Snatchers*, the movie Granddad's taking us to tomorrow night?" she whispered to Ian. "You know, the one where people get taken over by these bizarre giant pods from outer space?"

"Nope, never saw it." Ian put in his vampire teeth and made a scary face.

Zoé leaned across the table, knocking over a jar of malt vinegar. "I think something's happened to Iris, because she looks and acts like Iris but she's not Iris anymore. Just like in the movie, when fake people hatch out of the pods! What if Iris is a pod person and we don't know it?" She gave a nervous snicker, realizing how silly she sounded. "Just kidding."

"Pod person is good," Ian lisped through his vampire teeth. "I vote for pod."

Zoé put in the vampire fangs and gazed around the room, watching Iris putter around behind the counter, working the handles and spigots of the ice cream machine like a mad scientist in slow motion.

Inspired, she opened her journal and wrote: "Ms. Iris Tintern, café owner, Tenby, Wales, once beautiful, proud and pitiless, swallowed a ground-glass sandwich and turned into a time-ravaged old crone. Then aliens invaded and·changed her into a pod person."

Not a bad start. As she slid the journal into her backpack, Zoé's fingertips grazed a small object rolling around at the bottom. "Hey, want to see what I found on Granddad's front steps?" She pulled out a chunk of blue glass that had been wedged between the stone steps of the cottage. Deep inside swirled a fiery light, intense and glowing—and profoundly mysterious—making her wonder if the light had the power to hypnotize. "Do you like my pirate's spyglass?" She held it up to one eye.

Before Ian could answer, Iris trundled over with two dishes, setting them down with trembling hands. "Ice cream's a bit off, dearies. My Electro Freeze seems to be on the edge of a nervous breakdown."

Yeah, thought Zoé, suppressing a giggle, *and so are you.*

"All those knobs and switches," Iris went on, her eyes moving to the side. "Terribly off-putting."

Zoé watched the oversized glasses slide down Iris's nose. What if she really was a different person?

"Guess they don't make ice cream machines like they used to," joked Ian, sounding like their granddad.

Zoé peered through her blue glass at Iris and felt the hairs crawl on the back of her neck. At the center of Iris's forehead, she could see a black craterous eye whirling crazily.

"What's that in your hand?" asked Iris in a threatening tone. Zoé could see the eye growing bigger. "Did you pinch one of my salt shakers?"

Zoé whisked the glass into her pocket. "It's not a salt shaker. It's not anything, just a piece of old glass," she said, shrinking back in her chair, heart pounding against her ribs.

She looked up at Iris. The eye had vanished.

"Thanks, Ms. Tintern," said Ian, winking at Zoé. "The ice cream looks delicious."

Iris doesn't have three eyes, Zoé told herself. *I completely imagined that. Must be some sort of trick glass.*

"Enjoy your softies, dearies," Iris said with a vapid smile, but Zoé could tell she didn't mean it.

Scuffing over to the window, Iris drew the green-and-black curtains, making the room even gloomier.

"This softie ice cream tastes like rubbish, don't you think?" grumbled Zoé.

But Ian, caught up with eating ice cream and looking at the photos on his camera, didn't answer.

Zoé peered through the glass at the room around her: the tables and chairs appeared oddly distorted, the daffodil wallpaper obscured by a blue haze. All of a sudden, the room swung to one side, and for a chilling moment she saw not Iris, but something that wasn't human: a primeval figure with massive wings, shimmering in the dark. On its forehead was a glistening eye that seemed to be expanding. The eye was a dark space ringed with green fire—the kind of space you could fall into and disappear.

Terrified, she dropped the glass, and Iris was instantly her old self again, humming an off-key tune and running a duster over a rack of postcards while the coffee urn burbled. The café seemed normal—as if nothing extraordinary had happened—and Zoé wondered if she could be losing her mind.

"Look through this," she whispered, handing Ian the chunk of glass. "Look at Iris and tell me what you see."

Ian wiped his mouth on his sleeve and held the glass to his eye. "Arrgghhh! Avast, ye mateys," he rasped, squinting through it, using pirate expressions Granddad had taught them. "Thar she blows!"

He moved the glass slowly in the direction of Iris Tintern and Zoé saw him go rigid with fear. "What the heck?" he croaked.

Zoé looked up to see the café owner advancing on them, her face twisted in fury, hands raised like withered claws. She was like something roused from a nightmare, a mummy come to life.

"Give me that glass!" snarled Iris. Behind the tinted lenses her eyes gleamed like chips of black ice. "Give it over or I'll—"

"Run!" yelled Zoé, grabbing Ian's arm and snatching the backpack and messenger bag as they fled.

They sprinted across the café, stumbling over chairs, bumping into tables, and eventually charging through the front door, jangling the overhead bell to escape into the fog-bound streets of Tenby.

CHAPTER THREE
THE GRYPHON AND THE PHOENIX

Zoé felt a cold rain sweep in from the sea as they raced up St. Julian's, dodging puddles and bicyclists and mothers pushing strollers, past the houses and shops that lined the cobblestone streets. Fog snaked through the lanes like a giant smoky caterpillar, swallowing signs and awnings, turning people into shapeless lumps. Goblinesque trees crouched on the cliffs, and from far below came the crashing of waves.

Every time she thought about the café, Zoé felt her heart crawl up into her throat. Had she imagined Iris Tintern's humongous third eye? And Iris turning into a creature with wings—what was that all about?

They slipped behind the Saracen's Head Pub, run by Granddad's friend Mirielle Tate. While passing through the seventeenth-century graveyard where pets supposedly had been buried, Zoé caught a glimpse of Ian running beside her, his face deathly pale beneath his hood.

"Tell me! What did you see?" she shouted, wheeling on her cousin and screeching to a halt. "Did you see the eye?"

"Yeah, and it was horrendous, like some kind of monster's eye, and it was getting bigger by the second," he panted. "I was never so scared in my life! Thanks for getting me out of there."

"No problem." She knew Ian was hopeless at making fast getaways. That was because he tended to overanalyze everything: obviously not good if you were being chased by pirates or monsters—or by Iris Tintern.

"Why did Iris want that old piece of glass?" he whispered. She could see him shaking all over.

"She thought it was a salt shaker at first," said Zoé. "But when she realized what it was, she went crazy."

Ian thought a moment. "But what is it exactly besides a broken piece of glass? Maybe the glass is valuable. Hey, what if it creates optical illusions?"

"It sort of did make everything in the café look different," said Zoé. "Everything was swimming around, and I saw Iris with this huge whirling eye. Then she turned into some awful creature with wings."

Maybe the glass had a curse on it, though she knew Ian would laugh at an idea like that, since he had a logical mind. Even though he loved horror movies and scary games, she knew that real-life monsters, curses and dark magic were way off his radar. Ian preferred neat grids, balanced equations and columns of figures that added up.

"Listen, we need to find out more about that glass," said Ian, fidgeting with the strings of his hood. "For starters let's ask Granddad. He's bound to know something. You found it on his front steps, so maybe he's been looking for it. Better not ask too many questions, though, or things could get complicated. Let's not mention the weird eye or anything."

"Okay, mum's the word," said Zoé. "We keep the King's Ransom a secret and don't tell Granddad."

"We don't tell *anybody*," said Ian firmly.

"Secret shake," said Zoé, and, crossing right arms over left arms, they shook hands—their secret handshake to seal deals that really mattered.

Fog, thick and cottony, closed in around them as they followed St. George's Street to a medieval stone archway called the Five Arches. One of Tenby's original gates, the Five Arches was part of the Old Town wall, with crenellated battlements, huge arrow slits and massive archways. To Zoé's and Ian's delight, Granddad lived two doors away, in a stone cottage squeezed between a fish-and-chips takeaway and a frame shop.

Lace covered the windows and a string of tiny white lights framed a door with diamond-shaped panes. A brass plate at eye level read: THE GRYPHON AND THE PHOENIX, ANTIQUE WELSH FURNITURE BOUGHT AND SOLD, JOHN LLOYD BLACKWOOD, PROPRIETOR. Zoé was entranced by the cottage, with its peaks and turrets, its tilting chimneys and a weathervane twirling on the highest gable. Who else in Tenby had a weathervane that was a Welsh goddess? Nobody, she was quick to say, just as she was quick to tell kids that Granddad consulted the goddess like an oracle, for everything from betting on the Triple Crown to predicting Tenby's spring tides.

Arianrhod (that was the goddess's name) was made of beaten copper, with starburst hair, eyes of blue glass and a fierce expression. She wore a flowing dress and looked as if she were flying like the wind, holding a shield embossed with a Welsh dragon. Imagining the goddess as an avenging warrior, Zoé often wished she could change her name to Arianrhod. It sounded kind of classy.

"Granddad!" she shouted, running up the high stone steps and bursting into the shop.

What a relief to be in a familiar place, a place she loved beyond all measure—just as she loved her grandfather—breathing in smells that were old and musty. Weighed down with time and heirlooms, the shop had what Granddad called *a quaint geometry*. There were windows of leaded glass, thick as the bottoms of soda bottles; a curved stairway was flanked by portraits of whiskered ancestors, and maps of medieval Tenby hung on the staircase walls.

"Hello, you two," said Granddad from his leather armchair, where he sat reading *The Count of Monte Cristo*, dressed in his usual tweed jacket. No matter what time of year it was, John Lloyd Blackwood always wore a tweed jacket. The only variation was that in wintertime he wore a waistcoat underneath. He seemed thinner and more fragile than last year, but Zoé thought her granddad cut an elegant figure with his silver hair and clipped mustache.

People said Zoé was the spitting image of her grandfather. They both had the same sea-green eyes and aquiline nose, the same square teeth with a gap in the front. His wife, Louisa, had died years ago, but Granddad often showed them photos of her, reminiscing about bygone days, and in a way, Zoé felt as if she'd known her grandmother.

"Everything all right?" asked Granddad. "You both look like a bit of chewed string. Had a rough morning, did you?"

The two cousins exchanged a knowing glance.

"That's because we were running like maniacs through the rain," said Zoé, flopping onto a worn velvet settee and leaning back on the cushions. "Nonstop from the King's Ransom to here." She closed her eyes, trying to block out the frightening image of Iris Tintern. "There's a new shop on St. Julian's, Granddad, did you know? Zival's Optical."

"Zival, you say? Zival's Optical?" Granddad often repeated things because he was slightly hard of hearing. "Never heard of him, Magpie." Magpie was his pet name for her, because she squirreled away last-century treasures like glow-in-the-dark skulls, magic decoder rings and Looney Tunes figures.

"I took a ton of pictures, Granddad," said Ian. "I got some real gems of the Tudor Merchant's House in the fog. Very atmospheric."

"Well done," said Granddad with an approving nod. "Extraordinary town, Tenby. It was once a Welsh stronghold, as you know, and in medieval times a Norman castle was built on Castle Hill where Tenby Museum now stands."

"I wish I'd been around when the castle was here," said Zoé, disappointed that only isolated fragments of the castle walls remained, along with a single watchtower, perched above the sea cliffs.

"Aye, in those days Tenby was safe from invaders, enclosed behind an impregnable ring of walls, towers and gateways," Granddad went on, "with a great castle on the headland to protect it."

"Just as well the pirates are gone," said Ian with a grin. "Today they'd overrun Tenby in no time."

"Yeah, but we'd escape down the tunnels and they'd never catch us in a million years," said Zoé. "Hey, Granddad, have they found the tunnel to Dragon's Mouth yet?"

Dragon's Mouth was a spooky-looking cavern on Castle Hill overlooking the sea, impossible to access—unless you went by boat and climbed hundreds of feet up the steep cliff.

"I know how fond you two are of the tunnels," said Granddad, knitting his thick brows, "but I'm afraid I have some bad news. The town council shut them down earlier this year."

Zoé's face fell. "Shut the tunnels down? But . . . *why?*" Whenever she came to Tenby, she always visited the tunnels. Not going down there was unthinkable.

"What with coastal erosion and unpredictable tides, they've declared the tunnels hazardous." Granddad closed his book. "Last winter a spelunker went down and lost his way, so the authorities have become hypervigilant. They've sealed off the entrances."

Zoé sucked in her breath. "Okay, so some of the tunnels are dangerous, like maybe the one to Dragon's Mouth, but not *all* of them!"

Her grandfather threw her a sympathetic smile. "Sorry, Magpie, but that's how it is. No one's allowed in and anyone caught down there will be fined."

Zoé silently counted up the things that were different this year: the new optical shop, the closing of the tunnels, and—oh yeah—Iris Tintern.

"Zoé, weren't you going to ask Granddad something?" said Ian.

She blinked at her cousin, confused, then noticed the blue glass in his hand. "Oh, right. I found some old glass on the front steps, Granddad, and I was wondering if you knew anything about it."

"Glass? Old glass?" he echoed, a puzzled expression on his face.

"This one." Ian's hand shook slightly as he gave it to their grandfather. "We were just wondering," he added. "Like, is it part of a computer game or something?"

The glass looked ancient, like a treasure handed down through generations of wizarding families, or maybe a secret brotherhood of monks. Staring at the light smoldering inside, Zoé felt strangely drawn to it.

Granddad produced a magnifying glass from his jacket pocket. "Let's have a look, then." Watching him examine the glass, she was reminded of how much she loved her grand-father's gentle, inquisitive nature. "Well, I'll be jiggered. You know . . . I have an entire box of these things!"

Zoé threw Ian a sidelong glance. There were *more* glass pieces?

"Could we take a look at them, Granddad?" Ian asked.

"By all means." Their grandfather rose gracefully to his feet. "Back in a tick."

Granddad's physical stature never failed to impress Zoé: John Blackwood was well over six feet tall. He had to stoop to fit through the doorways of his cottage, and his head often brushed against the low beams.

"Maybe it really is trick glass," whispered Ian. "I mean, what if it actually can create illusions? There's got to be a ra-tional explanation for what happened at the King's Ransom."

Somehow Zoé wasn't so sure.

Granddad returned with a box the size of a small bread loaf. It had a curved lid, and the outside was encrusted with seaweed, barnacles and dried mud, as if culled from the bot-tom of the sea. *Like something a king's messenger would carry across a battlefield,* thought Zoé.

"Hmm, I'd completely forgotten about this box," he said, opening it. "I purchased it recently under somewhat odd cir-cumstances."

Wondering what her grandfather meant by *odd circum-stances,* Zoé stared into the box, fascinated by the jumble of luminous blue shapes inside.

"I've no idea what they're for, but they're quite lovely

nonetheless: handblown glass by the look of it, reminiscent of Wythernsea glass. In fact, I've been meaning to show them to Dr. Thistle at the museum." His tone grew a bit wistful. "Louisa used to say there's old memory in glass."

"Could we keep this for a little while?" asked Ian.

"We won't break the pieces or anything," added Zoé.

"Certainly you may. After all, you two have always been responsible and trustworthy."

"We'll be extra careful," she promised, feeling lucky to have a grandfather with such a generous nature.

"What were the odd circumstances, Granddad?" asked Ian, and Zoé leaned forward, eager to hear what their grandfather had to say.

"A curious story," he said, placing the box on a small table with scrolled legs. "About three weeks ago, a schoolgirl—around your age, rather unkempt—turned up at my door saying she'd found the box in a tunnel and would I be interested in buying it. She seemed quite desperate to be rid of it and I hadn't the heart to say no. She left with a fistful of pound notes, saying she was off to buy poetry books. The glass piece you found must have fallen from the box."

"The girl found this box in one of the *tunnels*?" Zoé's voice was tense with excitement. "Who was she?"

"Didn't tell me her name." Granddad reflected a moment. "Quite thin and tall she was, dark eyes, brown hair, freckles. Her coat was shabby, I did notice that, and she was wearing a school uniform. And, oh yes, a black beret."

"A beret?" Zoé couldn't believe her ears. "That's *her*, the girl who crashed into me! She came barreling out of the Captain's Quill Bookshop and knocked me down flat! Didn't say sorry, didn't—"

Before she could finish, the shop door opened and an elderly couple strolled in, shaking out their wet umbrellas.

"Ah, Mr. and Mrs. Llewellyn," said Granddad. "Here about the oak-paneled coffer, are you?"

"Quick, the box!" hissed Ian, spinning around, but Zoé was already whisking it away.

CHAPTER FOUR
MESSAGE FROM THE PAST

While their grandfather chatted with the customers, Zoé and Ian raced up the staircase to the cottage's living quarters, which were above Granddad's shop. Rambling and untidy, the upstairs contained antique furniture and Victorian rugs, a cozy yellow kitchen with an Aga cookstove and bedrooms with dormer windows.

Ian stopped by his room to grab his headlamp before they climbed the back stairs to the attic. Zoé kept a tight grip on the box, afraid she might drop it.

While Ian flashed his light on the attic door, Zoé twisted the knob and they both kicked the door because it always stuck. It creaked inward and she peered inside, expecting someone—or som*ething*—to jump out, or for long, cold fingers to land on her shoulders. Instead she saw a room with sloping walls, wooden beams and a window at the far end, wide open from the wind. The room was pretty sparse, with only a few stacks of bundled papers, an old sea chest and an iron bedstand slumped under the eaves.

"Remember the stuffed owl that used to be up here?" she whispered, suddenly nostalgic for a time when they were younger.

"That owl was mega-spooky," said Ian. "I used to worry about it coming to life and attacking me."

"Me too! But after we made up Owl in the Dark, I wasn't scared anymore." Owl in the Dark was one of many elaborate games she and Ian had invented over the years, along with Tunnel Monsters and Caldey Ghost Pirates. Their games, brimming with adventure and danger, always involved quests and riddles, treachery and derring-do, explorations, secret codes, maps and drawings.

"After we examine the glass, we'll track down the girl who sold it to Granddad, yeah?" said Ian, sitting cross-legged on the floor. "Find out what she knows."

"That shouldn't be hard," said Zoé, setting down the box and shrugging off her backpack. "Tall and skinny, dandelion-fluff hair, wears a beret and a raggedy pink jacket. She's what my mom calls an oddball. This girl's got an attitude you wouldn't believe."

Fishing a wool sock from her backpack, Zoé began scrubbing the sides of the box. Clumps of dirt and barnacles fell away, exposing a silver surface encrusted with stones that gleamed in deep, rich colors.

"Holy moly," said Ian, leaning in for a closer look. "What a relic."

"Positively medieval," breathed Zoé, unraveling a thick strand of seaweed.

There were tiny crescent moons cut along the top of the box, and through them she saw a faint glow inside. Wiping the lid free of dirt, she examined a symbol pressed into the tarnished silver: a woman in a long dress, holding up a shield.

"Arianrhod!" she said. "The Welsh goddess!"

"Shiver-me-timbers awesome," said Ian. "It's the same as the one on Granddad's weathervane, right down to the dragon on her shield."

Zoé thought a moment. "Do you think this box and the weathervane are connected?"

"Naw, I've seen this type of thing at my mom's museum. The Welsh dragon is a *repeating motif*," said Ian with an air of authority. "The goddess, too. It means they're a recurring artistic theme."

Zoé nodded, storing the phrase in her mind to write down later. Ian's mother was the director of a small museum, so when it came to artifacts, he knew the lingo.

She lifted the lid, and eerie light, the color of spring snow just before sunset, filled the attic.

"Looks like something from a Harry Potter movie," she whispered.

"Or the fog in *Attack of the Giant Leeches*," said Ian in a choked voice. *Attack of the Giant Leeches* was one of Grand-dad's favorite 1950s films.

"Here goes," said Zoé, tipping the box on its side.

She felt a fluttering in her stomach, watching the chunks of semitranslucent glass tumble to the floor. *I bet there are spells inside that glass,* she thought, feeling her heart quicken, *dark spells and old enchantments.* Sifting through the pieces, she counted twelve, thick and uneven, with smooth edges, each one shaped differently.

"Don't you think this glass is unearthly?" she asked, wondering with a secret thrill if it was magic. *Unearthly* was a word she sometimes used in her journal, along with *ethereal* and *surreal.*

"Hmm," said Ian. "I'd sure like to know how the glass distorts images when you look through it." He arranged several pieces in a line, beginning with the smallest, then moved them around. "There must be clues somewhere . . . a set of instructions maybe?"

Zoé peered inside the box. "Nope, nothing in here."

"I mean, how did it make Iris Tintern look like she had a third eye? Or turn her into a monster with wings?" Ian had a habit of talking to himself when trying to solve a difficult problem. Tutored by his father, a math teacher, he favored a systematic approach. Zoé watched him slide two pieces next to one another, and they snapped together, as if magnetized.

"What the heck?" she said. "What did you just do?"

Ian looked up, his baffled expression turning to wonder. "I figured it out! This is a puzzle!"

Zoé sucked in her breath. "A puzzle made of *glass?*" Did such a thing exist? She'd never heard of a glass puzzle before. The word *scintillating* bubbled up inside her head, followed by *end-of-the-world amazing.* It was nearly as good as finding a secret tunnel under your house or a murdered pirate in your kitchen pantry.

Heads bowed, they began putting the puzzle together. Ian worked slowly and methodically, while Zoé was impatient to be finished, pushing the pieces this way and that with a fierce intensity. To her frustration, none of them quite fitted together.

Hearing the marine chronometer in the downstairs hall chime three, she realized they'd been working for an hour, yet only part of the puzzle was completed.

She sat up, arms clasped around her knees. "I've never seen a puzzle like this before. It's totally not normal."

"Hold on, I think this could be one of those no-picture-at-all puzzles," said Ian, sounding suddenly confident. "Last year I ordered one online. There's no picture and no design, and each piece is a different shape, so you have to figure out the pattern. Putting it together is like solving a complex equation."

Zoé threw him an admiring glance. She might be tougher and braver than Ian, but she had to admit he had extraordinary brain power. His fingers began to fly back and forth, the light turning them ghostly blue. *No wonder I had trouble,* she thought. *Math's my worst subject.*

Enthralled, she watched the last few pieces click together.

Ian placed one piece on top of another, creating what looked like a second layer of glass at the center. The finished puzzle was a perfectly round circle, the shape of a full moon, no larger than one of Granddad's dessert plates. She stared at it, breathless. She'd read somewhere that circles had magical significance—and moons, too, were steeped in ancient lore.

"Some of these pieces are fused," explained Ian. "Melted together at high temperatures, some more transparent than others. It's a technique to create multilayered designs. My mom's museum had an exhibition of fused glass last year."

"It's really beautiful," whispered Zoé, unable to look away.

She gazed into its mysterious depths, where twisting columns of fire swirled endlessly, creating patterns that seemed to change every few seconds. At the center of the puzzle was a delicate raised image: a Welsh dragon, light emanating from its wings.

"A dragon!" she said, feeling a rush of excitement.

"A dragon inside a circle," said Ian. "Very Celtic."

"Repeating motif, right?" said Zoé, grinning. "Nice work, Ian." She flopped down on her stomach. "Too bad we can't shrink ourselves and crawl inside." Gazing into its glassy depths, she thought of firefly light and halls of mirrors where you saw yourself reflected a hundred times. A salty-tasting wind brushed against her face and she felt the puzzle drawing her in.

"Something's down there," she murmured. "Do you see it?"

Through fathoms of glass she saw the outline of an

island, dark and dreamy, floating on an emerald sea. A forest spilled down to a rocky coastline, and there were towers, domes, spires and bridges, all jumbled together, surrounded by a wall of golden stone: a vision so stunning it made her heart ache.

"I can see some sort of island down there," she said excitedly. "And a town, and little boats!" Everything was so vivid and alive, she knew she wasn't imagining things. "I'm not kidding, Ian—take a look."

Ian pushed back his headlamp. "Glass can create optical illusions, don't forget. It's easy to fool people using light and refraction. I'd guess what you're seeing is computer generated."

"No way," huffed Zoé. "This is real!"

"Maybe it's a hologram—though the perspective is slightly off. I think someone's tinkered with it. Most likely they've inserted computer chips into the puzzle pieces. Are you sure there's no instruction book?" he asked, turning the box upside down.

Zoé saw a tattered brown envelope drift to the floor with *To Whom It May Concern* scrawled in thick letters across the front. Grabbing the envelope, she tore it open. Inside was a small sheet of paper, lined and yellowed, so brittle it might turn to dust at any second.

"Give me some light," she said. "Quick!" Ian focused his headlamp and she carefully unfolded the paper. "A secret message!" she gasped, staring at the spidery handwriting.

"Wow, that looks really old," said Ian, leaning over her

shoulder. "See how the letters are different thicknesses? And all those blobs of ink. I bet it was written with a fountain pen."

Zoé was impressed. Granddad was the only person she knew who used a fountain pen, when he recorded furniture sales in his accounts ledger. Fountain pens were totally last-century items.

She began to read out loud:

> "*Property of Wyndham S. Marriott. Keep Out! Tres-passers shall be prossecuted. And that meens you! Under no circumstances are you to put this together.*
>
> *Signed:*
> *George R. Marriott, Hero,*
> *Inventor, Mastermind*
>
> *P.S. If you find this box and open it, do not reveel its contents to any person. No one knows what it contains. It is yours."*

At the bottom someone had drawn a skull and crossbones.

"Nice skull," said Ian. "He's a better artist than a speller, that's for sure."

"It's a warning not to put the puzzle together," said Zoé. "Too late, right? We already did it." She wondered uneasily if they'd made a mistake.

"The note's not very enlightening," said Ian. "I mean, it

doesn't say anything about the glass distorting people's faces or making them look like monsters with wings."

"The mystery deepens," said Zoé. That was what they always said on the detective programs her mom watched. "Can I borrow your headlamp? I need to write this stuff down in my journal."

She stood by the window, where a light rain was blowing in, adjusting the lamp to fit her head, listening to a foghorn booming out over Carmarthen Bay.

"Who are George and Wyndham Marriott? Brothers?" she wrote with her ink gel pen. "Why did they hide the puzzle in a tunnel with a warning note? Must track down: first, the mean, quirky girl in pink jacket and beret and second, the mysterious Marriotts. Note to self: find out if the glass puzzle is magic."

"Granddad's probably wondering where we are," she heard Ian say.

"Oh yeah, he—"

Ian's scream cut her off. Zoé whirled around, breathing in the sharp scent of brine and fish. Ian was scrambling away from the puzzle on all fours, a look of terror on his face. She felt a sudden fear in the pit of her stomach.

"Ian!" she cried. He didn't answer.

Without warning, a dark clotted shadow burst out of the puzzle and her heart jumped into her throat. It was a wavering shape, chilling and distorted, bringing with it a cold light. Then two more flew out.

She saw Ian standing there, rigid and trembling, as more

menacing shapes rose out of the puzzle, and in the awful, heavy silence of the attic she listened to her own wild heart-beat. *This can't be happening,* she told herself, *I'm not really seeing these things—*

The creatures shuddered and convulsed. On their fore-heads were craterous eyes rimmed with fire, identical to the eye she'd seen on Iris Tintern. Zoé stared at them in horror, wishing she'd never come to the attic, never put the puzzle together—

Massive wings exploded from their backs, scales bounc-ing across the attic floor, and she let out a shriek as they rose into the air. Crouching down, Zoé put her hands over her face, and the attic shook with the sound of flapping wings as the creatures rushed overhead, buffeting past her like a strong wind, making her cringe.

Then, just as quickly, they flew out the open window.

CHAPTER FIVE
HERO, INVENTOR, MASTERMIND

Zoé woke suddenly, shivering beneath the thin blanket she'd pulled over her head. All night long she'd dreamed about creatures slithering out of the glass puzzle, chasing her down the streets of Tenby. She dreamed about the stuffed owl in the attic coming to life, shrieking and flapping. She and Ian were in a cold, dark, winding tunnel, running and running, when suddenly a monster grabbed her by the throat—and that was when she woke up.

Her body tensed as she remembered the creatures in the attic. They were *real*! She could see them now, rising out of the puzzle, eyes whirling on their foreheads, leathery wings unfolding.

Terrified that more creatures might escape, they'd taken

the puzzle apart using Ian's methodical approach, working from the outside to the center. Then they'd hidden the puzzle at the bottom of the sea chest.

Too wired to sleep, she leafed through a Beano that Granddad had left on her bedside table. The British comic usually made her laugh out loud, but not this morning. Not even her collections of beach glass and trilobites gave her much comfort today.

A rook flew past the window of her gabled room and vanished into the fog. Pushing the nightmare images from her mind, Zoé envisioned the high cliffs of Tenby, and the waves gray and wild, with Caldey Island floating dreamily off the coast. "The name means *Cold Isle*," Granddad had said, "from the Viking *Keld-Eye*." She'd immediately written that down in her journal.

Hearing voices in the hallway, Zoé put on her turquoise jeans with rhinestone pockets, a striped T-shirt (like pirates wore in the French films her mom liked to watch) and a shiny pink headband. There were boiled sweets stuck to the insides of her pockets, and other things, too: bits of sparkly paper, bottle tops and a dried-up moth. She'd always been a magnet for lost things.

In the dining room Granddad was carrying a tray of boiled eggs and toast to the table while whistling a cheerful tune. Plenty of grandfathers were crusty and irritable, but not Zoé's. Granddad always kept the conversation upbeat and lighthearted.

Ian stood there looking moody, hands in his pockets,

wearing shorts and his prized shirt: Tuscan red with yellow trapezoids. Zoé considered it the ultimate in cool. Ian liked clothes with geometrical patterns because his favorite subject was math, but his mom often had problems finding math-themed clothing for boys.

"Morning, Magpie," said Granddad. "Listen, I know you're both disappointed about the tunnels, so how about a boat trip to Caldey Island? You could take some smashing photos, Ian."

"Fantastic," said Ian. "I was hoping to go to the Old Priory and take some pictures of the Caldey Stone."

The Caldey Stone, Zoé knew, had been found on Caldey Island and was a tablet from the Dark Ages inscribed in Latin and Celtic Ogham script.

"Sounds like fun, Granddad," she said, slathering gooseberry jam on a slice of toast.

"I'll contact Arthur Angel, see if he can take us on the *Sea Kestrel*. Do you recall going there in his mail boat last year?"

Zoé nodded. Mr. Angel, a grizzled old fisherman, had ferried them back and forth to Caldey Island one cloudy August day. She remembered the squawking gulls and leaping fish, the salt spray on her face—and Ian, seasick, almost falling over the side.

"If the fog lifts, we might even see the rooftops and turrets of Wythernsea," added Granddad, his eyes bright.

Wythernsea. Granddad's stories about the island always sent chills up and down Zoé's spine. A mile east of Caldey, Wythernsea had been famous for two things: its talented glassblowers and its Retreat for the Rescued, the Lost and the Shipwrecked. Wythernsea had a history of saving people lost at sea. Whenever there were shipwrecks, the islanders would jump into their boats and search for survivors, taking them to the Retreat to recover.

Family legend had it that their ancestor, Captain Ezekiel Blackwood, crashed his ship, the *Black Swan*, on the rocks off Wythernsea in a storm in 1324. He and his crew were rescued, and when the ship was repaired and they were preparing to set sail, the townsfolk presented Captain Blackwood with a weathervane, "to protect him forevermore." It was the very same weathervane that spun on the roof of Granddad's cottage.

Sadly, Wythernsea was submerged and washed away a quarter century later, when a hurricane struck the west coast of Wales. It was said that at low tide the castle turrets could sometimes be seen and church bells heard clanging. But Zoé knew that couldn't really be true; Ian had told her that by now the bells would have corroded underwater. Even so, whenever they were near Wythernsea, she listened for them.

"Er, Granddad," she heard Ian say, "ever hear of anyone in Tenby called Mr. Marriott?"

"There's a Dr. Marriott on Crackwell Street," replied Granddad, dipping his spoon into a soft-boiled egg. "Why do you ask?"

Zoé and Ian exchanged wary looks.

"Is he a local historian?" asked Zoé, thinking fast. "Ian's, um, looking for historians to interview."

"For my history project," Ian chimed in.

That's sort of true, thought Zoé. After all, Ian really did want to talk to local people about Tenby's history.

"Dr. Marriott's a retired academic who runs an antiquarian bookshop," explained Granddad. "I bought my illustrated edition of *The Count of Monte Cristo* from George last winter. A rather unorthodox character, but extremely knowledgeable."

George Marriott lived in Tenby! Zoé wasn't sure what Granddad meant by *unorthodox*, but it sounded hopeful. They needed some unorthodox help right now.

"Hmm, maybe I'll drop by and see him," said Ian, throwing Zoé a look of suppressed excitement. "Dr. Marriott probably knows some interesting history."

Once they helped clear the table and did the dishes, the two cousins grabbed their coats and took off into the Old Town.

"It's not really a lie, is it?" said Ian, snapping pictures of the more antiquated hotels and cottages they passed along the way. "Telling Granddad I needed to ask this George Marriott character about Tenby's history?"

"Not a lie. Well, it's kind of a fib," said Zoé, buttoning her shiny purple raincoat and flipping her collar up like a detective. In one hand she carried a tourist map of Tenby, with an X penciled in halfway down Crackwell Street. "But maybe that's okay, because we made a pact not to tell him. Granddad's sensitive," she added, feeling protective of her grandfather, "and we don't want to go scaring him."

"Totally right, best to keep him in the dark," agreed Ian as they made their way along St. Julian's. "Hey, look over there! A neon sign in Tenby's historic district? How gauche is that? I'm surprised the town council allowed it."

Zoé's mouth dropped when she saw the electric sign flashing the words ZIVAL'S OPTICAL SHOP, in orange and green letters, the O looking like an enormous eye. Inside the window a smaller neon sign flashed: WE ARE NOW OPEN FOR BUSINESS—WELCOME, SPECIAL CUSTOMERS!

"That wrecks everything!" she said, outraged. "How could they get away with it? Why didn't they keep their quaint hand-carved sign?"

The giant eye gave her a sudden queasy feeling, maybe because it made her think of Iris Tintern.

"I had weird dreams last night, did you?" she asked.

"I don't remember," said Ian. "None of us Blackwoods remember our dreams. It's because we're all concrete thinkers."

Zoé decided to let that one go. Ian's parents were quirky egghead types who spent hours arguing over obscure topics like the beauty of fractals or how mapmaking shaped the course of history. Her mom said some of their kooky ideas were bound to rub off on Ian.

"I keep telling myself I imagined those creatures," he said. "But I didn't, did I? We both saw them come out of the puzzle, right? And—" He came to a stop and swallowed hard, pulling his hood over his face, like a snail retreating into its shell. "Can we not talk about it right now?"

"I think we should tell this George Marriott about them,"

said Zoé. "I bet he saw them, too, and that's why he wrote a warning note."

Whenever she thought about the creatures, she felt ripples of fear inside her stomach. They'd flown out the attic window, disappearing into the fog—but where had they gone? It made her skin crawl to think they might be hiding somewhere in Tenby.

They turned onto a cobbled lane of elegant Georgian houses painted in soft greens and lavenders and yellows, overlooking Penniless Cove Hill and the harbor below. Moments later the two stood before a black lacquered door attached to a tall pink house facing the sea, and Ian took a rapid burst of photos—thirty at one go.

Zoé thought the bookseller's house charming, with its tiers of multi-pane bay windows and ornamental cornices. A plaque next to the door read: NO. 36½ CRACKWELL— GEORGE R. MARRIOTT, ANTIQUARIAN BOOKSELLER—HOURS BY CHANCE OR BY APPOINTMENT.

"This is the guy," she said with an air of certainty, lifting the elegant brass knocker. "I just know it."

A lean, bustling woman with crinkly hair opened the door and ushered them inside. Zoé knew her mom would go bananas over the hairdo. Her mother adored retro hairstyles, and this one seemed retro-retro.

"Goodness, we weren't expecting you quite this early," said the woman, smoothing down her apron. "Never mind, children, this way." Zoé and Ian exchanged confused looks but neither said a word as they followed her into a high-

ceilinged room lined with shelves of books that looked su-
premely ancient—probably just as vintage as the old lady,
thought Zoé.

"I'm Mrs. Prosser, Dr. Marriott's housekeeper. The professor will be with you momentarily. Make yourselves comfortable." The door clicked softly behind her.

"What was that all about?" said Zoé. "How did she know
we were coming?"

"Maybe Granddad phoned to say we were on our way,"
said Ian, looking around with a puzzled frown. "Hey, there's
nowhere to sit in this place! No chairs, no sofa, just a bunch
of old books. Like a scene out of Dickens." Both Ian and Zoé
were familiar with Charles Dickens because Granddad had
collected all his books and often read out loud from them.

Having nowhere to sit didn't bother Zoé, who was standing before a gilded mirror checking out her reflection. Before
leaving the cottage, she'd sprinkled on extra fairy-sparkle glitter, and now she could see a thousand tiny stars twinkling in
her hair—and a few shining on her forehead and ears as well.
The overall effect was sort of *ethereal*.

While Ian thumbed through an old history book, Zoé
began writing down impressions of Dr. Marriott's house in
her journal. Then, without warning, the door flew open and
a bulky shape filled the doorway.

"Hello and welcome," boomed a deep voice. "A fine day
for June, wouldn't you agree?"

"Oh, hello," said Ian.

With one glance Zoé took in the small walrus mustache,

the corduroy blazer and the T-shirt with the words IDEAS MAY BLOSSOM—HAYFESTIVAL.COM. The man was bald save for tufts of hair that sprang over his ears, giving him the appearance of a disgruntled owl. In one earlobe hung a tiny gold hoop. She hadn't expected the earring.

"Dr. George Marriott, at your disposal." He smiled, revealing a row of teeth gleaming like pearls.

They shook hands and Zoé liked him at once. Gazing down at his ink-stained fingers, she noticed a tattoo on one wrist: a fiery red Welsh dragon, so finely detailed she wondered if it was a stick-on.

"Nice to meet you, Professor," said Ian politely.

"Only Mrs. Prosser addresses me as Professor these days," said Dr. Marriott with a chuckle. "My academic career ended years ago. I prefer to be known simply as an antiquarian bookseller."

"You certainly have lots of old books," said Ian. "Very impressive."

"Indeed. First editions are my specialty."

"Our grandfather is John Lloyd Blackwood and he sells antique furniture," said Zoé. "But he likes antique books, too. You sold him *The Count of Monte Cristo*. It's his favorite novel in the whole world."

"Ah yes, I'm acquainted with your grandfather. I sold him an early edition. Sublime illustrations," said Dr. Marriott in what Granddad would call a *cultured voice*.

They trailed him out of the room and down a hallway that smelled of old books and boiled cabbage. Ian started peppering Dr. Marriott with questions when he saw the old-fashioned wallpaper depicting schooners and merchant ships and British seaports. *My cousin's a real history geek*, thought Zoé. She found his enthusiasm contagious, even when he got stuck on dates and other boring topics, and she admired his knack for unearthing obscure historical details.

Once on the top floor, Dr. Marriott escorted them into another room crammed with seemingly endless shelves of books running from floor to ceiling. Through the bay windows, Zoé could see thick fog rolling past, enveloping the boats in the harbor.

"Apologies for the chaos," said Dr. Marriott as they sidestepped stacks of magazines and crates filled with books. "I'm in the midst of rearranging my office, but it seems to be taking ages. Mrs. Prosser refuses to clean the room—can't say as I blame her."

Zoé had somehow imagined the grown-up George Marriott to be a frail, reclusive academic wearing rimless bifocals and a dark suit with patched elbows, his office filled with Victorian armoires and maps of galaxies pinned to the walls. The real version of George Marriott was much more intriguing.

"Make yourselves comfortable," said Dr. Marriott, unfolding two wooden chairs. "The *Tenby Observer* said they were sending their finest junior reporters, and I see they've done just that." He eyed Zoé's journal. "I see, too, you have your notebook at the ready. Well done."

"I think maybe—" Ian began.

Dr. Marriott rubbed his hands together enthusiastically. "Yes indeed, you strike me as inquisitive types."

More confused than ever, Zoé watched the professor sink into a captain's chair behind a desk littered with sketches, photographs, scrunched-up wads of paper and cups of cold tea (she could see mold floating in one of them). At the edge of the desk, threatening to fall at any moment, was a hulking typewriter with most of its keys jammed.

"But, Dr. Marriott," she said, "we're not junior—"

"Here, my calling card," he cut in, handing them each a crumpled business card. Then he leaned back in his chair, hands clasped behind his head.

Zoé smoothed out the card. *George R. Marriott, Professor Emeritus* was embossed at the top in scrolled letters. The next lines read: *Medievalist, Archivist, Seller of Antiquarian Books and Fine Manuscripts.* She wondered what a medievalist did but felt too shy to ask. In smaller print, at the bottom, it read: *Honorary Member of the Society of Astercôte.* She had no idea what that meant, either.

"Not to seem rude," said Ian, surveying the room with a curious expression. "I was just wondering . . . where's your computer?"

Dr. Marriott grinned and Zoé watched his mustache flip up at the corners. "You young folks will think me daft, but I'm extremely attached to my outdated typewriter. Lovely old thing—a 1940s Underwood—and I refuse to replace it." He gave an exaggerated wink that made Zoé giggle. "Here you go, kids, compliments of the house." A candy bar landed in her lap. "Brain food, stimulates all that gray matter."

She tore off a wrapper that read: "Pimms' Health Bar: If it isn't Pimms, it isn't healthy." *Definitely not from Maisie's Sweet Shop*, she thought, nibbling on it. It tasted a bit like cardboard (she'd once eaten cardboard on a dare), with a hint of coconut.

Dr. Marriott rummaged through his desk drawers and whipped out a pen, twirling it like a miniature baton. Zoé couldn't believe it. He was holding a fountain pen! "Before we get started, perhaps you'd like me to sign one of my books? *Doctor Doom and the Starchild* has just come out: a dystopian thriller for ages ten and up."

"You're an *author?*" gasped Zoé. She'd met plenty of journalists and bloggers before, because of her mom's profession, but this was the first time she'd met someone who'd actually written a *book*.

He nodded modestly. "I was a keynote speaker at last year's Hay-on-Wye literary festival." His hand swept past a stack of books on his desk, all with colorful covers. "Some of my earlier novels."

Tilting her head, Zoé read the titles: *Toxic, Gothic Werewolf, The Sea of Liquid Iron*, and a fourth that was composed of weird symbols.

"Wow, those are super titles," she said. There were hundreds of questions she wanted to ask, like whether he'd seen creatures come out of the puzzle and if so, whether he'd written about them in his books.

"Does the Captain's Quill Bookshop sell your novels?" asked Ian.

"I believe so," replied the professor, "but tell you what, I'll give you each a signed copy of *Doctor Doom* to take home with you."

"Super! Thanks, Mr. Marriott," said Ian. "I love thrillers." He paused, his expression growing serious. "But we didn't come here for an autograph."

"And we're not junior reporters," said Zoé, blushing. She hadn't meant to be dishonest, she'd just gotten a little carried away, charmed by this odd bookish professor and his fascinating old house.

George Marriott's eyebrows, fine as moth wings, shot straight up. "But the *Tenby Observer* rang yesterday and said—"

"Sorry," said Ian. "There's been a mix-up."

"We wanted to ask you about a puzzle," Zoé blurted out. "See, this totally off-the-wall Welsh girl dug it up in one of the tunnels here and sold it to our granddad and—"

"And we think maybe there's a hologram inside," Ian cut in.

"Or maybe not," said Zoé, slightly annoyed. "Anyway, it's a glass puzzle inside an ancient silver box and there's a warning to stay away."

"Somebody drew this cool skull and crossbones," added Ian, "and signed it 'George R. Marriott: Hero, Inventor, Mastermind.'"

"Hero, Inventor . . ." Dr. Marriott's voice faded to a croak.

"Oh, my giddy aunt," he murmured, knocking over a cup of cold tea.

Zoé leaned forward, suddenly anxious, seeing the stricken expression on his face. "It is you, isn't it?" she said. "It *has* to be!"

CHAPTER SIX
THE SECRET SOCIETY OF ASTERCÔTE

"Yes, I wrote the message," said Dr. Marriott, his trembling freckled hand mopping up the spilled tea with the *London Review of Books.* "You're saying that you actually have the glass puzzle? I mean . . . you know where it is?"

"Well, the puzzle belongs to our granddad," said Zoé. "But he said we could keep it for a while. We hid it inside a sea chest in his attic."

"After all these years," murmured Dr. Marriott as he slumped back into his chair looking distraught. "I never imagined." He tugged nervously on his gold earring. "This is all rather devastating. . . ."

"I really liked your message," said Zoé, trying to cheer him up.

"The skull and crossbones were nicely drawn," added Ian.

"Thank you. I was about your age when I wrote that warning. The message was intended to be a fierce and proper Keep Out notice."

Zoé thought she detected a guarded excitement in the professor's eyes, reminding her of Granddad when he talked about the past.

"It was fierce, all right," she said, "like something a pirate would write in the tunnels to protect his treasure! You know, to scare robbers away."

She could almost see Dr. Marriott as a young boy, his pockets stuffed with sweets, sauntering down the streets of Tenby in a porkpie hat, reading Sherlock Holmes and whistling bits of jazz.

"But you spelled a couple of words wrong." Zoé clapped one hand over her mouth. Maybe she shouldn't have said that to a professor emeritus.

Dr. Marriott didn't appear insulted. "Always was a dreadful speller." He threw her a crooked smile.

Ian cleared his throat politely. "So . . . where does the glass puzzle come from?"

"And why did you bury it in a tunnel?" asked Zoé.

She watched the antiquarian bookseller grip the arms of his chair, as if bracing himself for a roller-coaster ride. "Would you like to hear a cracking good tale?" Not waiting for an answer, Dr. Marriott launched into his story. "The puzzle goes back to my uncle and guardian, Wyndham Marriott."

"Wyndham Marriott's not your *brother?*" said Zoé, feeling a twinge of disappointment.

"Heavens no, I was an only child. Wyndham raised me from the age of eighteen months, after my parents' untimely death on a plane to Madagascar. They were anthropologists, you see. Traveled all over the globe studying primitive societies."

Zoé sat very still, absorbing every word, thinking how she was an only child, too, and *her* father had disappeared when she was little. But her father was merely *in absentia,* as her mom often said, while George Marriott was a true orphan. She'd never met a real orphan, having only read about them in books, and now here was one sitting next to her. In her opinion, orphans were a cut above the average kid: inventive, fearless and resourceful, battling against all odds to survive.

"Wyndham was an ornithologist and a marvelous illustrator of birds," Dr. Marriott continued. "He smoked Woodbines, two every evening, and smelled of Wildroot hair oil and peppermints. I was immensely fond of him."

Uncle Wyndham sounds real old-fashioned, thought Zoé, *sort of like Granddad.*

Dr. Marriott's voice dropped to a whisper. "Have you ever heard of the Society of Astercôte?"

"Not until I read it on your business card," said Ian.

Zoé looked down at the professor's card. *Honorary Member of the Society of Astercôte* sounded a bit exotic.

"But *honorary* means you're not a full-fledged member, right?" said Ian.

"Indeed. The society was a highly secret organization founded by Sir Harold Astercôte, an alchemist from Inverness, who possessed arcane knowledge. In particular, how to construct gateways to parallel worlds," Dr. Marriott explained. "Members of the society, including Uncle Wyndham, were all scientists of one sort or other—and all practiced alchemy. I was *honorary* by virtue of being Wyndham's nephew. The Astercôtes believed our world was one of many; they traveled not only to Wythernsea but to several alternate worlds. With me so far?"

"I— I guess so," said Zoé, her head spinning. But why was he telling them about the Society of Astercôte if it was supposed to be secret?

"So this is about, hmm, portals to other dimensions?" said Ian, sounding skeptical. "Like in science fiction?"

"Precisely," replied Dr. Marriott. "There are hidden gateways all over this planet, all leading to other worlds. The puzzle was made in Wythernsea and presented as a gift to the Astercôtes, who used their powers to transform it into a gateway."

Zoé's eyes went even wider. Granddad's puzzle was a door to *another world?*

"And what exactly is alchemy, Dr. Marriott?" asked Ian. "Changing metal to gold, right?"

"Simply put, yes: that was the goal of medieval alchemists and mystics," replied the professor. "They also sought a universal cure for disease, as well as the *elixir of life*, a medicine to extend life indefinitely. You see, alchemy is the power to transform something ordinary into something special, and that is exactly what the Astercôtes did: they turned the glass puzzle into a portal to Wythernsea. As far as I know, it is the only puzzle in existence that serves as a gateway."

"But how could the Astercôtes travel to Wythernsea?" asked Ian, incredulous. "The island sank in the fourteenth century!"

"I am well aware of that fact, young man," said Dr. Marriott in an arch tone. "In *this* world Wythernsea no longer exists, but ours is not the only world out there. Wythernsea is one of countless places that have been transported elsewhere— islands trapped beneath primeval bogs, cities buried under silt and muck, villages swallowed by desert sands—all lost in this world, all resurfacing in *other* worlds."

With her chin in her hands, Zoé sat imagining walls crushed between layers of mud and rock, spellbound relics, petrified bones, tunnels leading everywhere and nowhere, and Wythernsea, an island under a dark enchantment.

"So Wythernsea sank, then it teleported to this alternate reality," said Ian, obviously not believing a word of it. "And did this puzzle take them to lots of different worlds?"

"No, it was a gateway only to Wythernsea."

Zoé opened her notebook and wrote: *Ours is not the only world out there* and *Transported elsewhere.*

"But how did the Astercôtes get to Wythernsea in the first place?" persisted Ian.

"A hidden portal, some sort of Coptic urn, as I recall— but it was flawed," said Dr. Marriott. "A flawed portal invariably spells danger, so the Astercôtes destroyed the urn and replaced it with the glass puzzle." Dr. Marriott slowly rose to his feet. "Have a look at this watercolor." He gestured to the wall behind them. "Birds weren't the only things Uncle Wyndham illustrated."

Zoé turned to see a painting inside a wooden frame, obscured by a potted fern and a glass-fronted cabinet overflowing with books. The faded colors gave it a weathered look, like a drawing from an old story. Richly detailed, the painting depicted odd-shaped buildings, whorled towers, spiraling roofs, crenellated walls, boats moored in a harbor, and a green sea next to a dark, brooding forest.

A zing of recognition flashed through her: this was the same image she'd seen inside the puzzle!

"The fortifications around the town are awfully high, like almost twice the height of Tenby's old walls," observed Ian. "Is there some kind of enemy they're keeping out? Giants, maybe?"

Zoé stepped closer to the painting, examining the wall that encircled the town. Made of golden stone, it completely surrounded Wythernsea, cutting it off from a forest that hinted at something primal and possibly dreadful. Obviously the wall was intended to discourage someone, or some*thing*, from getting in.

"A complex story," said Dr. Marriott.

Noticing his anguished expression, Zoé hoped they hadn't upset him too much.

There was a rap at the door and Mrs. Prosser called from

the other side: "Dr. Julian Thistle from the museum to see you, Professor. He has an appointment."

"I must leave you now," said Dr. Marriott, shifting uneasily from one foot to the other. "My housekeeper will show you out."

"But you didn't tell us why you buried the puzzle!" protested Zoé.

Dr. Marriott's expression turned even grimmer. "The Astercôtes made an error when they transformed the puzzle into a gateway. You see, it was flawed. One night all the members of the Society went through the puzzle to Wythernsea—all except Uncle Wyndham, that is. Whenever the Astercôtes traveled, one member stayed behind to keep an eye on the gateway, and on that particular night it was Wyndham's turn." With his thumb and forefinger, he massaged the bridge of his nose. "But the Astercôtes never returned."

Zoé gave a little gasp.

"Uncle Wyndham waited weeks, months, years, but they didn't appear," he continued, his voice heavy with sadness. "Then one evening he noticed several dark shapes flying inside the puzzle—great winged beasts they were, unspeakable in nature—and he realized they were trying to enter our world! Terrified, he deconstructed the puzzle, as he'd been told to do in an emergency. Shaken to the core, having lost all hope of his friends returning, he asked me to throw the puzzle into the sea."

Feeling a cold uneasiness creep over her, Zoé glanced at

Ian. Her cousin's thin frame was taut as a wire. Wyndham Marriott had seen the same creatures they had—only the ones they'd seen had *gotten out!*

"I stood on the cliffs behind the Fourcroft Hotel looking out over North Beach, planning to toss the box into the waves. But I was young, extremely shy—and extremely naïve," said Dr. Marriott with a wry smile. "I couldn't bring myself to destroy something so rare and mysterious."

"So you put the puzzle together?" asked Ian.

"I did not. Chalk it up to my timid nature as a twelve-year-old: the thought of setting monsters loose on Tenby made me quake in my boots." He gave a loud sigh. "Turning my back on the sea, I went down into the tunnels, wrote a warning note and buried the puzzle, thinking that was the end of it."

Before Zoé could utter a word, the door opened and Mrs. Prosser stuck her head in. "Dr. Thistle is asking for you, Professor," she trilled, tapping a finger on her watch. "These children will have to come back another time."

Zoé's heart sank. Why did they have to leave now, with all these unanswered questions hanging over them?

"Promise you'll leave the puzzle alone until we can talk again," said Dr. Marriott in a conspiratorial whisper. "Don't mention it to anyone and, whatever you do, *don't put the puzzle together!*"

"This way, junior reporters," said the housekeeper, steering them out of the room.

Holding the door open, Dr. Marriott winked at them.

As they trooped through, Zoé noticed a small tattoo on his other wrist: a skull and crossbones.

"Shall we meet for tea, the day after tomorrow?" he asked. "The King's Ransom Café. Always quiet there. Say four o'clock? I'll bring *Doctor Doom*. Cheerio."

"We can't go to the King's—" Zoé started.

But by then the door was closing and Mrs. Prosser was nudging them down the stairs with her bony elbows.

CHAPTER SEVEN
THE MYSTERIOUS BLUE GLASS

In the evening, following a take-out meal of fish and chips, Zoé and Ian waited in line with Granddad outside the Garibaldi Pavilion Theater on High Street to buy tickets for the original version of *Invasion of the Body Snatchers*, what Granddad called "a quintessential black-and-white sci-fi B-movie."

Ian aimed his camera at the distant headland, taking pictures of the ruined castle and the ferry landing that jutted out into the harbor. Zoé admired the way he was so intense and professional, yet always willing to show her the finer points of photography. That was one reason she liked Ian so much: like Granddad, he had a generous nature.

"So if Dr. Marriott is, say, fifty years old," said Ian, pocketing his camera, "and he buried the puzzle when he was twelve. . . ." He furrowed his brow, doing a quick mental calculation. "Whooee, that means the glass puzzle was down in that tunnel for thirty-eight years!"

"My mom and your dad were going to school here thirty-eight years ago," said Zoé. "Hey, do you think all the Aster-côtes had dragon tattoos like Dr. Marriott's?"

"Maybe," said Ian. "But I like the skull-and-crossbones one better."

Granddad turned to them, waving three tickets. "Here we go, kids, my treat," he said merrily. "You're going to love this motion picture. It's classic science fiction!"

"Thanks, Granddad," said Zoé.

Over the years, she and Ian had come here often with Granddad, a horror and sci-fi movie enthusiast who was keen on films dating back to the 1950s and '60s. Ian was always eager to analyze the special effects, curious to know how films like *Godzilla* were made in the days before computer technology. Zoé simply loved being frightened.

The Garibaldi Pavilion Theater was a relic from a dying age, one of many threatened theaters in Britain, covered in vines and vegetation, crumbling from the outside in, yet Zoé adored it. The interior was so retro: a vast arching space with scrolled columns, worn velvet seats, an ornate balcony, and wall sconces shaped like castles and knights on horseback. The owner, Garibaldi Pooke, specialized in science-fiction films during the summer and vintage noir crime films in winter.

As always, Granddad chose front-row seats in the balcony. Zoé sat swinging her feet, waiting impatiently for the lights to dim, while images tumbled inside her head: Iris Tintern chasing them out of the café, the way the glass puzzle shimmered, and the eerie painting of Wythernsea by Dr. Marriott's uncle. Then she heard the whir of the projector through a window in the back wall and her attention was riveted on the screen.

Less than fifteen minutes into the film, the picture shuddered to a halt and the lights went on. Far below, a group of teenagers started throwing candy and boxes of popcorn into the air.

"Ladies and gents, the film will recommence shortly," announced Garibaldi Pooke, stepping out from behind the curtains. "And I'm asking you youngsters down in front to refrain from throwing popcorn: we'll not tolerate hooliganism in this theater."

"What's that he's saying?" asked Granddad, fiddling with his hearing aid. "Hooligans in Tenby? Well, I never."

"I'm popping off to the loo," Zoé told her granddad. *Pop off to the loo* was one of her favorite British expressions. "Be right back."

"Fine, Magpie, just steer clear of those troublemakers."

"Righty-o," she said, then whispered to Ian, "I'm taking my puzzle glass and checking things out in the lobby."

Curious to find out what else they could see through the

blue glass, Zoé and Ian had returned to the attic and taken a puzzle piece each from the silver box.

"Copy that," Ian whispered back. "I'll look for clues here in the balcony."

The downstairs lobby, carpeted in red and painted with Italian frescoes, was teeming with people buying snacks and beverages. Zoé waved to her friend Fritha Pooke, one of a few girls in Tenby she occasionally hung out with when she came here for the summer, who was working behind the counter, filling boxes of popcorn with a martyr's bleak expression, her barrettes sparkling in the glare of the lights. Fritha's dad owned the cinema and sometimes gave her free tickets to hand out to friends.

Squeezing between a gigantic fern and a soft drinks machine, Zoé held the glass to her eye and stealthily looked through it, but the recessed lighting made the wall fresco people overlap with the real people until they all blurred together. Disappointed, she headed upstairs to the ladies' water closet (WC for short), more commonly known as the ladies' loo. Although a modern WC had been built off the lobby, the upstairs ladies' loo had an old-fashioned water fountain that Zoé loved, and she found the room oddly charming.

Over the years the ladies' loo, pungent with soap and air freshener, had always been pink: pink walls, pink floor tiles, pink frothy curtains. Even the electric radiator was pink, though most of the paint had flaked off over time. Opposite the porcelain sink was a dressing table painted a soft rose, with a pink ruffle and an oval mirror. Zoé was captivated by the tiny shells glued around the mirror's edges, though each year she noticed a few more had fallen off.

Standing at the window, curtains rippling in the breeze, she gazed down at the cobbled street lined with benches, and the gray waves in the distance, thinking how her mom used to come here when she was Zoé's age. This time of year it didn't grow dark until late, but just before the darkness the air grew hazy—the *gloaming*, Granddad called it—and fairy lights strung from lampposts flickered on.

While she gulped water from the fountain, the door banged open. Wiping a hand across her dripping chin, she saw another girl she knew from past summers in Tenby: Catherine Beedle.

Catherine had a round face and white-blond hair pulled tight against her head and twisted into a ponytail down her back. Her dress, patterned in red-and-black checks, was sort of a cool vintage look, along with her glasses, which had tinted blue lenses and rhinestone cat's-eye frames.

"Hi, Catherine," said Zoé. "I like your new glasses."

"Hiya, Zoé. Thanks," said Catherine. "My mum bought them for me at Zival's." Behind the bluish lenses of her glasses, her eyes looked small and dark.

"I really like the rhinestones," added Zoé, thinking how there was something different about Catherine. The hollowness of her voice perhaps, or the way she kept looking to one side.

"Me too." Catherine set her glasses on the rim of the sink

and turned on the taps, splashing water over her face. Tiny beads of water sprayed across the mirror.

Something's off, thought Zoé, feeling the hairs stand up at the back of her neck. *Why is she wearing blue-tinted glasses the same as Iris Tintern?*

"If I get glasses someday, I'm getting pink frames with tiny shells around the edges," said Zoé. Acting casual, she reached into her pocket for the puzzle-glass, closing her hand around it, anxious to look through the glass at Catherine. "What's Dr. Zival like, anyway?"

"I didn't see Dr. Zival," murmured Catherine, turning off the taps and inspecting her face in the mirror. "Some bloke named Dr. Brown tested my eyes."

Now! thought Zoé, and whisked out the glass piece. When she stared through it, her knees buckled: reflected in the mirror, on Catherine's forehead, was an enormous whirling eye. She stood frozen to the floor as the room seemed to tilt at an angle. In the pale pink light of the ladies' loo, gills appeared on Catherine's neck, and scales began erupting up and down her arms.

Zoé took a step back, her breath coming in short, strangled gasps. *Time to go*, she thought, almost knocking over the dressing table as she bolted past Catherine and out the door. Clattering down to the lobby, she thought she heard Catherine shouting after her.

Diving into the velvety darkness of the theater, Zoé collapsed into the seat next to Ian.

"You're just in time," he whispered.

On the screen, people in fifties-style clothes stood around a table inside a cellar, staring with frightened eyes at a giant alien pod slowly ripping open, revealing a waxen face, smooth and half formed, not quite fully human.

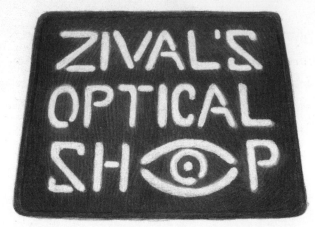

CHAPTER EIGHT
PIPPIN

"You're not getting me back inside that ghastly café tomorrow," declared Ian the next morning as he and Zoé walked through the Old Town, coins jingling in their pockets. It was Saturday, and Granddad had sent them off to buy a loaf of bread and a treat for themselves. "She's a complete lunatic, Iris Tintern. I'm never setting foot in there again."

Exasperated, Zoé rolled her eyes. "But you just said you'd never set foot in the Garibaldi Pavilion Theater either!" After watching *Invasion of the Body Snatchers* and hearing about Catherine Beedle, Ian was becoming super jumpy. "Well, it's no good going to Dr. Marriott's house with Mrs. Prosser bothering us all the time. If we go to the café, we can dress incognito," she added, using one of Ian's secret agent words.

Ian looked thoughtful. "Okay, you've got a point. Dr. Marriott needs to know about the creatures we saw—and about Iris and Catherine, too. Maybe he can explain why all these weird things are happening."

"Nobody else would believe us," said Zoé, "not even Granddad."

"Especially not Granddad," said Ian. "And, oh yeah, there's something else we have to do: find the girl who sold him the puzzle. Hey, look at all those people lined up outside Zival's."

Beneath the orange-and-green neon sign, a new sign flashed: SPECIALIZING IN CUSTOM-DESIGNED, LIGHT-SENSITIVE LENSES. Zoé stared at the dozens of people waiting in a line that snaked past a jeweler's store and a shop selling rare prints, all the way around the corner.

"Catherine Beedle got her blue-tinted glasses from Zival's," she said, shuddering at the memory. "I wonder why so many people are getting them."

There's definitely a creepiness factor here, she thought. Was the sudden popularity of blue-tinted glasses linked to the creatures from the puzzle? Both the glasses and the creatures had appeared in Tenby around the same time. But . . . what exactly was the connection?

Ian shrugged. "Simple: tinted glasses are all the rage. Last summer my dad bought glasses with gray light-sensitive lenses that go dark in the sun. I guess blue's the popular color this year. Hey, know what would be awesome? Dark glasses made of lightweight titanium and you hook tiny mirrors to the sides of them and see who's following you. My friend Jackson back home has a pair."

"Wow," said Zoé, "that's icy cool."

Ian had his career as a code breaker/spy all mapped out. The only obstacles, Zoé knew, were his fear of heights, a tendency to get food poisoning and a habit of falling out of boats—all of which gave Ian's future a complicated edge.

"I need to buy some postcards to send to Mom and Dad," said Ian, heading up the steps to the Captain's Quill Bookshop. "I also want to send some funny ones to Jackson and some of my other friends."

"I'll get one for my mom," said Zoé.

But as she sorted through the postcards, she remembered her mom was traveling all summer without a fixed address, and email was a no-go because Granddad didn't own a computer. She didn't have the addresses of any of her friends with her, either—not that she had many friends.

Oh, kids liked her all right, everywhere she went, maybe because she was good at telling stories and organizing adventure games. But she and her mom moved so much that she never had a chance to make close friends. It used to make her feel like an outsider, but now that she was eleven she thought of herself as an *independent spirit*.

Coming out of the bookshop, Zoé saw a wiry shape run past, wheeling around the corner to Bridge Street: head lowered, elbows pumping, hair streaming from under a black beret. The girl was wearing the same pink jacket with torn pockets over a gray pleated uniform.

"That's her!" cried Zoé. "The girl who found the puzzle!"

Ian whirled around. "Hey!" he shouted. "You in the pink jacket!"

The girl skidded to a stop at Castle Square, crashing into a placard advertising island cruises, as Zoé and Ian raced over.

"What's the problem?" said the girl, setting the placard upright. Narrowing her eyes at Zoé, she added, "Blimey, I remember you."

"I remember *you!*" Zoé shot back. "You're the one who knocked me down and got my special journal all wet and you didn't even say *sorry.*"

"We have a question to ask," said Ian, sounding more like a detective than an eleven-year-old, at least in Zoé's opinion.

"Do you, now?" The girl wiped her nose on her sleeve.

"You bet we do," said Zoé, lowering her voice. "It's about something you sold to our granddad, Mr. Blackwood. He sells antique furniture over by the Five Arches."

"A puzzle," said Ian. Zoé saw a wary expression flit across the girl's face. "You were in a big hurry to get rid of it."

"It was made of glass," added Zoé, "inside a box covered with mud."

"What of it?" said the girl, appearing to recover a bit; she threw back her shoulders. "Mr. Blackwood buys and sells antiques all the time. It was a business deal, that's all."

Zoé glared at her, trying to look fierce.

"We know why you sold the puzzle," said Ian. "You did it because you were afraid."

"You put the puzzle together, didn't you?" said Zoé accusingly. "And something scary happened."

The girl's face turned bright red.

"We put it together, too," whispered Zoé.

"So let's not pretend it's nothing," said Ian. "We're all in this together now."

"I moved here last September from Bargoed," said the girl as they walked beside a ruined wall covered in vines and creepers that was part of the old castle, climbing uphill toward the headland. "I live on Upper Frog Street with my Auntie Gwennie and Uncle Dai; they run a shop filled with all sorts of rubbish they sell to tourists. He's a bit of a horror, Dai, sort of pale and pickled-looking, like he was stuffed in a jar and left overnight." The girl grinned. "Actually Dai's not a bad old sort."

Zoé giggled. Then she frowned, remembering something the girl had said earlier. "Hey, you're not from Tenby, you weren't even born here! If I'm a foreigner here, then so are you."

The girl bristled. "Am not a foreigner. I was born in Nantyglo, Wales, and that counts for something. I'll bet you don't have a British passport."

"I could if I wanted."

"Er, know anything about Zival's?" asked Ian, clearly trying to change the subject. "It's a new optical shop across from the Captain's Quill, and they've put up this garish neon sign. I bet the town fathers are turning in their graves."

Zoé smiled to herself. *Turning in their graves* was one of Granddad's favorite expressions.

"Zival's a mystery, I've heard," said the girl. "Some say he's over seven feet tall, but Mrs. Larkin the postmistress claims no one's ever set eyes on the man."

"I'm Ian Blackwood, by the way," said Ian as they passed beneath a stone archway. "And this is Zoé Badger."

"We're cousins," added Zoé. She was always proud to associate herself with Ian. Even though they didn't look much alike, they had similar ideas and adventurous spirits; to use a phrase her mom was fond of, they were *coconspirators in the game of life.*

"I'm Philippa Jenkyn Thomas." The girl wrinkled her nose. "Everyone calls me Pippin."

Zoé nodded, thinking that Pippin's nickname fitted her perfectly.

They skirted around Tenby Museum, following the path along the headland, a cold wind at their backs.

"Our ancestor was a sea captain," Zoé boasted. "And there's a famous lady pirate who has the same last name as mine."

"Er, why do you live with your aunt and uncle?" asked Ian as they wandered past the ruined castle watchtower.

"Do your parents travel a lot?" Zoé asked. "My mom does. She's a journalist."

For a moment Pippin seemed to be lost inside her thoughts. "My mum took off years ago, and we've not seen her since, and Da lost his job at the factory, so now he travels around, picking up work where he can find it. Last year he ran the Sizzler Twist at the Barry Island funfair."

"Where does your da live, then?" asked Zoé, thinking how unhappy she'd be if she didn't live with her mom. She was lucky, too, having Ian and Granddad, even if she only saw them in the summer. It sounded as if Pippin didn't have anyone.

"Oh, here and there. I fell behind at school because we moved so much, and Auntie Gwennie said I needed a stable home, so that's how I ended up in Tenby. Da visits when he can. I never know when he'll turn up, but he always does—and he always brings me something nice."

Zoé could hardly believe it: Pippin was a borderline orphan, with no mom and her dad away all the time, shipped off to live with distant relatives. How sad was that?

A soft drizzle started as they climbed up onto the cannons outside the coast guard house and looked out across the slate-gray waves.

Pippin described the dusty three-room flat where she lived over her uncle's shop, eating tinned baked beans and watered-down tea (her aunt was a dreadful cook) and licorice humbugs from a jar in the pantry. School was a dead loss, she said, because the headmistress had it in for her, as did her biology teacher, an old geezer named Bascomb.

Zoé could hardly get a sentence in edgewise. When at last Pippin stopped to take a breath, she asked, "But don't your aunt and uncle worry about you?"

"Sure they worry, but they're ever so busy this time of year. They trust me to do my schoolwork and not get into trouble." She ran a grubby hand through her hair. "Even so, sometimes I think about going off with the gypsies, so I could be writing poems instead of studying for biology exams."

"Are you a *writer*?" Zoé looked at her in surprise. "Me too! I'm going to publish runaway bestsellers when I grow up. Thriller novels!"

"Zoé writes real zingy stories about Tenby," said Ian. "Spine-tinglers about evil ghosts and pirates who are bad to the bone."

Hearing this, Zoé puffed out her chest a bit. She could always rely on Ian to be her steadfast fan—well, her *only* fan, actually.

"I'm going to be a poet," said Pippin. "Bronwyn Gilwern at the Captain's Quill Bookshop says I ought to be a poet if I'm not one already, and she should know, she's an expert on runes. See, Bron finds ancient writings in the tunnels and copies them down—even though the tunnels are deadly dangerous—then she plugs 'em into her computer and it spits out translations."

"Your friend goes down into the tunnels?" said Zoé, impressed.

"Hmm," murmured Ian. "I thought they shut down the entrances."

"Oh, Bron isn't fazed," said Pippin airily. "Just the other

day she found a pattern of triskeles; she says they were carved into the rock millennia ago along with a mythic figure she thinks is a goddess."

"Is it Arianrhod?" asked Zoé. "Our granddad has a weathervane with Arianrhod on it." *What is a triskele?* she wondered. It sounded like a breakfast cereal.

Pippin shrugged. "She didn't say. Bron has sort of, well, *mystical* connections. Some call her a seeress, though others say she's right bonkers. Personally I think she's somewhere in between. Bron can float in space if she sets her mind to it: I saw her with my own eyes, one winter's eve, drifting out past Caldey Island."

They jumped off the cannons and Zoé exchanged a dubious glance with Ian as they headed toward the bandstand. Granddad, she knew, would describe Pippin as one of those kids who were *prone to exaggeration.*

"Are you serious?" said Ian. "You saw her *levitate?*"

"Think I'd lie about a thing like that?" said Pippin from the edge of the headland. "Look here, a hidden stairway!" She kicked aside a tall leafy plant, revealing a flight of stone steps overgrown with vegetation.

Going single file, they started down; the steps curved sharply and Zoé nearly fell, Ian grabbing her just in time. She'd worn sandals today, yellow ones with daisies, but maybe next time she'd stick to sneakers.

"Does this Bronwyn Gilwern know spells?" she shouted to Pippin.

The girl shot her an exasperated look. "Dull as foggy

weather, you are. Course Bron knows spells! Shutting spells, maze spells, fog spells, vanishing spells—there's heaps of them. It's a forgotten art, spell conjuring. Has to do with the lost enchantments."

"The lost enchantments?" said Zoé, intrigued. "What are those?"

But Pippin had already vanished down the twisting stairway.

CHAPTER NINE
INTO THE PUZZLE

The crumbling steps spilled out onto Castle Beach, where Zoé, Ian and Pippin walked beneath the cliffs, staring up at the dark, forbidding gap that was Dragon's Mouth, while Ian gave a running commentary on Tenby, pointing out deteriorating sections of the old wall and castle, and St. Catherine's Island with its ruined Victorian fort, so near you could walk there at low tide. Caldey Island, wrapped in fog, was hardly visible.

Ian's tales evoked thrilling scenes of adventure and, as always, Zoé yearned to live in swashbuckling times. It was easy to picture herself and Ian high on the mast of John "Calico Jack" Rackham's pirate ship, the *William*, keeping watch for sea lords and marauders.

They strolled along a dune-backed stretch of golden sands as Ian continued snapping photos. Giggling, Zoé and Pippin made silly faces and posed for him, Zoé turning cartwheels and Pippin throwing her beret into the air. By now the two girls had forged an uneasy truce. And although Pippin annoyed her at times, Zoé was fascinated by her talent for pulling images from thin air and tossing out colorful phrases.

"Here you go," said Pippin, reaching into her torn pocket. "Almost forgot." From a squashed paper bag she extracted three sticky buns, made with doughy pastry and covered in sugar, nuts and cinnamon—a local specialty. "Time for elevenses." She handed one each to Zoé and Ian. "Mrs. Owen the baker gives me her day-olds."

"Wow, thanks," said Zoé, suddenly realizing her stomach was rumbling. She loved what the Brits called *elevenses*, that time of late morning when Granddad turned up with a sweet roll and a cup of milky tea.

"Famished, I am," said Pippin, biting into her sticky bun, looking to Zoé like a street urchin from a Charles Dickens novel. "A bit stale, but never mind."

Ian cleared his throat the way Granddad always did when he had something important to say. "Right, then, the puzzle."

"Tell us, Pippin, tell us what happened, and don't leave anything out," said Zoé as the three sat in the sand above the high-tide mark.

Pippin began, "I was roaming the tunnels, see, back in March, right before they shut them down, keeping an eye out for triskeles and runes and whatnot, so's I could tell Bronwyn Gilwern."

"What's a triskele?" asked Zoé.

"A pre-Celtic symbol made of three curved lines: sort of a triple spiral," said Ian before Pippin could answer. "There's a silver Greek coin in my mom's museum with a triskele on it."

Zoé smiled, impressed as always by Ian's ability to conjure up little-known nuggets of information.

"So I came to a tunnel below Tudor Square," Pippin continued, "when all of a sudden my candle fizzled out and I tripped over something in the mud. It was ever so dark, stinking of low tide and dead fish and all. I'd a trowel in my rucksack, so I started digging and pulled out a box covered in gunk. Popped it into my rucksack and off I went." She tugged at her beret. "I knew straightaway the box was ancient. And it was filled with bits of glass—lovely they were, all blue and glowing like. Real beauties."

Zoé loved the way Pippin pronounced the last word: *bewties*. That's how Granddad talked.

"Did you look through the glass pieces?" asked Ian. "At people, for instance?"

He blushed as Pippin furrowed her eyebrows together, acting as if he'd asked an idiotic question.

"Forget it," he muttered, digging his toes into the sand.

"What did you do then, Pippin?" asked Zoé. "Did you take the box to your friend Bronwyn?"

"I did, but Bron was visiting her sister in Porthcawl, so I went back to my auntie and uncle's flat, straight up to my room. Took me a while to figure out it was a puzzle. Then I wanted to put it together."

"Did you see the island inside the puzzle?" asked Zoé, anxious to know. "And the town with a forest all around it?"

"Aye," said Pippin, scooping up a handful of sand. "But all of a sudden I felt something cold and clammy on my skin." Her expression darkened and Zoé braced herself for what was coming next. "Then these horrible shadowy things came bursting out of the puzzle, with massive eyes on their heads and great huge wings! Gives me the collywobbles just thinking about 'em."

Gazing out at the waves, Zoé felt her stomach turn to lead.

"We saw them, too," she whispered with a shudder.

"How many, Pippin?" asked Ian.

"Just the two, and that were enough. Scared beyond anything, I was, screaming and kicking the puzzle. Then I dropped to my knees and took it apart. Wasn't easy, mind. By then Auntie Gwennie was banging on my door, shouting like a fishwife—'What's all the ruckus?' she wanted to know—and them shadowy things went flapping out the window."

"The creatures we saw flew away, too," said Zoé, her thoughts in turmoil. "We hid the puzzle in our granddad's attic—just in case."

"How many got out when you put it together?" asked Pippin.

"Six or seven, maybe more," Ian replied. "It was too dark to count."

It was too dark and we were too scared, thought Zoé.

"Six or seven?" said Pippin in a choked voice. "Plus my two? Crikey, that's nine of them things! So where did they go?"

"Search me," said Ian. "Out to sea, I hope."

"I don't think so," said Zoé. "I think they're hiding in the tunnels."

Wide-eyed, they stared at one another, their faces ashen.

After stopping at the Old Bakery, Zoé and Ian headed back to their grandfather's cottage. On the way they told Pippin about Iris Tintern and Catherine Beedle and how they'd tracked down Dr. Marriott.

"It's like one of them horror movies at the Garibaldi," said Pippin, waving her arms in a melodramatic manner. "Iris and Catherine with them great horrid eyes, just like the monsters, what's that all about? What sort of evil's creeping into this town?"

"There *is* something evil, isn't there?" whispered Zoé. "I can feel it in the air. It's like a cold tingling all around me."

"I wish we hadn't put the puzzle together," said Ian. "If we'd seen the warning message first, maybe we wouldn't have—"

"I didn't see any message," Pippin cut in. "Then again, I was in a hurry and didn't want Dai to find it. Auntie Gwennie's all right, but he'd take the box and puzzle and sell 'em for a few quid."

The pathos in her voice tugged at Zoé's heart. She couldn't imagine having a relative who'd steal your only treasure.

"So you never see your mum?" she asked Pippin.

"She cleared off, she'll never be back. Da says Mum's a wild spirit and wanted her freedom more than she wanted us, so he let her go."

"My dad jumped ship, too," said Zoé in a small voice. "You know, cleared off." She saw Pippin's eyes widen in surprise.

Nobody's life is ever what you think it is, Zoé reflected. *Isn't that what my mom always says?*

"See you," said Pippin as they turned onto St. George's Street.

"Wait a minute—you can't just leave," said Ian.

"I've homework," said Pippin. "Heaps of it."

"I thought you hated school," said Zoé.

"Yeah, but Da says I need to make something of myself. I'm already in trouble for handing assignments in late and being rude to a teacher. Next time it's detention with old Bascomb—a fate worse than death." Pippin made a gruesome face, causing Zoé to laugh.

"Meet with us tomorrow, okay?" said Ian. "Four o'clock, the King's Ransom. Dr. Marriott's going to be there and you can ask him about the Society of Astercôte and how his uncle saw monsters like we did when he put the puzzle together."

"That's why Dr. Marriott buried it in a tunnel," added Zoé. "He was afraid."

Pippin straightened her beret. "I s'pose this Dr. Marriott will want to meet me, d'you think, seeing as I found the puzzle and all. Right, then, see you tomorrow."

Inside the shop, Granddad was showing a parquetry table to a gentleman in a straw hat and white blazer. Waving, Zoé hurried past, running up the stairway two steps at a time and rushing into the kitchen to place the loaf of wheat bread on the counter.

Moments later the two cousins were standing in the attic doorway, munching on Eccles cakes and debating whether to go inside.

"It's not like we're going to put the puzzle together," said Ian.

"No way," said Zoé, her scalp prickling. "We took it apart to stop those creatures from coming through."

Amid the gloom, she could see the outline of the sea chest, where they'd hidden the puzzle. The chest was authentic, with iron bindings and leather handles, stamped with the name of the owner and that of his ship: CAPTAIN EZEKIEL BLACKWOOD, THE BLACK SWAN.

"Maybe we should check to see if the puzzle's okay," said Ian.

Springing to the chest, they lifted the curved lid and rummaged through layers of wool coats and World War II–era blankets reeking of mothballs.

"Here it is, safe and sound," she said, lifting out the silver box.

They sat on the floor, watching shimmery light flow out

as they opened the box, filling the attic with an eerie glow. It gave Zoé the shivers, but in a good way. Tipping out the puzzle, she noticed tiny bubbles floating inside the glass, winking at her like phantom eyes.

"That light is sort of hypnotizing, isn't it?" murmured Ian.

"Yeah," said Zoé dreamily. *But nothing scary's going to happen,* she told herself, *because we're not going to put the puzzle together.* A radical thought popped into her head. "Wouldn't it be awesome if we started up a *new* Society of Astercôte and all the members were kids?"

"Hey, cutting edge! How cool would that be, traveling to another world?" Ian absentmindedly began moving some of the pieces around. "We could pull Pippin in, make her a member and take her with us."

"I guess," said Zoé with a shrug. "She talks an awful lot, though."

"We could ask everybody we know here," he went on. Having spent so many summers in Tenby, they'd made friends with several kids their age. "What about Philip Fox and Derek Owen? And oh yeah, Fritha Pooke, the Jones twins and Trevor Beedle."

"But we're not asking his sister Catherine," said Zoé with a shiver.

"Hey, y'know what's strange?" Ian went on. "I haven't seen any of those kids around this summer. Hmm, guess they're busy with school and stuff. But I bet you anything they'd be interested in joining."

Zoé heard a soft *click!* as two pieces snapped together, and, forgetting Dr. Marriott's warning, she joined Ian in fitting the other pieces together. The odd thing was she couldn't stop herself. It was as if the puzzle was compelling them to finish it.

Slotting in the final piece, she felt her hair bristle with static. Leaning forward, the two cousins stared into the eerie blue light, thick as a cloud of fireflies, swirling inside the glass.

From deep inside the puzzle came a high, whistling wind, bringing with it the smell of salt air. Zoé heard strange cracking sounds, as if her body were flying apart like the frame of an old house. Then the wind was pulling them through the glass, and, terrified, she grabbed Ian's hand. The next instant the room fell away and they were being swept into the puzzle.

She opened her mouth to scream but nothing came out. Spilling and twisting, they plummeted, deeper and deeper, down a bottomless tunnel. She could no longer feel Ian's hand in hers: there was nothing left to hold. He was disintegrating atom by atom.

Zoé felt lighter than air, streaming through time and space, exploding into motes of light. She realized she was coming apart, too, her body dissolving into molecules, glistening like shattered stars.

CHAPTER TEN
TIME ROVERS

The walls of translucent glass were like cold water flowing over her. Zoé's heart thudded as she heard screams all around, echoing back and forth, and then she realized they were *her* screams. She'd always imagined herself to be fearless, like Spider-Girl or Pippi Longstocking, but it was impossible not to panic.

There was no way to tell how long she'd been falling or whether she was going backward in time or forward. If her heart was beating, didn't that mean she was alive? Alive but transformed. She pictured her atoms being crazily rearranged. What if she wasn't Zoé Badger anymore, but a collection of tumbling particles streaming into infinity?

Warm, clammy air wafted over her and there was an

overpowering scent of seaweed. Lurching and rocking, she spun in circles, capsizing in the air, turning over and over, hair blowing sideways, her T-shirt flapping.

A voice shouted beneath her—it was Ian: "We're losing speeeed!"

Zoé felt herself slowing down, her body turning solid once again. Reflected in the glass walls, she saw her arms and legs, her entire body, still spinning. *I'm still in one piece!* she thought with a thrill of amazement. *I'm still me!*

Through a hazy light she saw a patch of green rising beneath her, telescoped by the walls of the tunnel. Perhaps it was water, or maybe a field of grass. Whatever it was, she hoped it would cushion her fall.

Landing with a hollow thump and curling into a ball, Zoé rolled over moss and ferns and flowers with sharp leaves. Her stomach was still churning as she lifted herself up on her elbows, catching her breath and looking around for Ian. Tiny shells and fronds of seaweed were stuck to her arms and legs; her knees were bleeding, but she hadn't broken any bones.

"Ian!" she yelled, panicking when she couldn't see him anywhere. What if he'd gotten lost on the way down? Her heart started to race. "Ian, where are you?"

"I'm here!" he shouted back, and relief flooded through her. "Are you okay?"

Peering into the mist, she watched him lurch to his feet, dwarfed by giant ferns and bushes, looking like the same Ian she'd always known.

Feeling a lump in her throat, Zoé suddenly realized how much he meant to her. Ian wasn't just any ordinary cousin; he was her friend and confidant, the kid she double-dared to jump from high places, her technical advisor for secret codes and her accomplice in devising cool adventure games. He was the brother she'd never had. Life without Ian, she knew, would be totally drab and boring.

"I'm okay, I just skinned my knees!" She jumped up, shaking her head, watching shells fall from her hair.

"This is total madness. It's unbelievable! Did we really get pulled into the puzzle?" Ian stared at her in baffled amazement. "That means Dr. Marriott was telling us the truth after all."

"I knew that." Zoé had never doubted the professor for a moment.

"We're not on terra firma anymore!" shouted Ian, waving his arms around. "This is absolutely mind-boggling! We're not on planet Earth, Zoé—we've been teleported to another dimension!"

The immensity of what had happened suddenly hit her. Zoé gaped at him in disbelief, wondering what exactly they had gotten themselves into.

"We're in Wythernsea," she whispered.

The landscape held a strange, almost mystical energy, a force so intense she could scarcely breathe. She felt like a traveler without a map, a watcher from another time.

"We're like sea rovers, right?" she said, infused with a wild exhilaration. *Sea rovers* was another term for *pirates*, according to Granddad. "But instead of roving the high seas, we rove through time and space to Wythernsea."

"Time rovers, yeah, that's us," said Ian, brushing leaves and shells from his shorts. "Now . . . where exactly on this island are we? Hmm, that high wall over there must be the one surrounding the town. See, there's the forest over there, on the other side."

Zoé followed his gaze through the mist, to an immense wall of pale gold stone with looming turrets, sweeping down a hill and vanishing into a copse of trees. She recognized it as the wall in Wyndham Marriott's painting. What was different were the thick shards of glass along the top, their jagged ends pointing skyward, interspersed with odd mechanized objects that resembled giant metal claws, turning and snapping at the air.

"Look at those weird machines," said Ian. "Sort of steampunk medieval, yeah? I knew they were keeping something out."

"Enemies," said Zoé with a shiver of alarm, aware that they were thinking the same thing: *I'm sure that's where the creatures we saw come out of the puzzle live . . . over there, on the other side of the wall.*

Beyond the wall, tendrils of fog swirled through dense unyielding vegetation. Overarching trees spilled one over the next, strung with thick moss, forming dark tunnels, their spiked branches sharp and menacing. Inside her head Zoé filed away words like *impenetrable forest, antediluvian* and *primeval,* to write down later in her journal.

"Hey, look!" she shouted, pointing excitedly to a figure of beaten copper: a goddess in a flowing dress, brandishing a shield, stood atop one of the turrets. "It's Arianrhod! Just like Granddad's weathervane!"

"I can see more on the turrets down there," said Ian. "Hmm, strange that they're not moving. The weathervanes look sort of damaged, don't you think? The wall's not in great shape, either; I hope it's strong enough to keep out whatever's on the other side."

"Sure it is," said Zoé, trying to sound upbeat. "That's one tough wall."

On closer inspection she could see the stone had worn away in certain areas, leaving small gaps where vines snaked through from the other side.

Then she heard a burst of distant voices.

"Shhh, someone's coming!" hissed Ian, both of them dropping to the ground.

The voices were getting nearer; marching through the trees were three men in leather boots and shirts the color of corroded tin. One was leading a silvery-white dog on a chain—at least it looked like a dog, but Zoé couldn't be sure.

Keeping low, the two children fled, flinging aside brambles and creepers, trampling over ferns and damp squishy plants. As they plunged headlong into a thicket of gnarled branches, Zoé felt thorns tearing at her skin.

Huddled next to Ian, she held her breath, studying the men's flinty expressions as they inspected the mechanical claws. Their tunics were made of small metal rings linked together, and they carried wooden crossbows like the ones she'd seen at the British Museum. The dog had a wolfhound's face, white crinkly fur, a long snout and webbed paws. Zoé swallowed hard, hoping the animal wouldn't pick up their scent.

Apparently satisfied, the men continued striding along the wall, crossbows drawn. Zoé and Ian crawled on their bellies commando-style through the thicket, emerging on the other side covered in mud and insects.

Sprinting off, they clambered up a steep path lined with trees that shut out the light. As Zoé ran over spongy moss and plants with waving fronds, flaming red petals, thick as leaves, floated down, landing in her hair. She breathed in the salty tang of the sea. Mist turned the air wet and glittery, and more than once she sensed someone watching them through the trees.

The path ended at a wide grassy square on a headland with tall, spreading trees, stone benches and a burbling fountain.

"Water!" gasped Ian.

"Who were those guys in the silver shirts?" asked Zoé as they gulped down handfuls of water. "Did you see their crossbows? Maybe they were olden-day knights."

"Yeah, they looked totally medieval. I think they were wearing chain mail."

Gazing down at the town below, Zoé was instantly charmed by the tiny streets lined with gardens and trees and courtyards, the half-timbered houses with sharp slate roofs and latticed windows. Here the scent of fish was stronger, mixed with the smell of low tide. There were inns and taverns and warehouses, a ruined castle and rows of white pavilions, all leaning over the waterfront. And on every roof spun a goddess weathervane.

With its blurred colors, the port struck her as an otherworldly version of Tenby, evoking the same feeling as Wyndham Marriott's watercolor. On the piers fishermen were unloading their catch, while women with baskets hollered, "Eels for sale!" and "Mussels to buy!" She took mental notes on the crates, wooden barrels and coils of rope; the workers hammering; the market stalls where people in rough clothing milled about. Long narrow boats, painted in bright colors, bobbed up and down in the harbor.

"See their clothes?" said Ian. "Not exactly modern."

"They look like characters out of *Treasure Island*." Zoé had read *Treasure Island*, a birthday gift from Granddad, at least half a dozen times. "Does that mean we traveled to the past?" She was sure they'd landed in some unimaginably distant era.

"Hard to say," he answered with a shrug. "It could be the past, but we can't rule out the future, either. Time's bound to be different here."

"I feel woozy, the way I do when I swim underwater," she said. "It's like I'm floating through layers of time and nothing seems real."

"A timeless watery underworld," murmured Ian, flopping down on the springy grass.

Exhausted, Zoé collapsed on the ground beside him, staring up at the sky, thinking how spookily cool Wythernsea was, her eyes fluttering shut.

When she woke, the light had changed. She bolted upright, heart pounding. Through the falling water of the fountain, a boy in homespun clothes stood staring at her with a curious expression. As he edged nearer, she noted his reddish-orange hair, all shaggy around his face, his mud-covered feet and almond eyes, dark and pensive. His skin seemed almost luminous.

"Wake up, Ian," she said, shaking her cousin. "There's a kid over there!"

Ian's eyes flew open and he sprang to his feet. "What the heck?"

Assuming an aggressive stance, Zoé glowered at the boy. "Hey," she said in her tough-girl voice—the one she used whenever she started a new school. "I saw you sneaking around back there. Why are you following us?"

The boy nodded, his eyes bright. "Yes, I followed." To her surprise, he didn't seem intimidated. "You be travelers? From where do you come?"

"We're rovers," said Zoé. "We come from somewhere really far away." They had traveled not only distance-wise, she realized, but also through time, and there was no way she could explain that.

"If we told you the name of our town, it wouldn't mean anything to you," said Ian. "We're here from a whole other world."

The boy's mouth dropped open.

"This is Wythernsea, yeah?" said Zoé. "Do you live in the town?"

"Course I lives there," said the boy, as if she'd asked a silly question. "There's nowt else but the sea." He inched closer, and she could see his eyes were bright with curiosity. "Can't go to the forest, now can I? Nobody goes there. Not no more, not never."

Zoé fixed him with her gaze. "And that's because ...?"

He gave her a strange look. "Monsters is there, that's why. Them things with glitt'ry eyes that crawl and fly through the trees, staring out at you from their deep, dark swampy caves. Half dead and half alive, they is. They wraps you in their wings and suck the breath right out of you. No one goes to the forest. Leastways, no one with any sense."

"What do you mean, they suck out your breath?" asked Zoé, feeling her stomach turn over.

"They fold their wings right round you and swallow your every breath. And they keeps on swallowin' till there's no more left."

Zoé blinked hard, his words chilling her to the bone.

"Is that why there are those crazy machines and men with crossbows along the wall?" asked Ian, his voice shaky. "Are they protecting everyone?"

"Aye." Cupping his hands, the boy scooped up water from the fountain. "But you daren't mess with them, oh no, not the Defenders. They're a prickly lot, working long hours and always overtired: the stress gets to them." With a start, Zoé noticed webs stretched between each of his long pale fingers, like a frog. "And never mess with their animals. Especially not the barkers. High-strung, they is."

The dog I saw, thought Zoé, *that must've been a barker.*

"Those guys with crossbows, they're Defenders?" asked Ian.

Wiping his mouth on his sleeve, the boy said, "Aye. See, parts of the wall are coming down and they've sent the Defenders to keep the monsters out."

Zoé and Ian exchanged worried glances. *What if the monsters managed to get through?* she wondered. *What would happen then?*

"Name's Gwyn," he went on. "I'm a Messenger. Who be you?"

"I'm Zoé and this is my cousin Ian," said Zoé.

"So . . . where's your house?" asked Ian.

"I lives at the Retreat," said the boy. "We all lives there."

Zoé couldn't believe her ears. "The Retreat for the Rescued, the Lost and the Shipwrecked?" she said excitedly, remembering Granddad's tales of Wythernsea rescues, including their sea captain ancestor. "*That* retreat?"

She saw Gwyn's face light up. "Aye, that's the one," he said, looking surprised. "I'll take you there. Happens I knows a shortcut."

Wythernsea
Retreat

for the rescued, the lost
& the shipwrecked

no one shall be turned
away from this door
as per order of
...

CHAPTER ELEVEN
RETREAT FOR THE RESCUED, THE LOST AND THE SHIPWRECKED

*Z*oé and Ian followed Gwyn down a muddy path and over a bridge. Beneath the wooden boards flowed a river where dragonflies skimmed the water and heron-like animals waded in the shadows near the bank. They weren't birds, exactly, because they didn't have wings. Their necks were long and thin like small giraffes' and they had dense, white glistening fur. *Cute*, thought Zoé, wishing she could take one back with her to Tenby.

"Do you know the date by any chance?" asked Ian as they turned onto a path overhung with moss-laden trees. When Gwyn didn't respond, Ian said, "Er, the year, then. What year are we in?"

Zoé saw a puzzled look cross the boy's face.

"No idea what you're talking about, mate," said Gwyn.

"A timeless watery underworld," murmured Zoé, throwing Ian a crooked smile. Maybe time didn't exist here after all. How freaky would that be?

Gwyn guided them onto a narrow path lined with swaying beeches and tall poplar trees, up a great stone stairway covered in barnacles and seaweed, each footstep crackling the shells beneath them.

"Mind your step," said Gwyn. "These old weeds are right slipp'ry."

Zoé kept glancing at his webbed fingers (she hoped he didn't notice her staring), wondering if he had webs between his toes as well. She couldn't tell because his feet were too muddy.

The stairs led to an impossibly tall structure wreathed in mist, with towers projecting at odd angles and balconies curved like the prows of ships: a strange, fantastical building with a gleaming archway and a great main door of polished wood. Zoé gazed up at the turrets and domes, the copper roofs with different-sized chimneys and goddess weathervanes, and rows of arched windows glimmering with blue light. There was no drawbridge or moat—she was a little disappointed about that—then again, this was a retreat, not a castle.

"There be our entrance," said Gwyn as they passed beneath an archway.

"Know what we're walking under?" Ian said to Zoé.

"A whale's jawbone! See how it's bleached by the sun, and look at all the rows of teeth."

She stared at the teeth, yellow and sharp, protruding from the curved bone, imagining herself being swallowed by a whale.

Gwyn pointed to a sign over the front door. "Cracking brilliant, ain't it? Painted by Miss Glyndower herself."

Zoé read the slanting gold-and-black letters: WYTHERN-SEA RETREAT FOR THE RESCUED, THE LOST & THE SHIP-WRECKED, and, in smaller script: NO ONE SHALL BE TURNED AWAY FROM THIS DOOR, AS PER ORDER OF E. MORWENNA GLYNDOWER.

The three marched up to the door, through which light shone dimly, and Zoé's heart thrummed faster, seeing the life-sized image of Arianrhod carved into the dark wood. The goddess held her shield in a warrior pose, waves rippling beneath her feet.

Reaching up with a froglike hand, Gwyn lifted the worn silver knocker shaped like a crab and let it drop. At the bottom of the door, a square of wood flapped open and Zoé saw two round eyes peer out through a grille.

"That you, Gwyn?" said a high, reedy voice.

"Course it's me. Now open up."

From the other side came the sounds of multiple locks clicking undone. Gwyn rushed forward as the door swung wide, revealing a girl in a cream-colored dress with a scalloped eyelet hem. She wasn't much more than six or seven,

Zoé guessed, with thick braids tumbling down her back and webs glistening between her fingers and toes.

Seeing Zoé and Ian, the girl jumped back with a little gasp.

"Travelers," said Gwyn. "I've brung travelers."

"Never!" whispered the girl, looking frightened and excited all at the same time.

"Quick, Tegan, fetch Miss Glyndower," said Gwyn. "Tell her we've visitors." Zoé watched the girl spin around and race down the hall, braids flying.

They entered a hallway where light fell through narrow windows, illuminating patterns of shells on the walls. Here, too, the smell of the sea was strong and fresh, and Zoé had the same sense of floating underwater. The ceiling was made of glass mosaics: ships sailing across waves, fish leaping, seabirds whirling. There were no square corners anywhere—the edges of the windows and doors were curved—making the Retreat seem welcoming, and more mysterious, too.

At the end of the hallway, through the luminous light, a regal figure stepped forward, garments billowing, reminiscent of the image on the door.

"That be her!" whispered Gwyn. "Our Miss Glyndower!"

The woman striding toward them was surreally tall, taller even than Granddad, with golden eyes and hair streaming in a flaxen cloud. She struck Zoé as a cross between a goddess and a pirate queen, with a hint of lioness thrown in. Whispers echoed down the hallway as a gaggle of children appeared, all dressed in summery colors, among them Tegan.

"Welcome to our Retreat. I daresay this is entirely un-expected," said Miss Glyndower in a formidable tone. Zoé found herself shrinking a bit under the woman's penetrating gaze. "I thought never to see travelers again in Wythernsea."

Behind Miss Glyndower the children murmured to one another, blinking up at Zoé and Ian with curious expressions.

"Haven't been travelers for donkey's years," said Gwyn.

"Long before your time, Gwyn Griffiths," said Miss Glyndower, and Zoé saw the boy flinch at her stern voice.

"I am Miss E. Morwenna Glyndower, overseer of this Retreat," she continued. "Caretaker of lost children, guardian of the Messengers, keeper of all who wash up upon our shores. A distant ancestor of mine was Owain, the last native Welshman to hold the title Prince of Wales."

"I'm Zoé Badger," said Zoé, impressed that this woman was descended from royalty. She thought Miss Glyndower beautiful in a grave, unsettling way, and terribly elegant.

"My name's Ian Blackwood," said Ian, surprising Zoé by bowing with an elegant flourish.

"We're from America," said Zoé, wondering how much Miss Glyndower knew about other worlds. "But we spend summers with our grandfather in Tenby, Wales."

"They's cousins," Gwyn added. "I followed them from the wall." He puffed out his chest. "Then I brung 'em here."

"Nicely done, Gwyn Griffiths," said Miss Glyndower, and Zoé saw the boy's chest expand a bit more.

More children spilled out through doorways and down

staircases, giggling and tumbling onto the floor, one or two waving shyly, all with webs between their fingers and toes.

"Who are the Messengers?" asked Ian.

"You're lookin' at one right 'ere," said Gwyn.

"The Messengers are these children," explained Miss Glyndower. "Their task is to deliver letters and communiqués throughout Wythernsea. They know every nook and cranny of this island—save for the Harshlands, of course."

"I see. Sort of like the postmen in Tenby," said Ian. "Makes sense, I guess, since you probably don't have computers or cell phones."

Miss Glyndower glared down at him. "Whatever are you talking about, young man?"

"Nothing," he muttered, staring at his feet.

"Our grandfather told us all about this retreat," said Zoé, trying to contain her excitement. "He says Wythernsea was famous for rescuing people from the sea, including our great-great-great- . . . well, I'm not sure how many greats—"

"Our ancestor, who was alive before Wythernsea went under the waves," said Ian. "Ezekiel Blackwood."

"*Captain* Ezekiel Blackwood," Zoé went on, hoping to impress Miss Glyndower. "His ship hit the rocks and they saved him, and when he left Wythernsea they gave him a goddess weathervane to take home. She's really beautiful and her eyes are made of blue glass."

Miss Glyndower gave a knowing nod. "Wythernsea glass: handblown glass from this island, renowned for its rich blue color and mystical properties."

Mystical properties? thought Zoé, the words reeling inside her head. Did that mean the weathervane was magic?

"Wythernsea glass is famous in our world, too; you can find it in all the museums," said Ian. "Er, if you don't mind, I have a question about the goddess weathervanes on your town wall, because their copper's oxidized and they've all turned green. Have they been damaged? None of them were turning on the battlements."

"They looked ready to fall off," added Zoé, watching Miss Glyndower's expression grow even more fearsome.

"The weathervanes were sabotaged. We've tried to repair them, but they are quickly deteriorating." Her voice shook with fury. "Thus the mechanized claws were erected and the glass shards put in place. Until now the goddess weathervanes have guarded Wythernsea, deflecting any evil that threatens us, especially our enemies in the Harshlands."

"The Harshlands? That's the forest?" asked Ian.

"The forest, yes, although the Harshlands is no fairy-tale woodlands. Rather it is a bleak, forsaken, no-man's-land of twisted trees and bottomless swamps."

Zoé felt a shiver go through her. What if they'd landed on that side of the wall, where the monsters lived? Not a pleasant thought.

A boy with light red hair brittle as icicles appeared with a tray, handing out apricots, plums and goblets of water.

"Fresh water drawn from our well," said Miss Glyndower.

Zoé couldn't help staring at Miss Glyndower's intense golden eyes, her long fingers strung with webs, and the voluminous mane of hair that seemed woven from strands of light. As with everything else in Wythernsea, thought Zoé, she didn't appear to be quite real—at least, what *used* to seem real.

"We've all webbed hands and feet: vestiges of drowned Wythernsea," said Miss Glyndower, and Zoé blushed, realizing she'd been caught staring. "Over time we humans have had to adapt to this damp, misty world."

"We's all got webs," said Gwyn. "You's the ones who's diff'rent."

"I know," said Zoé, smiling sheepishly, and he grinned back at her.

"If you will follow me," said Miss Glyndower.

The younger children laughed and cheered as they formed an uneven line, trailing Miss Glyndower down the hall like ducklings, then up a spiraling stairway.

"She's taking us to the grand balcony," Gwyn whispered.

Zoé walked out onto a terrace of gleaming stone entwined with plants; it had a carved balustrade and silk awnings that fluttered in the wind like the sails of a ship. Standing on her toes for a better view, she looked down over the sloping rooftops of Wythernsea. Some of the smaller kids edged next to her, touching the hem of her T-shirt and staring with inquisitive eyes, making her feel like a celebrity.

"The young ones have heard tales of travelers, but never have they seen one," said Miss Glyndower. Hair drifted around her face in glassy filaments, and Zoé thought again how she resembled a lioness. "Sadly, the last travelers who came to Wythernsea fell prey to Scravens."

"You mean . . . the *Astercôtes?*" said Ian, glancing at Zoé. A look of understanding flashed between them.

"Then there really are monsters in the forest?" asked Zoé, struck by an icy numbness. "You call them *Scravens?*" It was an ugly-sounding word. But monsters weren't real, she told herself, everybody knew that; they were just . . . made up. Weren't they?

"Monsters, Scravens, call them what you will," replied Miss Glyndower, waving a dismissive hand. "Their his· tory is devastating. You see, Scravens were once human— Wythernfolk, like us."

Zoé gasped. The creatures they saw fly out of the puzzle had been *human?*

"Scientifically speaking," said Ian, "I'd say that's impossible."

"In your world, perhaps," said Miss Glyndower. "As you know, centuries ago Wythernsea was lost beneath the waves. What happened next was beyond imagining: our island was transported to this far-flung sphere, placed within a confluence of light and mist. To everyone's astonishment, many Wythernfolk acquired healing powers, and we shared our knowledge with travelers from your world and other worlds."

So what Dr. Marriott told us is true, thought Zoé. *There must be all kinds of different worlds out there, with their own secret gateways, and travelers going back and forth between them!*

"One group of Wythernfolk was violently opposed to sharing our knowledge of the medicinal arts with outsiders. So they formed a secret society and made a pact amongst themselves," Miss Glyndower continued, her voice growing melancholic. "When travelers to Wythernsea began to mysteriously disappear, it was discovered that this secret group had done away with them."

Zoé swallowed hard. She was pretty sure that *done away with* meant *killed*.

"Under the high laws they were banished to the Harshlands, living as exiles in the swamps, growing gills and wings, transforming from light-filled beings into creatures of darkness, attacking any travelers who passed this way." Miss Glyndower paused, staring into the distance. "However, do not mistake Scravens for beasts: they are highly intelligent and extraordinarily devious."

I had a feeling the Scravens were smart, thought Zoé. *That explains how they figured out a way to go through the puzzle.*

Miss Glyndower rubbed her finger against her forehead, and Zoé gaped in wonder as an eye of smoky quartz appeared. "All Wythernfolk have *shallows*—what you call third eyes—and through them we take nourishment from the light. Our shallows connect us to spiritual beings in other realms. But the Scravens' shallows have lost this connection, instead drawing energy from the dark. They seek not enlightenment but evil."

"We saw them!" Zoé burst out. "We saw Scravens in our grandfather's attic and they had these horrible whirling eyes!"

"We have this glass puzzle, see," explained Ian. "It belonged to the Astercôtes, but now our granddad owns it, and when Zoé and I put it together these Scravens came flying out."

"The puzzle's a gateway to Wythernsea," said Zoé as Miss Glyndower's expression grew stormier. "But Dr. Marriott says it's flawed and he warned us not to put it together, but that was after we already had! And we didn't know anything about the Scravens! I think they're in the tunnels. There are *heaps* of tunnels in Tenby," she added, using Pippin's expression, "and I really think that's where they're hiding."

"But why do Scravens want to come into our world?" asked Ian.

Miss Glyndower reflected. "You may not know this, but time is not a constant here. In Wythernsea, time passes slowly in the light and we Wythernfolk hardly age at all, whereas the Scravens age quickly, since time passes extremely fast in the darkness of the Harshlands."

Zoé glanced at Ian, certain that Miss Glyndower was probably far, far older than they'd first imagined.

Leaning forward, Miss Glyndower went on, "In Tenby, the Scravens will be able to slow down their aging process and extend their longevity. By exposing their third eyes to the light, they'll regain the powers they've lost—including the ability to connect with other realms—not spiritual realms, but ones that are corrupt and malevolent." She gave an anguished sigh. "Tenby will be for them a new beginning, the chance to spread evil into another world."

CHAPTER TWELVE
THE DARKNESS OF NO RETURN

Zoé gripped the balustrade as a cold wave of fear broke over her. The Scravens were planning to live in Tenby? She and Ian had to go back—*pronto*, as her mom would say—because Granddad was in danger. So were Pippin and Dr. Marriott, and everyone else who lived in Tenby. The whole town was at risk of being invaded by Scravens.

"But Scravens like the dark," she argued. "There's too much sunlight in Tenby, they'll hate it there."

"They fear the light, it is true," replied Miss Glyndower, "but I suspect they'll gradually infiltrate your world. Remember, they are sly—and extremely clever."

Ian blanched. "You mean they'll worm their way into Tenby?"

Miss Glyndower nodded and Zoé felt her throat go hollow as she remembered the creatures from the puzzle—and Iris and Catherine, too.

"Why don't the Scravens infiltrate the town of Wythernsea instead?" she asked.

"They've no desire to live here. This place and its people symbolize a catastrophic chapter in their history," Miss Glyndower explained. "The Scravens seek revenge for being exiled to the Harshlands: they want only to destroy Wythernsea and everything in it—leaving nothing behind."

Zoé sucked in her breath, thinking how devastated she'd be if Wythernsea was torn apart by Scravens.

"Do you think our granddad's safe?" she asked, feeling more anxious by the moment. "Will the goddess weathervane protect him?"

"So long as the weathervane is on the roof of your grandfather's house, Scravens cannot enter."

That was a relief to hear—sort of. Still, Zoé was terrified. After all, Granddad loved going for walks by the sea and stopping by the Saracen's Head Pub for cider and vinegar crisps. The weathervane wouldn't protect him then.

Miss Glyndower held them with her severe gaze. "When you return to Tenby, you must track down the leader of the Scravens—otherwise known as The First—because he or she was the initial Scraven to escape into your world. The First is the mastermind behind the invasion and is extremely powerful. We need to identify who it is to plan our counterattack."

Zoé felt panic rising within her. *Track down the Scravens' head honcho? How are we supposed to do that?* And what could she and Ian actually do? They couldn't go looking in the tunnels because the entrances were closed, and, aside from Pippin and Dr. Marriott, who would believe that Scravens existed? She had a hard time believing it herself.

As if reading her mind, Miss Glyndower said, "I understand that what I'm asking of you may seem an impossibility. It is undoubtedly a dangerous venture. But you should think hard if you feel you cannot do this. Scravens are invading your world, and so the burden falls onto you."

Too upset to speak, Zoé stood fighting back tears, while all around her the web-fingered, web-toed children played, oblivious to their conversation, singing songs and wrestling and hanging over the edge of the balcony.

Miss Glyndower reached into the folds of her gown, extracting two glass-topped bottles. They looked like small perfume bottles, the kind Zoé's mom kept on her dresser, only these were filled with a silver liquid.

"Vials of mist from Wythernsea, extremely rare and extremely potent. There are but a few left in existence." She handed them each a bottle. "The mist will hold off an attacking Scraven."

Zoé cringed at the phrase *attacking Scraven*. Not exactly warm and fuzzy words.

"Uncork the stopper and mist will flow out," said Miss Glyndower. "Choose your moment wisely: once a vial is broken, you must use it all."

This is it? thought Zoé, throwing Ian a worried glance. *We're going to defeat the Scravens with two tiny bottles of mist?*

"Look, the sun's going down!" said Ian. "We've got to get back."

Zoé felt a fresh stab of panic. "Oh no, I hope Granddad isn't wondering where we are."

"There is no need to worry. In your world only a few minutes have passed," said Miss Glyndower reassuringly. "Be warned, however: it is during this brief time that the Scravens have a window. And although they are weakest in daytime, they are still capable of escaping through the puzzle into your world."

"There's no way we can stop them?" asked Ian.

"Unfortunately, no. Not if the gateway is flawed."

How many Scravens are getting through the puzzle this very minute? wondered Zoé. *And how on earth are we supposed to fight them off? Forget it, this whole quest is totally hopeless.* After all, she and Ian weren't unstoppable superhero kids with magical powers who could fend off Scravens and save the world. Not in real life, anyway. They were just ordinary kids who liked to play scary games.

"While you are gone, I shall devise a strategy to rid both our worlds of the Scravens forever," said Miss Glyndower, walking with a vigorous step down the hallway. "The Scravens are treacherous foes and you must anticipate their every move. They will try to drag you down into their darkness—a darkness from where there is no return."

"But how do we fight them?" asked Ian. "We're just kids."

"There is an ancient runestone in your world which the Astercôtes took back with them from Wythernsea, rather small as runestones go. Inscribed on it is the Incantation of Arianrhod. You must find this stone: it is crucial to defeating the Scravens."

Oh great, thought Zoé, *one more impossible task.*

"Our granddad told us that there are thousands of runestones in the British Isles," said Ian. "Remember, Zoé?"

"Umm, not sure," she said. Those kinds of things tended to slip her memory, whereas Ian always remembered historical facts down to the minutest details. She looked up at Miss Glyndower. "Did you give the runestone to the Astercôtes?"

"I did, yes, as a protection against the Scravens. The incantation has far-reaching powers, for it was written by the goddess herself."

"Arianrhod was *real?*" Zoé felt as if the top of her head were flying off. She never realized that deities such as Arianrhod had actually walked the earth.

"Most definitely." Miss Glendower thought a moment. "The Astercôtes had connections with the Tenby Museum, as I remember, and to ensure the runestone's safety they kept it on display within one of the smaller locked cabinets. As far as I know, the stone is still there."

"Wait a minute," said Ian. "You want us to *steal* the runestone from the Tenby Museum? But everything's behind glass! Not to mention all the surveillance cameras. We'll get arrested!"

"If the Scravens are devious, you must be twice as devious," Miss Glyndower shot back. "You must find a way. And we have to move quickly. Midsummer's Day approaches, the longest day of the year: we shall strike then, when the Scravens are at their weakest. We've only six days left."

Wow, thought Zoé, *this is getting more complicated by the minute.* Through a row of arched windows she glimpsed the Harshlands, and the sight of the gloomy forest filled her with dread.

"So you think Arianrhod is the Scravens' Achilles' heel?" Ian was asking Miss Glyndower.

"You could say that, yes."

Zoé had only a vague idea what *Achilles' heel* meant—it sounded mythical. "What's an Achilles' heel?" she whispered to Ian.

"Achilles was a Greek god," he whispered back. "He had one weak spot and that was his heel."

"Got it," said Zoé as Miss Glyndower ushered them through an archway made of a small whale's jawbone, into a soaring chamber with a domed glass ceiling through which light filtered down. Zoé could see faint patterns of starfish, shells and sea horses embedded in the walls, and again she had the sensation of floating beneath the sea.

"This is the original gateway to Tenby, made of Wythernsea glass," said Miss Glyndower, pointing to the ceiling. "It is the way back to Tenby."

Zoé stared up at the glass, which gave off waves of swirling blue light.

"Holy moly," said Ian.

"The Scravens are weakest in the day, because of the light, but remember: the moment you return, take apart the puzzle, for they are still capable of escaping," said Miss Glyndower, placing a hand on each of the children's shoulders. "May the goddess Arianrhod give you strength," she whispered, kissing Zoé and Ian in the exact spot where, if they had one, their third eye would be.

"How exactly do we get through there?" asked Ian, frowning up at the ceiling, looking like he was trying to solve a difficult math problem.

"Follow the light," she whispered.

Then she was gone.

"Miss Glyndower sure likes to talk in riddles," said Ian. "I hope she hasn't made any serious miscalculations. What if—"

"Hey, how old do you think she really is?" asked Zoé. "Like, a hundred years? Two hundred?"

But Ian wasn't listening. Instead he was staring open-mouthed at the ceiling, which was lowering, coming closer and closer, until it was only inches above their heads. Zoé felt a tingling through her body, her hair bristling with static, as she watched Ian slowly come apart, condensing into fine sparkling dust. Then she began to dissolve, too, atom by atom.

The glass closed over her and Ian, pulling them in as the room fell away, sweeping them down a tunnel of glass. Zoé's last thought was tinged with regret: they hadn't said goodbye to Gwyn and Tegan.

CHAPTER THIRTEEN
PIRATES, WRECKERS AND RUSTED DAGGERS

Zoé felt the floorboards beneath her and knew at once she was back in her grandfather's attic. Ian sat nearby, rubbing the back of his head, his wiry hair sticking up all over the place.

Leaning on one elbow, she stared up at the vaulted beams arching into darkness. Outside the window the fog had thickened, graying the light. Nothing seemed to have changed and she wondered how long they'd been gone. A half-formed thought nagged at her: Miss Glyndower telling them to do something when they returned. But . . . *what?*

"Was I hallucinating?" asked Ian, sitting up and looking

around. "Did we really go through the glass puzzle to Wythernsea?"

"The puzzle pulled us in," said Zoé, feeling light-headed. "And we met Gwyn and Tegan and Miss Glyndower. They're all *real*—well, sort of—and Wythernsea is real, too." She held out the vial of mist from Miss Glyndower. "Look, here's proof."

Ian reached into his pocket and, pulling out the second vial, stared at it in disbelief.

"Oh no!" cried Zoé, scrambling to her feet. Dark twisted shapes were rising out of the puzzle, eyes glowing, whirling up into the air. "We're supposed to take the puzzle apart!"

They sprinted over and in a wild panic Zoé wrenched away one of the pieces, sending it flying across the room.

"Careful, you'll break the glass," said Ian, his voice taut. "I showed you, remember? Work from the outside."

Zoé tried to work methodically, but it was hard to concentrate with the Scravens circling overhead. If she looked up, she could see the leathery undersides of their wings—the sound of them scraping the beams made her want to crawl out of her skin—and cruddy black scales kept falling onto the floor next to her.

As Ian dropped the last piece into the box, the Scravens gathered into a quivering mass, shrieking madly. Hurtling out of the window, they flapped away into the mist.

"This is our fault! We let them in," said Ian, placing the box at the bottom of the sea chest. "We shouldn't have put the puzzle together."

"I know," whispered Zoé. "I didn't mean to, really. I think the light hypnotized me."

The cousins exchanged guilty looks. How many Scravens had they just set loose on Tenby?

"I wonder what the time is." Ian secured the wooden lid. "I hope Granddad didn't notice we were gone."

"Zoé, Ian!" Granddad's voice floated up the stairwell. "Time for a cup of tea!"

"That answers your question," said Zoé. Granddad, she knew, always served tea at exactly four o'clock in the afternoon—which meant they'd been gone less than fifteen minutes.

The next morning, umbrellas aloft, Zoé and Ian trooped behind their grandfather up a cobbled lane bordered on one side by the castle ruins, heads bowed against the pelting rain. Their trip to Caldey Island had been called off due to stormy weather, so Ian had suggested spending the morning at Tenby Museum. In the afternoon the two cousins would be meeting up with Pippin and Dr. Marriott.

Inside their pockets they carried the vials of mist—"just in case," they whispered to one another—and a puzzle-glass each. Ian joked around, calling them Scraven-Detector Kits, as if this were one of their made-up adventure games. Zoé knew he was trying to keep her from being frightened: a typical Ian gesture, which she appreciated. After all, he was probably just as scared as she was.

Zoé gazed up at the high rocky headland before them, rising out of the sea like a green-humped dragon. Since leaving the cottage she'd been keeping an eye out for Scravens—or anyone who might have been tainted by the evil infiltrating Tenby. So far she'd encountered two little kids floating homemade boats in a gutter and Mrs. Owen from the Old Bakery walking her Welsh terrier.

Finding the runestone would be tricky, she knew, but how were they going to track down The First? It seemed that Miss Glyndower had given them an impossible task.

Granddad, in a long raincoat, scarf and galoshes, stopped to catch his breath halfway up Castle Hill. "This time of year, we're never certain of the weather. Glorious one minute, then ghastly the next," he puffed. "I expect you won't be taking many photos today, Ian my boy."

"That's okay," said Ian. "I'll spend my time in the museum soaking up Tenby's history."

"You'll find some rather bleak moments, I daresay," said Granddad. "In the tenth century, bands of Vikings stormed the coast. Right terrors they were, too. The pirate John Paul Jones met his fate on Caldey Island, where his bones were found wedged between the rocks."

Zoé gave a low whistle. The pirate bones story was Granddad's favorite tale, and it never failed to give her the creeps.

"Don't get me wrong, real pirates were in no way romantic," Granddad went on, striding once more up the hill. "They were vicious and deadly—and a good number of them were Welsh."

"And did kids like me and Ian run away to sea?" she asked, as she often did.

"Most certainly, little Magpie," he replied, steering them through the crumbling stone archway to the museum. "Back then there were more child pirates from Wales than you could shake a stick at."

They left their umbrellas and coats in the museum entryway, and Granddad gravitated to his favorite exhibit—the birds of prey—while Zoé and Ian stood on either side of him, gazing solemnly at the rooks, ravens and carrion crows. Zoé never tired of hearing Granddad talk about the ravens in the Tower of London, and how for centuries they'd guarded it day and night. If ever the ravens abandoned the tower, Granddad declared, the tower would most certainly fall.

Hmm, she thought, *Wythernsea could definitely use a few ravens.*

"Anyone keen on fossils?" said a high, nasal voice. "We've an exceptional specimen on display in our fossils collection."

"Ah, Julian, nice to see you," said Granddad, shaking hands with a tall, thin man in a tweed jacket and old-fashioned trousers, hair brushed neatly back. "I've my grandchildren with me today. Zoé and Ian, you remember Dr. Thistle. He's head curator here."

Dr. Thistle nodded distractedly and Zoé noticed with a start that he wore rimless round spectacles with blue-tinted lenses, exactly like Iris's and Catherine's. *Uh-oh*, she thought, looking over at Ian, *this could be enemy territory.*

"Hello," he said, his eyes sliding past them. Zoé could see

he was clearly more interested in his fossils. "You're in luck," he continued, guiding them over to a glass-topped cabinet. "Look here: five fossilized brittlestars with arms interlinked. Found in a peat bog near the River Usk."

"Peat bogs preserve things marvelously, don't they?" murmured Granddad.

Pressing her face to the glass, Zoé studied the handwritten cards describing a Cenozoic crab, a prehistoric egg, two Usk beetles and a trilobite. She took out her notebook, writing down the names of the specimens, taking care to spell them correctly, and drawing trilobites and beetles in the margins. She loved fossils, especially small, delicate, ethereal-looking ones.

"Excuse me, Dr. Thistle," said Ian, his voice quavering a little. "Do you have any runestones? I'm doing a special history project on Tenby and I think old medieval runestones are fascinating." He held up his camera. "Would it be all right if I took some photos?"

"I'm his fact checker," said Zoé importantly, but already she could see Dr. Thistle shaking his head, lips set in a tight line.

"Photos are not allowed," said the curator. "In any case, we haven't any runestones. You'll have to inquire at the National Museum in Cardiff."

"I was sure there was a small runestone here," Ian persisted, "in one of your glass cabinets."

Zoé grinned. She'd always admired her cousin's stubbornness, probably because she had a stubborn streak, too.

"Maybe it's locked in a closet somewhere," she suggested.

Dr. Thistle gave a dry laugh. "Not very likely. I would be aware if we had such a prominent artifact on the premises. However, we have an ancient reliquary on display, discovered by a man digging up a wild cat on Caldey Island." He pointed in an abstracted manner, adding dismissively, "Permanent Exhibits, next room over."

He walked off and rejoined their grandfather, who had moved on to the mammoth teeth. Zoé and Ian exchanged disappointed glances.

"Think he's hiding something?" Zoé whispered. To her, the curator came off as one of those superior-acting Brits her mom was always going on about.

"He acted a bit cagey," Ian whispered back. "Wouldn't even look us in the eye. I'm wondering, what if Miss Glyndower had it wrong about the runestone? Old people are forgetful sometimes, and maybe she's mixed up."

"No way," huffed Zoé. "Miss Glyndower is ageless and brilliant and her brain's in perfect shape. She'd never forget something as important as a runestone."

"I guess not," said Ian, scratching his head. "I just hope she's being straight with us. I mean, how does she know so much about Tenby when she lives in a totally different universe? What if Miss Glyndower's mixed up with the Scravens and we don't know it?"

Zoé threw him a withering look. "I trust Miss Glyndower, that's all. She seems, well, *authentic.*"

Authentic was a journalistic word her mom used, along

with *verifiable* and *factual*. Zoé felt a sudden pang, realizing she missed her mom. If her mother were here, she'd tell her about all the peculiar things going on in Tenby. Zoé imagined her mom going wide-eyed, pretending to be scared, though of course she wouldn't believe a word of it.

"Let's split up," said Ian. "I'll stay with Granddad and check out the first floor, maybe get a look at Dr. Thistle through the puzzle piece. You can investigate the second floor."

"I'm on it," she said, leaving Ian and Granddad to browse through models of old ships and climbing up to the Maritime Gallery. It was her favorite exhibit, filled with compasses and sextants and foghorns, a swivel saker gun and the figurehead of a knight from a sunken ship.

When she saw the case marked *Pirate Trove*, Zoé felt a thrill go through her like an electric charge, certain that if this were the sixteen hundreds she'd be running off to sea. Inside were coins flattened by time, rusted daggers, and a pistol with a mother-of-pearl handle. RECOVERED FROM THE WRECK OF THE BLUE SPEEDWELL, LOST OFF CALDEY ISLAND, ASH WEDNESDAY 1602, read the placard. THE REMAINS OF THE CREW WERE NEVER FOUND. She wondered if the inhabitants of Wythernsea had tried to rescue them.

Zoé leaned against the case writing in her journal, imagining pirates with uncombed beards and pitted skin, cursing and spitting fish bones through gold-plated teeth. Dressed in bold colors, they creaked about the ship in leather boots; on rainy days, which were frequent, they sat around cheating at dice games, quick to lose their tempers.

"A bloodthirsty era, to be sure," said a splintery voice.

Spinning around, she saw in the doorway a short man wearing an official-looking jacket over a rumpled sweater. His mouth looked as if it had been drawn with the flick of a pencil.

"Piracy flourished for centuries in these waters, John Paul Jones being the most notorious pirate of all. One of his officers, known as 'Leekie' Porridge, was Tenby born and bred." There were creases around the man's eyes, like a child's scribbling, and his hair hung in oily curls. "The seas were dangerous, what with them pirates and the wreckers," he added in an ominous tone.

"My granddad has heaps of books about pirates, like Charlotte Badger and Calico Jack, and I've read every single one. He's told me stories about John Paul Jones, too." Noticing a badge on the man's lapel, she asked, "Um, do you work here?"

"I do. Happens, too, I know local history better than most." Sidling into the room, he glared at her from beneath his thick brows. "The name's Stokes. I'm assistant curator."

"I'm Zoé." *Maybe this Stokes can help me find the runestone,* she thought. "What are wreckers?"

"Thieves, for want of a better word." The man's voice was like something rusty being scraped with a knife. "Stood on the cliffs of Caldey in the dead of night, swinging lanterns to lure passing ships. Afore long a ship sails past and makes for the light, then . . . *crack!*" A tiny spray of spittle flew from his lips, and Zoé's stomach turned over. "The ship breaks up on the rocks and, like horrible crabs, the wreckers scuttle down, picking the wreckage clean."

"But . . . why didn't the Wythernsea people stop them?" asked Zoé, confused. "Why didn't they fight off the wreckers?"

"Now, that's rich." Stokes gave what Zoé considered a rude snigger. "Wythernsea fell beneath the waves in 1349."

"Oh yeah," she said. "I forgot." Ian, of course, would have known that. And she'd known the date, too—but this Stokes character was throwing her off guard.

"Folks in Tenby turned a blind eye to the smuggling that went on here, and I daresay there were some who profited handsomely," he said with a smirk. "Very handsomely indeed."

"What did the wreckers do with all the stuff they took?" asked Zoé. "Did they hide their treasures in the tunnels?"

"Heard about the tunnels, have you?" Stokes's eyes glittered, as if he'd been waiting for her to mention them. "Bleeding treacherous, the tunnels. Many an unsuspecting soul has gone down there, never to be seen nor heard of again. You don't half know what goes on in the tunnels."

As he spoke, the light shifted and a stillness fell over the room. The only sound Zoé heard was from her own heart, which thudded steadily against her ribs. She wouldn't be surprised if Stokes was working as a spy for the Scravens. He definitely seemed like what Granddad called an *unsavory character*.

A smile worked its way into the corners of Stokes's thin, dry lips. "And when the fog comes rolling in, no one dares go down the tunnels."

"The tunnels don't bother me," said Zoé, determined not to be frightened. "My granddad's taken me down plenty of times and never once did I get scared." She gazed at Stokes's sweater, which was riddled with holes, the wool unraveling around his neck. "Anyway, my cousin Ian's doing a history project on Tenby and he's trying to find an ancient runestone so he can take pictures of it and stuff. We know it's in this museum, but we can't find it anywhere."

Stokes's eyes grew flinty. "The *runestone?* How d'you know about that, then, eh? I can't rightly say where it is, as we've no end of storage rooms and closets filled to overflowing. Museum's not large enough to hold all the relics and artifacts, so we have to rotate."

"But the runestone's real, right?" *What a breakthrough,* she thought. *I can't wait to tell Ian!* "And it's here, in the museum?"

"What's it worth to you, eh?" said Stokes in a sniveling voice. "If I tell you, how much will you give? Information like that don't come free, y'know. Around these parts, old secrets are the equivalent of gold."

Was he trying to blackmail her? Before Zoé could say a word, she saw Dr. Thistle appear in the doorway with a trolley stacked with boxes.

"Stokes, are you in there? Give us a hand, will you, old fellow?"

Without a backward glance, Stokes limped out of the room, knees cracking like dry twigs, and left Zoé on her own, wondering how much the old man actually knew.

CHAPTER FOURTEEN
THE KEY TO THE TOMBS

"So the runestone exists—somewhere. First-class detective work, Zoé," said Ian as they walked down Lower Frog Street to the sea. She beamed; praise from Ian was always hard-earned.

The rain had eased up, and Granddad was back at the cottage taking a nap. This was the first chance she'd had to tell her cousin about Stokes.

"Did you look at Dr. Thistle through your puzzle piece?" she asked.

He shook his head. "Zero opportunities. Sorry."

"I wish I could tell my mom we were searching for a runestone, because she likes things that are mysterious and offbeat," she said wistfully. "My mom would think a hidden runestone was the ultimate in cool, and she'd write a front-page story about it, with lots of color photographs and a catchy headline." She pushed back her dark fringe of hair. "Well, maybe not, because she'd have to come to Wales to write it."

"My mom and dad would ask a million questions. I can hear them now," said Ian. "But even if I told them about Wythernsea and the Scravens, they'd never believe me. When I called them the other day, all they talked about was some boring river cruise in Prague. They couldn't handle it if I told them Tenby's about to be invaded."

"Parents, hmph," said Zoé, but still she felt a twinge of envy. She hadn't talked to her mother since coming to Wales, because her mom had lost her cell phone right before Zoé left and there was no way to get in touch with her.

"If we're to believe this Stokes character, the runestone exists, but he can't tell us where it is. Or maybe he knows and he's not saying," said Ian. "So it's up to us to track it down."

"Right," said Zoé. "And, oh yeah, we have to find The First and destroy the Scravens. *No problemo*, as my mom would say." She thought a moment. "I've never met anybody as peculiar as Stokes."

"Yes, you have," said Ian, grinning. "Iris Tintern!"

"Hah! Those two would make a right pair," she said with a giggle—*right pair* was one of Granddad's phrases—and they both laughed. "Stokes kept going on about the tunnels and pirates and wreckers. He tried to scare me, but it didn't work. When I asked about the runestone, he said 'What's it worth to you?' Then he said old secrets are like gold."

"He sounds shady," said Ian. "Stokes could be lying."

"I have a feeling he was telling the truth about the runestone. His eyes lit up when I mentioned it."

"Stokes is our only lead so far," said Ian, going into secret agent mode. "Better keep communication lines open."

"Hey, why would Iris and Catherine be in cahoots with the Scravens?" mused Zoé. "They were *born* in Tenby!"

"No idea," Ian replied. "I wonder if they have information on where the Scravens are hiding? Maybe they're spying for them."

"Maybe they know who The First is!"

Moments later they were sitting at a recently vacated table amid the bustle of the King's Ransom Café. Zoé had dressed up for their meeting with Dr. Marriott in a long Indian skirt stitched with beads and tiny mirrors, a T-shirt embossed with CAT WOMAN STRIKES AGAIN! and a short-sleeved pink hoodie. To top it off, she wore a bracelet made from typewriter keys. She was sure Dr. Marriott would love it, seeing as typewriters were right up his alley.

She had her hood flipped up, and Ian was wearing his Red Sox baseball cap. Ian had taken up her suggestion that they arrive incognito, so that Iris Tintern wouldn't recognize them. It would be a disaster if she did, since last time Iris had gone berserk and chased them out of the café.

To Zoé's surprise, all the seats in the café were filling up fast, and she realized extra tables had been squeezed in wherever there was room. Iris scurried from one customer to the next, rattling off menu choices of "sausages and . . . ," "bacon with . . ." and "mushrooms or . . ." and slamming down pots of tea with the food. *Iris sure has a unique style,* she thought.

A long queue had formed, snaking out through the front door. All the times Zoé had been to the King's Ransom Café, she'd never seen more than a handful of people, but today the place was jam-packed. Odder still, everyone was wearing blue-tinted glasses.

"Look through your puzzle-glass," she whispered to Ian. "But don't let anyone see you."

"Copy that," he said. "A good CIA operative is always discreet."

"Hiya," said Pippin, appearing out of nowhere, hair fluttering beneath her beret. "Crikey, what's going on? Where did all these people come from? And everyone's got specs on! This café is usually zombie land. How'd you get a table?"

"I saw a group leave and we rushed in," explained Zoé.

"Maybe there's an optometrists' convention in town," joked Ian. "Hey, I know: they're all beta testers! Dr. Zival's paying them to try out his tinted glasses."

"I don't think so," said Zoé. Ian was sometimes a bit over the top. Still, the sight of all those blue lenses gave her an uneasy feeling.

"Hey, would you like to meet my friend Bronwyn Gilwern?" asked Pippin, pulling up a chair. "Bron's off work tomorrow, says she'll be at her favorite hangout by the sea and we can stop by after I get out of school."

Ian nodded enthusiastically.

"I'd love to meet a real seeress," said Zoé, thinking how Pippin was turning out to be a good friend after all.

"Pippin, do you know a Mr. Stokes?" asked Ian.

"He works at the Tenby Museum and tells frightening stories about wreckers crashing ships on the rocks," added Zoé.

Pippin shook her head. "Never been to the museum."

"Are you kidding?" said Ian. "You don't know what you're missing!"

"My cousin's a history maven," Zoé said to Pippin—*maven* was a favorite word of Granddad's. Ian turned bright red, but secretly she knew he was pleased.

As Ian launched into Tenby's past, Zoé looked through the puzzle-glass. But each time she held it to her eye, the people around her shifted in their seats, turning their faces away, until with an exasperated sigh she gave up. Suddenly she glimpsed a shiny round head with tufts over the ears coming through the door: Dr. Marriott was elbowing his way into the café, looking startled by the crush of people.

"Over here, Dr. Marriott!" she called, waving to him.

"I'll be gobsmacked," he said, setting down a plastic shopping bag. "What's this, eh, a costume bash? The place is absolutely *heaving*! And I'll be jiggered: everyone here is wearing spectacles." He noticed Pippin and reached over, shaking her hand. "Hello, I'm George Marriott."

"Hiya. I'm Philippa Jenkyn Thomas, but call me Pippin."

"Pippin's the one who found the glass puzz—" Zoé

started, but Ian nudged her with his foot as Iris Tintern scuffed over in her crepe-soled shoes. They'd agreed not to say anything about Wythernsea or the puzzle in front of Iris, just in case.

"Special today for lunch: toad-in-the-hole," Iris announced, pencil hovering over her order pad. "For tea I've gooseberry scones and clotted cream."

Ian pulled down the peak of his cap and Zoé drew her hood lower, ordering an orange squash using the fake English accent she'd perfected over the years, while Ian mumbled, "Same for me." Iris was so rushed she wrote their orders without looking up and dashed off.

Zoé shook her arm, jangling the typewriter keys. "What do you think of my bracelet? My mom gave it to me for my birthday last month. I got to wear a tiara and eat a chocolate cake with my name on it."

"It's gorgeous," said Pippin with a lopsided smile, and Zoé felt a pang of guilt, recalling how Pippin's mum had run off and that she lived with relatives who probably never remembered her birthday.

"Very nice indeed," murmured Dr. Marriott. "You appear to have a mother who encourages creativity. Most commendable."

"Sometimes she does," said Zoé, who chose her words carefully whenever talking about her mom. "But she doesn't always get it right."

Her mom had a *cut-and-paste* history—something Zoé had overheard one of her teachers say, though she wasn't sure exactly what it meant. Zoé knew only that her mother tried hard to be a good mom, though it wasn't always easy.

"No one gets it right all the time," said Dr. Marriott with a kind smile, and Zoé relaxed a bit. "Oh yes, I nearly forgot." He reached into the plastic bag, identical to the one Granddad used for food shopping, and pulled out two books. "For you." He handed one each to Zoé and Ian. "As promised."

Doctor Doom and the Starchild read the bold letters on the cover, *by George R. Marriott.* The book jacket depicted a girl Zoé's age standing in a barren wasteland, with tiny spiders parachuting down from a blasted-out yellow sky.

"Gosh, thank you," said Ian. "I've never owned a book signed by the author."

"I love the cover," said Zoé, opening her book to inspect Dr. Marriott's signature, all loopy and unreadable—not at all like his handwriting when he was a kid. He'd used a fountain pen, which made it even more special.

"I'll rustle up a book for you, too, if you like," Dr. Marriott said to Pippin.

Zoé saw her eyes light up.

"Oh yes, please," said Pippin, "that would be smashing."

"My pleasure," said Dr. Marriott, turning back to Zoé and Ian. "If you don't mind my saying, you look extremely bleary-eyed today. Too many late shows on the telly?"

"Granddad doesn't have a TV," said Zoé. "He says it rots your brain."

"He listens to the BBC on his 1937 Ekco Bakelite radio,"

added Ian. "If we look wrecked, it's because there's a lot of unbelievable stuff going on."

They had a million things to tell Dr. Marriott, but Zoé wasn't sure where to begin. "It's like this: Ian wanted to see the puzzle again, to double-check his hologram theory." She glanced sideways at Ian, realizing that was an out-and-out lie. Still, it probably wasn't a good idea to mention their plan to start a new Society of Astercôte. "We didn't mean to, but we, um, put the puzzle together. It just sort of happened."

"There was this blue light swirling around us," said Ian, "and we got blasted apart—*whammo!*—it was giga-awesome—and the puzzle pulled us through a glass tunnel and we landed in Wythernsea."

Zoé heard Pippin take a deep breath. "Never!" she gasped. "You didn't tell me that!"

"It's the same Wythernsea that sank under the waves centuries ago—well, sort of," said Ian.

"But it's in a completely different world now," added Zoé, watching Pippin's eyes grow so big they seemed to pop out of her head.

"You went to another *world*?" whispered Pippin.

Dr. Marriott leaned forward. "You traveled to Wythernsea through the puzzle?" Zoé could see his complexion going from crimson to pasty white, fading to shadows beneath his eyes. "Oh dear, I should have warned you of the dangers." His gaze held a mixture of anguish and guilt. "I told you not to assemble the puzzle, but I failed to explain what you were up against."

"You didn't give us all the information, that's for sure," said Ian. "You didn't tell us about the Scravens."

"Them's the creatures, right?" said Pippin, suddenly animated. "Them things that came flying up out—"

"Here you go," said Iris, slamming down three glasses of orange squash and a cup of tea. Judging by her distracted expression, Zoé was sure she hadn't overheard their conversation.

Once Iris was out of earshot, Dr. Marriott turned to Pippin. "You've seen the creatures as well? And what did they look like?"

"Same as the creatures they seen, great horrid shrieking things with wings," said Pippin matter-of-factly. "Came flapping out of the puzzle when I put it together, same as what happened to them."

Seeing a look of alarm creep into Dr. Marriott's eyes, Zoé said quickly, "We wanted to tell you about it, but we didn't get a chance because your housekeeper made us leave!"

"The Scravens are infiltrating Tenby so they can get back their lost powers," said Ian in an ominous tone. "Then they'll be able to connect with other worlds: *evil* worlds!"

"We met this lady—well, she's kind of a giantess—and her name's Miss Glyndower," Zoé explained. "She said the Scravens were banished to the Harshlands and they hate it there because time goes by too fast and they age quickly."

"They want revenge on Wythernsea for exiling them. Basically they want to decimate it," said Ian, and Zoé saw the professor flinch. "The town wall is falling apart and the weathervanes won't turn and there's all this dangerous stuff we have to do before Midsummer's Day or else the Scravens will conquer Tenby."

Looking miserable, Dr. Marriott began dropping sugar cubes into his tea. Zoé had a funny feeling he wasn't counting. On all sides of the table, customers were shouting and joking and laughing uproariously. More people were crowding in through the door, all of them wearing blue-tinted glasses.

"Stuffy, isn't it?" said Ian, swallowing the last of his orange squash.

"Absolutely suffocating. This noisy lot is rather more than I can take," said Dr. Marriott, dropping a five-pound note on the table. "Shall we make a dash for it? The harbor is lovely this time of day."

"Blimey, look at the queue over there," said Pippin as they pushed their way out of the café. "It's unnatural-like, all them people wearing specs."

At the bottom of the street, Zoé saw a crowd milling around outside the optical shop, some lined up and others peering through the window.

"Very curious," said Dr. Marriott. "Why this sudden interest in Dr. Zival's shop? I wonder. And Iris Tintern's café? I suppose there's no predicting what the public will clamor for next."

"Hey, maybe Dr. Zival's a sleeper agent for the Scravens," said Ian, and Zoé rolled her eyes, knowing what was coming next. Her cousin read far too many spy novels, in her opinion. "I bet he's got a secret identity and carries silencers and poison bullets, and cyanide pills in case he's caught. Not to mention cutting-edge gadgetry and meticulously constructed cover stories."

"Zival's a *spy*?" said Pippin, looking confused.

"Anything's possible," replied Ian, pulling down the bill of his hat.

They followed the lane along Penniless Cove Hill to the harbor, past the old Seaman's Rooms (now tourist rental flats) and the fishermen's chapel, built of stone from Caldey Island, weaving their way past tiny cottages and overturned boats.

"What's with the hood?" Pippin asked Zoé. "Is it a new gangster fashion from America?"

"It's not a fashion. Ian and I are traveling incognito."

"We're keeping close to the ground," said Ian. "We don't want Iris Tintern recognizing us."

"No chance of that," said Pippin. "Iris Tintern never looked once at us, did she? Her eyes kept going off to the side, like."

"I don't understand," said Dr. Marriott. "Why shouldn't Iris recognize you?"

Walking beside the water, Zoé and Ian explained how Iris had chased them out of the King's Ransom Café when she saw them looking at her through the puzzle-glass.

"Catherine Beedle, too," added Zoé. "I looked at her through the glass at the movie theater and she had a scary third eye—like the Scravens!"

"Makes me guts shudder," said Pippin. "I mean, what's Iris doing with an eye in the middle of her head, eh?"

"A rather unsettling image," agreed Dr. Marriott.

"Yeah, but guess what?" said Zoé. "People in Wythernsea have extra eyes, too! Eyes on their foreheads!"

"They call them *shallows*," said Ian.

"Crikey," said Pippin, "they've all got three eyes?"

"Hmm, I seem to recall Uncle Wyndham talking about the Wythernfolk having third eyes linking them to far-flung realms, which explains their deep knowledge of medicinal practices," said Dr. Marriott. "Of course, after the Astercôtes vanished into the puzzle, Wyndham no longer talked about Wythernsea. My uncle became a haunted man: he died while I was away at college. The doctors said his heart had weakened and finally given out, but my theory is that grief got the better of him and his heart broke in two."

"That's really sad," said Zoé.

"Miss Glyndower told us that Scravens have shallows because they were once Wythernfolk," said Ian. "They were exiled to the Harshlands for doing away with travelers. Deprived of light, they deteriorated in the swamps, attacking any travelers who passed through there."

Zoé watched Dr. Marriott freeze midstep.

"Scravens *murdered* travelers," he said quietly. "Ah yes."

Feeling tears prick her eyes, she suddenly regretted bringing up Scravens in the first place.

"My uncle always claimed that Scravens were behind the Astercôte disappearances. It seems now that he was right."

"I'm sorry," said Zoé, her heart aching for him, and she wished she could give him a hug.

"You mustn't be sorry," said the professor. "The Astercôtes were explorers, adventurers, high-level alchemists; they knew full well the risks they were taking."

Zoé knew that she and Ian had been reckless and foolhardy to go into the puzzle (anything might have happened), but, like the Astercôtes, she and Ian were adventurers, too. They were rovers by nature, impetuous and brave—well, sort of brave—and sometimes they had no choice but to plunge headlong into danger.

"Miss Glyndower says it won't be easy to rid Tenby and Wythernsea of Scravens, and she's sent us on a two-pronged mission," Ian told Dr. Marriott. "We have to find The First—the leader of the Scravens—and we have to find the Runestone of Arianrhod."

"The Runestone of Arianrhod rings a bell, but of course there are hundreds of such runestones in the British Isles. Hmm, I seem to remember seeing one at the museum years ago: a slight, rather delicate stone, no more than twelve fingers' breadth—that's nine inches wide—and thin as slate, with the most esoteric symbols one could ever imagine. It seemed to glow from within."

"It *was* in the museum," said Ian glumly, "but not anymore."

"I've every confidence you will find it. Or perhaps the stone will find you. Nothing of such magical significance can ever truly be lost."

"We only have until Midsummer's Day," said Zoé. "That's no time at all!"

"You've a difficult task ahead of you, no doubt about it. This Miss Glyndower evidently has high expectations." Dr. Marriott glanced at his watch. "Oh dear, I must be off, I've a buyer coming for a signed edition of *The Gorilla Hunters*. Dare we return to the King's Ransom tomorrow to continue our conversation? Perhaps in a day's time the café will be back to normal."

Zoé winced at the idea of seeing Iris again, and she noticed Ian tightening his jaw. But in the end they agreed: same place, same time.

"We forgot to tell him about Stokes," said Zoé as the three took off their shoes and waded into the sea, the damp fog curling around them. "Stokes knows about the runestone but he won't tell me where it is." Before she could lift her long skirt, a wave fell, soaking the hem.

"Won't he now?" said Pippin in a defiant tone. "This Stokes sounds like a right little horror. Then there's nothing for it but to find him and let him know we mean business, eh?"

Bursting into the museum, Zoé could see Dr. Thistle bent over his collection of fossils, flicking a feather duster over the brittlestars.

"Hello, Dr. Thistle," said Ian. "I'm wondering where we can find Mr. Stokes. I'm doing historical research on Tenby and I'd like to ask him some questions."

Dr. Thistle shot them a cursory glance. "Stokes?" he said, wrinkling his nose as if contemplating something unpleasant. "Try the Maritime Gallery; Stokes is setting up the Black Barty exhibit. But be quick about it, we're closing soon."

There was no sign of Stokes in the Maritime Gallery, aside from a wooden stepladder Zoé found leaning against the wall. Hanging from the ceiling was a colorful banner: LEARN MORE ABOUT PEMBROKESHIRE'S MOST FAMOUS PIRATE! BARTHOLOMEW ROBERTS, ALSO KNOWN AS BLACK BARTY.

"Hey, look, pirate trove!" said Ian excitedly, and they all rushed to the display case.

"Cor blimey," said Pippin, pointing to a silver dagger. "Imagine having that thing pointed at your throat."

"Happened more times than not, what with the pirates and all," rasped a voice as Stokes limped into the room, wearing his official jacket, carrying a hammer and a box of nails. "A snick of the knife and some poor sod's bought it. No second chances for the weak."

"You must be Mr. Stokes, the assistant curator," said Ian.

"Stokes is the name," he said, gazing suspiciously at the three children.

"Remember me? I was here this morning," said Zoé. "This is my cousin Ian, the one who's looking for the ancient runestone, and this is our friend Pippin."

"You've brung your crew of marauders, is it?" said Stokes with a chilly smile. "Thick as thieves, I see. No doubt you *are* thieves."

Zoé tried not to giggle. *Does he think we're pirates?*

"I'm doing a history project on Tenby," said Ian. "I wanted to interview you about the old days."

Stokes peered down his nose, mouth set in a menacing sneer. "All depends what you want to know." Zoé wondered if he was curling his upper lip to scare them. "Plenty of history in these parts, but ever'thing comes at a price—if you get my meaning."

"What do you mean, a *price*?" asked Ian. "That sounds like bribery."

Zoé stepped forward, hands clenched at her sides. "You should be ashamed of yourself, a town employee like you, asking for a handout."

"I weren't asking for no money," Stokes huffed indignantly. "I were just—"

"Get a move on, Stokes," said a familiar voice. Zoé turned to see Dr. Thistle stick his head through the door, blue lenses flashing in the overhead lights. "Off with you kids, then, it's closing time."

The moment Dr. Thistle left, Pippin whirled around. "Stop playing games with us!" she hissed at Stokes, looking so furious Zoé thought she might attack him. "It's the runestone we're here for, so get on with it and tell us where it is."

"Should've known the blasted thing'd come back to haunt me," muttered Stokes. "Time passes and people forget, see? But old Stokes remembers. Stokes has a mind like a steel trap."

"Tell us," said Zoé, closing her fingers around the puzzle piece in her pocket.

"Won't be easy finding it, mind; been hidden down there for ages."

"Down where?" asked Ian.

"In the Tombs, is where." Stokes gave a self-satisfied grin and Zoé could see his ratlike teeth, yellow and chipped at the edges. "Down in the dark bowels of this museum all manner of things is stored, and among them's your precious runestone."

"That's absurd. The runestone's a valuable artifact!" said Ian. "It should be exhibited in your museum for everyone to see. I ought to know, my mom's a curator, and it sounds to me like something fishy's going on here."

"Don't you go accusing me of stealing artifacts or I'll have your guts for garters, boyo," said Stokes, his dark eyes flashing. "Wasn't me who was paid a pretty sum to hide the runestone out of sight, oh no, but I watched money change hands and I know where it's gone."

"Are you talking about Dr. Thistle, the head curator?" asked Ian. "Somebody *paid* him to hide it?"

"Who?" demanded Pippin. "Who was it paid him?"

"What's in it for me?" growled Stokes. "And why should I tell you lot, anyway?"

"What are the Tombs?" asked Zoé. "Are they down in the tunnels? Can you take us there?"

"The Tombs lie directly below the museum," said Stokes. "A pity the Tombs are locked. A pity the key's been lost."

Zoé's heart sank. She should've known he'd been stringing them along.

"Stop your mucking about, Stokes," said Pippin. "You've the key, so's you'd best hand it over—or you'll be right sorry."

"This isn't a game we're playing," said Ian. "Give us the key."

"Say no and I'll set Bronwyn Gilwern on you," added Pippin in a threatening tone.

Stokes's grin evaporated, and a look of trepidation crossed his face. To Zoé's surprise, he reached into his jacket pocket and pulled out a ring of keys, grumbling under his breath something about "the witch."

He took his time, sorting calmly through them, choosing at last an intricate, old-fashioned key. It looked like a key to the door of a castle. Or maybe, she thought with a shudder, the key to a dungeon.

"Take it," snarled Stokes, dropping it into Pippin's outstretched palm. "Take the key to the Tombs. But if it's not back in my hands within twenty-four hours, you'll regret you were born!"

CHAPTER FIFTEEN
THE SILENT SEERESS

Zoé stood at her bedroom window, gazing out at the boiling black clouds sweeping in from the sea. Last night she'd lain in her four-poster bed, hands crossed over her chest mummy-style, listening to the rain drumming on the roof, matching the hectic beat of her heart. She'd fallen asleep to the sound of foghorns booming out over the dark storming waters, and all night long she'd had terrifying dreams.

On her bedside table lay Dr. Marriott's book, unopened. She couldn't wait to read it, but too much was happening. Zoé sighed. It would have to wait.

She dressed quickly, hearing pots slamming in the kitchen. Granddad was doing a big fry-up, most likely laverbread, a Welsh delicacy—mixing seaweed with oatmeal into patties and frying them in bacon fat. With her mom, meals were strictly vegetarian, but in Wales she ate everything Granddad set on her plate. Laverbread was Zoé's favorite breakfast, along with the Welsh Glengettie tea that he brewed in a china pot.

Dropping the key to the Tombs into her pocket, Zoé tried not to think about the Scravens or Iris Tintern or oily old Stokes.

In the steamy kitchen her grandfather was frying laverbread cakes on the Aga cooker while humming what sounded like an old Welsh hymn. Ian, wearing a shirt patterned with triangles and looking like he hadn't slept either, was pouring orange juice into sturdy glasses. *Ian and Granddad look a lot alike,* Zoé thought. *I never noticed that before.* They had the same tall frames, the same proud stance and similar faces, long and solemn, like Norman knights carved on tombs in medieval churches.

"A card arrived from your mum," said Granddad, pointing to the fridge, where he'd stuck it up using magnets shaped like teapots and double-decker buses.

Zoé's mom liked to send silly postcards that made her laugh, but they usually dwindled as the summer wore on. She knew it wasn't that her mother forgot about her, it was just that she had important deadlines.

This postcard showed prairie dogs in the desert, lined up like a barbershop quartet, above the words GREETINGS FROM

PARADISE, ARIZONA. On the other side her mother had used a glitter pen (her mom was really into glitter) to write a spiral of words that ended with a sparkly star at the center.

> *Having a blast, Paradise is hot, hot, hot, found a gecko*
> *in my shoe, have fun with Ian, take care of Granddad,*
> *I miss you, 1,000,000 kisses, xxo.*

"Your mom sure writes tiny," said Ian, peering over her shoulder.

"Yeah, my mom's artistically inclined," said Zoé, noticing that her mother had forgotten to write down a phone number where she could be reached. Maybe that was the price of being creative: artistic people like her mom tended to be forgetful.

If she were in Arizona now, she'd be basking in the sun in her pink bathing suit with turquoise dragonflies. She might even help out at the beauty salon, streaking teenaged girls' hair sixteen shades of red and rolling curlers on old ladies' heads. But soon her mother would move on, taking on new assignments: back on the road again.

The truth was, Tenby was Zoé's number one choice. There was nowhere she'd rather be than hanging around with Ian and Granddad, her two best friends in the world.

"Seems there's been an accident over near Caldey Island," said Granddad as he dished up breakfast. "A merchant ship crashed in the fog last night and got hung up on the rocks."

Zoé's eyes went wide. "How awful, Granddad!"

"A tragedy, for sure. Hasn't happened in these parts for ages."

"Was everyone rescued?" asked Ian.

"Far as I know, captain and crew are safe, but it's a worry all the same. According to the weather prophets, more rain and fog are on the way. Arthur Angel's in a fine fix: he's having trouble making deliveries to the monks. Guess we won't be going to Caldey Island today. Sorry, kids."

Zoé leaned over her plate, breathing in smells of laverbread, bacon and cockles. "That's okay, Granddad, we like it here no matter what the weather. Even if it rains frogs!"

Across the table, Ian snickered. He always appreciated her jokes, even the goofy ones.

"Nice triangles, math wizard," she said, pointing to his shirt, and they both started to laugh.

Gazing out through the window, Zoé felt safe and peaceful here with her cousin and grandfather. At this very instant, while she scoffed down handfuls of laverbread, the Scravens seemed like imaginary players in one of their extravagant monster games.

"Granddad, do you know Mr. Stokes?" asked Ian, interrupting her reverie. "He's the assistant curator at Tenby Museum."

"Stokes is in charge of the Black Barty exhibit," said Zoé. "He likes to scare kids with stories about wreckers and pirates."

"Ah, Black Barty, the pirate who declared he wanted

'a short life and a merry one.' He got his wish, too." Granddad poured himself a third cup of tea. "As for Stokes, I know the gentleman by sight. He's a singular chap, the sort that keeps to himself. Hasn't any family that I know of. Stokes lives alone in a flat on Lower Frog Street."

"That's kind of sad," said Zoé. If Stokes weren't so sneaky, she might even feel sorry for him. "What about Bronwyn Gilwern? Do you know her?"

"Oh aye, everyone in Tenby knows Bron," said her grandfather. "Bron was born in Tenby, lived here until she was fifteen or so, then her family moved to Crickhowell in the Black Mountains. She comes here summers to work in her uncle's bookshop. Extraordinarily gifted, Bron; they call her the Silent Seeress of Tenby. Some say she has a deep knowledge of magic and sorcery, and a knack for deciphering runes. Mirielle Tate at the Saracen's Head Pub claims she's seen her glide across the Irish Sea at midnight." Granddad chuckled. "I'm not so sure about that, but I know Bron Gilwern's got a mind with a twist of its own."

Zoé's mouth dropped. Pippin hadn't been exaggerating after all.

"Our friend Pippin's taking us to meet Bron today," said Ian.

"Splendid," said Granddad. "She's Welsh and she's fierce. You'll like her."

"So, Granddad," said Zoé. "Do you believe in magic?"

Their grandfather considered. "Centuries ago, people believed in all sorts of things. Driven by fear, plagued by superstition, they believed in curses, spells and ghosts—and in the power of unearthly creatures. Fortunately for us"— he nibbled on the edges of a fried tomato—"we live in enlightened times."

🐉

Zoé and Ian threaded their way through the arcaded shops of the Old Town with Pippin in the lead. Zoé was wearing a yellow batik cotton dress, her typewriter keys bracelet, plaid sneakers, and glitter in her hair, in honor of meeting such a luminous personality as Bronwyn Gilwern.

They passed one of her favorite spots, the old apothecary, with MEDICAL HALL inscribed over the arched doorway. Zoé stopped, as she always did, admiring the handblown glass bottles in the window. Each one was filled with a different-colored liquid.

"Hey, Pippin, if we tell your friend Bronwyn about Wythernsea and the Scravens, think she'll believe us?" asked Ian.

"Doesn't matter," said Pippin. "We need her help and she won't let us down. Bron's the only one who has a map of the tunnels—a map that shows all the secret entrances."

"*Secret* entrances?" said Zoé, impressed.

"I'm surprised that sort of thing is public knowledge," said Ian. "I've looked everywhere online and I never found a map of the Tenby tunnels."

"Oh, there's a map, all right, but the authorities keep it locked away." Zoé watched the corners of Pippin's mouth lift into a smile. "Bron hacked into the town archives two years ago and found a digital replica of a map some bloke drew in the seventeenth century," she said, striding off down Quay Hill. "Bron printed it out and now she takes it with her whenever she goes down the tunnels."

"Your friend is a *computer hacker?*" said Ian, his eyes going wide.

"Wow," said Zoé. "I never met a cyber criminal before."

"Bron's not a criminal," said Pippin defensively. "She's just clever."

They turned onto Crackwell Street, following a stone wall overlooking the harbor. Pippin came to a sudden stop, pointing to a break in the wall, and Zoé looked down a flight of rough stone steps half hidden by lush greenery. *Tenby sure has a lot of hidden stairways,* she thought.

"Hey, aren't these Dead House Steps?" said Ian, pulling out his camera. "I've been trying to find them so I could take photos! That's what they were called in the eighteen hundreds because drowned sailors were carried up from the harbor to the Old Town mortuary under cover of night."

"Dead House Steps, that's them," said Pippin. "Look for the stone building with a round door: that's the mortuary."

Zoé scribbled *Dead House Steps* into her journal, then clattered after Pippin and Ian down steps worn smooth from the wind and salt air, gray mist clinging to her arms and legs like cobwebs. Silently they wound their way past the old mortuary with its bright green circular door, until at last Pippin stopped beside an ivy-choked wall.

"This is it," she said, pointing to the other side. "Bron's allotment."

Standing on tiptoes, all three peered over the top of the wall into a wind-wracked vegetable garden. Zoé could see rows of bright flowers and rangy bean stalks leaning in the wind, and stunted Welsh oaks crouched low on the ground. Amid the elderflowers stood an upright figure, stark against the sea, holding a small brass telescope to one eye.

"Bron lives on Cob Lane but she spends her free time gardening here by the harbor," whispered Pippin. "That's a spyglass she's looking through."

"The Tenby Museum has a whole collection of spyglasses," Ian whispered back. "I'll show you next time we go there."

"Pirates used spyglasses to keep a lookout for treasure galleons," said Zoé, who prided herself on knowing all the pirate jargon.

"C'mon, then." Pippin scrabbled up and over the wall, shouting, "Bron, Bron!" as the two others followed close behind.

Bronwyn Gilwern was muscular and tough, with a wide-eyed, fierce expression, like a female pirate, and it struck Zoé that Bron was a seeress, pirate and computer hacker all rolled into one. An unbeatable combination. Bron's short spiky hair was pink, with streaks of purple, and her eyes were purple, too.

Zoé made mental notes of all the things that were pirate-like about Bron so she could record them later: silk blouse with fringed sleeves, multicolored embroidered vest, gold nose ring. Her red leather skirt seemed to fall into another category, though Zoé wasn't sure what.

"These here are my chums, Zoé and Ian," announced Pippin.

The young woman held out a hand cluttered with silver rings and shook hands first with Zoé, then with Ian. "Bron," she said simply. Up close she smelled faintly of licorice.

"Comes here every summer, Bron does, to work at the Captain's Quill," said Pippin.

"We've been in your uncle's shop lots of times," said Zoé, awed and slightly afraid.

"I bought a book from you once," added Ian. "A history of Tenby filled with old black-and-white photographs. Real stunners, they were."

Bron said nothing. Her metallic earrings, threaded with brass nails, twirled in the wind. Now Zoé knew why Granddad had called her a silent seeress. At the base of Bron's throat was a tattoo in the shape of an elaborate Celtic symbol. It looked magical. *Someday I'll get a tattoo like that one*, thought Zoé.

"Happened accidental, the way we met," said Pippin. "Zoé and I, we crashed head-on in the street, just as I was coming out of the Captain's Quill. My books and papers were dripping wet, and when I got to school—late as usual—old Bascomb had seventy fits."

Bron lifted her pointy eyebrows. "Nothing in this life is accidental, Philippa."

Pippin grinned. "I knew you'd say that."

Zoé opened her mouth to say it was actually Pippin

who'd crashed into *her*, knocking her flat on her back and getting her sparkly notebook all wet. Then again, maybe it was better to keep quiet. *It's not a good idea to start things off on a down note*, that was what her mom always said.

"We've something important to ask you," said Pippin, and Bron's eyebrows shot up again.

Zoé watched Bron listening intently as Pippin talked about the glass puzzle, not seeming the least astonished to hear that the drowned island of Wythernsea had resurfaced in a different world and that the people there had extra eyes on their foreheads. Bron sat completely stone-faced and unruffled while Pippin explained the fate of the Astercôtes, describing how monstrous winged creatures were escaping into Tenby through a leaky portal.

"We need your help, is why we're here," concluded Pippin. "This is a war and we're fighting the Scravens."

That last bit, *fighting the Scravens*, was Zoé's cue. She reached into her pocket and waved the ornate key they'd wrested from Stokes.

"The key to the Tombs, given to us by Mr. Stokes," said Pippin in a dramatic voice. "And the Tombs are secret, hidden somewheres beneath Tenby Museum—in the tunnels is what I'm saying—and I'll wager the Tombs are marked on your map."

"We have to go down to the tunnels, no matter how dangerous," said Zoé. "The problem is, they've closed all the entrances and we can't get inside."

"There's something terribly important we need to find,

but we can't do it alone," Ian chimed in. "Otherwise we wouldn't be asking."

"An old, old stone," said Pippin, "down in the Tombs beneath the museum."

Bronwyn Gilwern turned to face the sea, her violet eyes fixed on Caldey Island. For several moments she was quiet.

"There've been signs of late," she said at last. "Signs, shadows, omens . . . I've heard just now of a second ship caught on the rocks off Caldey. Then there are the Ogham runes alluding to a dark being who will appear out of nowhere and threaten Tenby. 'Beware the Measurer of Sight who comes in darkness, moving unseen through Tenby, stirring up chaos and fear.'"

Gazing at the rows of stalks tipping in the wind, arching golden against the sky, Zoé felt an icy chill creep into her heart.

"So the runes are a prediction, yeah?" said Ian. "But who wrote them?"

"Aye, a prediction," said Bron. "See, there lived long ago beings far wiser than ourselves—the Enchanters—who saw far into the future and inscribed the lost enchantments on the tunnel walls. The most ancient runes come from them."

"Is that what you are, an Enchanter?" Zoé blurted out, her face turning red. Maybe that hadn't been the right thing to say.

"The Enchanters were here but a short time: they exist no more. I'm a seeress," said Bron. "We're all seers and seeresses in my family. Runs in the blood." Before Zoé could ask more, Bron went on: "I suppose Pippin's told you about the map and how I came by it. If we go, there are risks. They've hired security guards to keep folks out."

All three children nodded gravely.

"We're not afraid of the tunnels," said Zoé, setting her jaw in what she hoped was a brave expression.

"Nor the guards," said Ian, sounding defiant.

"We'll face whatever's down there," added Pippin.

Running her fingers through her stiff hair, Bron frowned. "The way I see it, they've no right closing the tunnels. Heaps of folk need to go down there—geologists, historians and harrowers, archaeologists and rune interpreters like myself—and now they're stopping us all from going."

"What's a *harrower*?" asked Zoé.

"Questing heroes, departing kings. Kids like you, off on important missions."

Zoé's eyes lit up. *We're on a quest,* she thought, *we're harrowers!* The word had an adventurous ring; it was even better than *time rovers.*

"So that's why I'm saying yes, I'll take you down to the Tombs. Just don't let it be known I've a map of the tunnels," said Bron. "Meet you tomorrow morning: five o'clock at the Gaslight building on Tor Lane. It's quietest then."

All three of them began to cheer and shout, giggling wildly and jumping up and down, pounding each other on the back and chanting, "To the tunnels, to the tunnels!"

Then Bron Gilwern raised her pirate's spyglass to the sky and gave the loudest and deepest belly laugh that Zoé had ever heard.

CHAPTER SIXTEEN
THE BOOK OF ASTERCÔTE

"He's late again," said Zoé, sitting at a table outside the King's Ransom Café with Ian and Pippin, waiting for Dr. Marriott. They'd come straight here from seeing Bron, arriving in high spirits just as the bells of St. Mary's Tower began chiming four.

Inside, the café was overflowing, so Iris Tintern had set up tables on the front sidewalk. "Long as no rain threatens," she muttered, too busy arranging chairs to notice Zoé and Ian among her customers. "Nothing to worry about, see."

"So . . . is this Bron Gilwern truly a bona fide seeress?" asked Ian.

Zoé had no idea what *bona fide* meant and she could tell Pippin didn't know, either. But as usual, Pippin bluffed her way through, saying, "Why else d'you think Stokes gave us the key to the Tombs? He's *deathly* afraid of her powers."

While Ian and Pippin talked on, Zoé took out her journal and pretended to write. Then, making sure no one was watching, she held the puzzle-glass to one eye and looked through the café window—the perfect way to spy on people, she realized, because no one seemed to notice her sitting outside.

Suddenly her heart jumped into her throat: all the people wearing blue-tinted glasses had eyes on their foreheads rimmed with green fire, exactly like Iris's!

"Put the glass away," hissed Pippin, squeezing Zoé's arm. "Quick!"

"They're watching you," said Ian. He tilted his head and spoke without moving his lips—one of his favorite spy techniques. "Over there."

Zoé dropped the glass into her pocket, acting casual. Across the street four kids were leaning against the wall of the hardware store, all of them wearing blue-tinted glasses. With a jolt she recognized Fritha Pooke, Catherine and Trevor Beedle and Philip Fox. Her insides shriveled.

"I think they're spying on us," whispered Ian, still not moving his lips. "That's why we haven't seen them around this summer. They've gone over to the Scraven side."

"Act normal," whispered Pippin. "Hiya!" she yelled, waving at them, but none of the kids waved back.

"Listen, you guys," whispered Zoé, "I have to tell you something! Those people inside the café—"

"Hello, hello," boomed a voice as George Marriott came bouncing along the sidewalk, a worn leather briefcase under his arm. "Sorry I'm late. Up half the night, I was." He eased into a chair and set down his briefcase, flipping the latches intently. "I suddenly awoke, remembering that in my attic was a book written and self-published by the Society of Astercôte. Haven't opened it since Uncle Wyndham's death."

He reached into the briefcase, pulling out a copy of *Doctor Doom and the Starchild*. "For you," he said with a boyish grin, handing the book to Pippin, who smiled delightedly back.

"Now, first of all, what's happening with the runestone?" asked the professor. "Have you found it?"

"Not yet, but we know where it is," said Ian. "Down in the Tombs, beneath Tenby Museum."

"We had to threaten old Stokes at the museum to give us the key," added Pippin. "Bron Gilwern's taking us down first thing tomorrow."

"Good, good," said Dr. Marriott, extracting a thin volume with a red leather cover from the case. "Priceless, this is. The only book of its kind in existence." He stared down at it with a reverent expression. Imprinted on a worn cover in ornate script were the words *The Book of Astercôte*. Below the title, Zoé could see a Welsh dragon stamped into the leather.

"The book contains ancient secrets, most of which were known only to the Astercôtes." Fascinated, Zoé watched Dr. Marriott's pudgy fingers riffle through the pages. "Here you have the history of the glass puzzle: its creation by glassblowers in Wythernsea and its presentation to the Astercôtes. It also explains in detail how the Astercôtes transformed the puzzle into a gateway to Wythernsea." He flipped to another page. "This chapter speaks of the Afflicted: 'Those who have succumbed to Scravens.' A fate worse than death, apparently."

"Sounds dreadful," said Pippin. "Like some kind of disease."

"I suppose it is, in a way," said Dr. Marriott. "You see, the Astercôtes realized Scravens could enter our world through flawed portals and infiltrate entire towns, scavenging energy from humans."

Infiltrate! There was that word again, the same one Miss Glyndower had used. Zoé made a mental note to record it in her journal.

"There's something else." Dr. Marriott stared down at the book, his mouth set in a taut line. "The Astercôtes believed Scravens had the ability to inhabit humans."

"Scravens can become *human?*" said Zoé in a strangled voice.

Looking skeptical, Ian said, "Hmm, sounds like a far-fetched theory. I thought these Astercôte guys were scientists."

"Indeed they were." What Dr. Marriott said next echoed the words of Gwyn Griffiths from Wythernsea. "They describe the process here: the Scraven enfolds a human within its wings, and there is a crossing-over of psyches as the two merge. The person is unaware of what has happened and appears to go about his or her life as normal. Physically the

Afflicted still look and act like people, but in reality they've undergone a radical transformation: their true inner selves have been totally submerged—and the Scraven is now in control. And this isn't the first time. Attempts by Scravens to take over humans have been recorded in at least three other worlds."

Zoé swallowed hard, exchanging frightened looks with Ian and Pippin. *This can't be happening*, she thought, struck by a sense of impending disaster. Yet suddenly she knew, beyond any doubt, that they were all in danger—terrible danger.

"So while we sit nattering away, them creatures are taking over our friends and families in Tenby?" said Pippin, gripping the edge of the table. "We've got to stop them!"

"Special today: bangers and mash!" shouted Iris Tintern. "For dessert we have lemon-and-orange-peel-flavored Mister Whippy–style ice cream."

Zoé jumped: it seemed as if the café owner had materialized out of nowhere, brandishing her pencil over their heads.

"Four hot cocoas, please," said Dr. Marriott.

Zoé watched him furtively slide the book under his briefcase, away from Iris's prying eyes. She had a sinking feeling about the café owner. Unlike the film *Invasion of the Body Snatchers*, it wasn't the pod people who'd gotten to her, it was the Scravens. She was almost certain Iris had joined the ranks of the Afflicted.

"Hey, listen, everybody—there's something I have to tell you. It's really important!" she said in a loud whisper, feeling feverish and light-headed. "I looked into the café through the puzzle piece, and all the people with tinted glasses have *shallows*! You know, eyes on their foreheads!"

The color drained from Dr. Marriott's face.

"Proper spooky that is," said Pippin.

"Miss Glyndower said the Scravens want to take over Tenby so they won't age as fast," Zoé told them. "And they want their lost powers back so they can connect with other worlds: *evil* worlds!"

"But why tinted glasses?" said Pippin. "Odd."

"The lenses are bluish, aren't they?" said Ian. "What if they're made of the same glass as the puzzle? Wythernsea glass has mystical properties, right?"

"Hmm, very astute of you, Ian." Dr. Marriott tugged one end of his mustache. "It's possible the Afflicted are wearing spectacles in order to identify one another. That would explain why they're congregating here in Iris's café. Wythernsea glass reveals their shallows, allowing them to identify who is a true Scraven. No second-guessing, see."

"And the tinted glasses cut out the glare of the sun," added Ian, "protecting their eyes while they adjust to the light."

Zoé was sure that Ian and Dr. Marriott had gotten it exactly right. "Is there anything else in the book we should know about?" Ian asked Dr. Marriott.

"Well, yes, actually." Zoé watched him slide the book back out from under his briefcase, flipping through the pages to a chapter entitled "The Thirteenth Piece." "When the Astercôtes turned the puzzle into a gateway, they left out one piece. The Thirteenth Piece is the key to sealing the puzzle, and once it is sealed the Scravens cannot enter our world."

"*Seal* the puzzle?" said Zoé, feeling a twinge of panic. "You mean it wouldn't be a gateway to Wythernsea anymore?"

"It would not," replied Dr. Marriott, shaking his head. "You see, flawed gateways are extremely dangerous. To begin with, you risk more Scravens escaping into our world. And if their leader—The First—ever got hold of the puzzle, a most unpleasant scenario would ensue. It would be, in short, the end of Tenby."

Her heart fell. That meant she'd never see Miss Glyndower or Gwyn or Tegan again.

"So where's the Thirteenth Piece?" asked Ian.

"This is where it gets tricky. One particular member of the Society of Astercôte, Edward Yates, was the designated Keeper of the Thirteenth Piece. After he disappeared in Wythernsea, Edward was declared dead, and in his will he bequeathed the Thirteenth Piece to his grandson Gwydion."

"Super," said Ian. "So . . . does Gwydion Yates live in Tenby?"

"Not exactly. Gwydion's a monk on Caldey Island." Dr. Marriott's moth-wing brows bunched up over his eyes. "Uncle Wyndham tried contacting him, of course, but Gwydion was unreachable: as a monk he'd taken a vow of silence and refused all visitors. That was why Wyndham asked me to destroy the puzzle: sealing it wasn't an option."

To Zoé's surprise, he suddenly smiled. "Enough of this morose talk," he said, closing *The Book of Astercôte*. "I didn't have time to read the chapter on the runestone, but according to this book it is the ultimate weapon against creatures of evil. So take heart. Because if anything will defeat the Scravens, it is the Runestone of Arianrhod. Finding the stone is what must first be done."

CHAPTER SEVENTEEN
THE TUNNELS OF TENBY

The sun was just coming up, washing the sky in shades of yellow, pearl and silver, when Zoé and Ian crept out of their grandfather's cottage. As arranged, they met Pippin outside the apothecary on Cresswell Street. Walking through a light mist, the three talked nonstop about their meeting with Dr. Marriott and *The Book of Astercôte*.

"So the Afflicted look and act like ordinary people, but in reality they're being controlled by Scravens," Ian was saying. "The only way we can identify them is by their blue-tinted glasses—and, oh yeah, they don't make eye contact."

Zoé kept thinking about the people in the café and their black whirling eyes. The Afflicted. Her stomach twisted into knots as she had a sudden, awful vision of Tenby, where everyone in town had been taken over by Scravens.

"Dr. Thistle has blue-tinted glasses," she said. "He's probably one."

"Yeah, but ordinary people wear tinted glasses, too," argued Pippin. "Blue lenses are popular, but not everybody wearing 'em is a Scraven."

"Good point," said Ian. "That's why we need the puzzle pieces to identify the Afflicted, because we need to know our enemy. That means we have to stay undercover: *strength lies in secrecy*, as they say."

"Because this is war," said Pippin.

"We fight to the death." Zoé raised her clenched fist.

Bron Gilwern was waiting for them, standing before a faded red door outside a derelict building at the end of Tor Lane, THE GASLIGHT COMPANY OF TENBY etched into the archway above her. Zoé thought Bron looked ageless and watchful, like a gatekeeper in a fairy story. Her hair looked even shorter and more brittle than yesterday; today it was flaming orange.

Ignoring their chorus of hellos, Bron turned the key in the lock, bumping her husky shoulder against the door and springing it open. Heart fluttering, Zoé stepped into a cavernous room littered with the remnants of desks and chairs, splintered glass, and machines piled in towering heaps. A thick layer of dust covered everything, and she began to sneeze.

"Smells like dried-up mouse guts," whispered Ian, wrinkling his nose.

"Petrified frog brains," said Pippin with a grin.

"Clotted monkey innards," Zoé snorted.

Their giggling was cut short by a scathing glance from Bron.

The three stood in silence as she lit a black lattice oil lantern and studied the printout of a map, creased and torn and marked with fingerprints. In the half-light Zoé could see spidery lines that she guessed were tunnels, running in the same direction as the streets of old Tenby, and hand-drawn squares that were no doubt the secret entrances.

Bron strode through a door falling off its hinges into a room shrouded in cobwebs, its single window overlooking an alley. For the first time ever, Zoé was wary of going down into the tunnels. What if there were Scravens down there?

"Stay invisible," said Bron, stuffing the map into her leather jacket. "Not a word out of you." She unbolted a door so tiny that Zoé wondered if it had been made for goblins.

"I hope there aren't rats," said Ian as they stared down into the darkness.

"Eels," came Bron's curt reply. "Sea creatures. Wheezy, bumping, soft-shelled things. So watch your feet."

Oh great, thought Zoé, *those sound even worse than rats.*

"If a guard turns up, the lantern goes dark. Total silence. Understood?"

The three nodded solemnly. Zoé, feeling a sudden thrill of fear, now understood Ian's obsession with spydom and danger.

Ducking through the door, Bron ushered them down a staircase that groaned with every step. At the bottom the air felt cool and dank. Zoé was glad she'd worn *Wellies* (short for *Wellington boots*) and a *wooly jumper* (what the Brits called a sweater), as Bron had instructed. They made their way through the cellar, sidestepping picks and shovels, piles of rubble, bricks and dirt, through an archway into a dark, narrow tunnel.

Zoé had always suspected there were ghosts in the tunnels, generations of them, and she sensed their menacing shadows all around. Ghosts could scare the wits out of you, but ghosts could be beaten and their secrets found out, that was what Granddad had told her. And once you knew their secrets, you could take their power away.

But when it came to Scravens, she had no idea what to do. Miss Glyndower's vial was in her pocket, but how long would the mist keep the Scravens away? After all, there was only a limited amount of it. She felt her skin crawl, picturing them huddled like bats inside the tunnels, wings neatly folded, ready to snatch their prey.

"There's loads of ancient runes down here," Pippin whispered, pointing to the dimly lit wall. "You just have to know where to look."

Zoé noticed for the first time the strange, archaic symbols etched into the stone, barely detectable unless you knew they were there. Although she'd been on guided tours of the tunnels, she'd never heard of any ancient writings, maybe because it had always been dark or, more likely, the runes existed in special tunnels where tourists weren't allowed. Yet she quickly understood that a hidden world existed inside this labyrinth of tunnels, vaults, passages, niches and stair-cases, all hollowed out from the earth below Tenby's old medieval town.

"See here. The language of the Enchanters," said Bron, shining her lantern across the wall.

The writings were incomprehensible, yet beautiful all the same. Zoé watched Pippin trace her chewed-up fingernails over the symbols, a contemplative look on her face. Pippin, she suspected, longed to be a seeress and interpreter of runes, like Bron.

"This stone you're after in the Tombs," said Bron, "what exactly is it?"

"I imagine it to be like the Caldey Stone," said Ian. "Though quite a bit smaller, according to Miss Glyndower. Our friend Dr. Marriott said he remembers it being twelve fingers' breadth—that's nine inches wide."

Zoé smiled, thinking how animated her cousin always became whenever history topics came up in conversation. After seeing the Caldey Stone last summer, Ian had talked about it nonstop for days afterward.

"No end of Ogham stones in Ireland and Wales, going back to the fifth century," said Bron. "Right, let's get a move on. This tunnel runs the length of St. Julian's; then we take another tunnel up Castle Hill. The Tombs lie beneath Tenby Museum."

Face set in a stony expression, Bron marched ahead, sloshing through puddles, map rattling in her hand. She boldly navigated the twists and turns, keeping the lantern low so as not to draw attention, long legs moving so swiftly that Zoé had to run to keep up with her.

Soon Zoé's bones began to feel loose and springy, but her teeth chattered from the deathly cold. They were deep underground, and she thought of Granddad's tales about townspeople hiding in the tunnels to escape the ravages of the plague. "Poor, tortured souls," he'd said. "Ach, there was no escaping it. In the end the Black Death was upon them."

At last Bron stopped before an elaborate wrought-iron gate with a rusted padlock hanging off it, its hinges embedded in stone. Above the gate hung a wooden sign with black lettering: ENTRY FORBIDDEN, PER ORDER OF THE MAYOR OF TENBY. PROPERTY OF THE TENBY MUSEUM AND ART GALLERY, CASTLE HILL, TENBY, EST. 1878.

This is it! Zoé thought excitedly. *The Tombs!*

"Wake up," said Pippin in a loud whisper, jabbing her elbow into Zoé's ribs. "The key, remember?"

Zoé fumbled for Stokes's key, fitting it into the ancient lock, turning it one way, then the other. Nothing happened. She twisted it again, but the padlock stayed firmly shut, while around her tension filled the air. What if Stokes had tricked them and this was the wrong key?

Bron gave an exasperated snort. "Give it over."

There was a scraping sound, then the click of tumblers as the key turned in the lock. Suddenly the padlock fell open and they trooped silently through the gate, into a cold shadowy space that reminded Zoé of crypts she'd seen in Ian's horror comic books.

"The orphaned treasures of Tenby Museum," murmured Bron, holding up the lantern, illuminating a passage lined with rough-cut stone shelves partitioned into sections, filled with an assortment of objects.

"I wonder how long all this stuff's been here," said Zoé. "And why isn't it in the museum?"

Ian spoke up. "Like Dr. Thistle said, museums often rotate their exhibits, and some aren't big enough to display everything at once. So museums like Tenby Museum and like my mom's keep an overflow room where relics are stored and documented—"

"Be quick and find your stone," Bron cut in. "I'll stand guard."

The search for the runestone was on. Going by Dr. Marriott's description, Zoé imagined it to be small and elegant as she peered into dozens of shelves, rummaging through the contents. There were globes and charts and atlases, pocket watches and hand-painted Indian silk, gold-plated cutlery, little coffers of spice, inlaid combs, silver fasteners, trinket boxes, blown-glass figurines, turn-of-the-century postcards with foreign stamps, and portraits of Victorian authors in elaborate frames. But nowhere did she discover a stone of any kind, with or without runes.

"I've looked high and low," said Pippin at last. "It's not here."

"We've scoured every corner," said Ian. "You know what? I think Stokes sent us on a wild-goose chase."

"We can't give up yet," argued Zoé, though secretly she was beginning to despair of ever finding the runestone.

"Hear that?" whispered Bron, and the lantern went out. Everyone froze. Zoé could hear footsteps echoing down the tunnel.

"Run!" gasped Bron, slamming the gate behind them.

As she sprinted off, Zoé heard an angry voice shouting, "Stop! Thieves!"

Stokes! He's followed us down to the Tombs, the sneak!

A few yards ahead, two figures advanced through the shadows: security guards in caps and uniforms, waving batons. Zoé felt the blood rush to her head.

"Stop right there," ordered one. "Don't move another step."

"We're here on urgent business," said Bron, in a voice that Zoé had never heard her use before: soft but with a persuasive undertone. "We've permission to be in the tunnels."

"No one's allowed down here under any circumstances," growled the guard. "Now clear off."

"Rules is rules," said the other. "The tunnels are strictly off-limits." He glowered at them. "Leave now or we'll bring charges."

Zoé saw Bron stiffen, arching her back the slightest bit. Turning to face the guards, she shot them each a piercing look. Their faces seemed to go doughy and their eyes went blank; Zoé heard the batons clatter to the floor as the men stumbled back, arms flapping, mouths forming perfect Os.

"Go!" Bron rasped.

Zoé took off, racing through the darkness, hearing a furious wail from a distant tunnel and Stokes shouting, "You won't get away with this, enchantress—you nor your young thieves! I see through your trickery!"

CHAPTER EIGHTEEN
THE CAVERN OF LOST ENCHANTMENTS

Racing through the mud and darkness, Zoé continued to hear Stokes yelling at the top of his lungs: "Yer rascally cutthroats!" and a string of other swear words, old-fashioned ones like "yer scurvy scallywags" and "mangy bilge rats," the kind she imagined pirates using.

At last Bron stopped running and leaned against the tunnel wall. The others collapsed around her, gasping for breath.

"Maybe we set off an alarm," said Zoé.

"Yeah, I bet that's exactly what happened, and Stokes came down hoping to catch us red-handed," huffed Ian, "except the stone wasn't there."

"Maybe someone stole it," suggested Pippin.

"Tell me more about this stone," said Bron, sounding exasperated. "You've been right frugal with details."

"Well, it belongs to the museum," said Zoé. "Stokes, the assistant curator, told us it was in the Tombs."

"Stokes hinted that someone paid Dr. Thistle to hide it," added Ian.

"Truth be told, I'm acquainted with Stokes, and I wouldn't put much faith in anything he tells you," said Bron with a sniff.

"And, oh yeah, it's called the Runestone of Arianrhod," said Pippin.

"Oh, *that* runestone," said Bron, the suggestion of a smile crossing her lips. "Why didn't you say? The Runestone of Arianrhod is back in its proper place, in Dragon's Mouth."

"Dragon's Mouth?" echoed Zoé. What was a valuable runestone doing in a *cave?* "How do you know that?"

"I ought to. I put it there."

"Huh?" said Ian. "You *stole* the Runestone of Arianrhod from the Tenby Museum?"

Bron yawned. "Wasn't difficult."

"But . . . *why?*" spluttered Ian.

"A fortnight ago I was tracing runic letters near the Tombs when I saw Dr. Thistle rush down a tunnel. He was carrying a mallet and an object wrapped in burlap: I knew straightaway he intended to smash it." Bron relit the lantern. "So I threw a spell over him, simple as that. Knocked the breath from me when I saw it was the runestone he meant to destroy."

"I knew it," said Ian. "Dr. Thistle's colluding with the Scravens!"

Once again they set off, taking a roundabout route to elude the guards. Ordinarily, Zoé would be wild with joy to be going to Dragon's Mouth—she'd often dreamed of exploring the legendary cavern above the sea—but the thought of possibly encountering Scravens made her stomach ache with dread.

The light from Bron's lantern sent shadows running up the rocky walls and across the roof of the tunnel. Black and dripping, the passageway echoed with a low, moaning wind. Smaller tunnels branched off; Bron said they led to dead ends, with other passages turning back on themselves, like a maze. For Zoé the moments seemed to stretch into an eternity, and her nerves were fraying fast. She felt that at any minute she could snap.

At long last she heard the muffled sound of waves pounding against the cliffs as the tunnel widened, opening into a vast round chamber with an enormous archway looking out to the sky and sea. From a domed ceiling hung dozens of stalactites. The sloping walls of black stone were veined with white rock that sparkled in the light.

"Absolutely cracking," breathed Pippin.

"Holy cow," said Ian, pulling out his camera.

"Put the camera away. *Now*." Bron's voice was sharp. "You're in a sacred space."

Zoé watched Ian sheepishly drop his camera back inside the messenger bag. Just as well she'd left her journal at the cottage.

Light, pale and misty, filtered through the great archway that was Dragon's Mouth.

"It really does look like a dragon's mouth," whispered Zoé.

The enormous gap was exactly as she'd imagined, with sharp stones jutting out like giant teeth. She pictured a dragon crawling out of the tunnels, its spiked tail lashing back and forth as it roared across the rooftops of Tenby, shaking the beams in everyone's houses.

Zoé raced to the archway, coming to a screeching halt when she realized there was no rail or barrier to stop her from falling hundreds of feet down. The edge of Dragon's Mouth seemed to spill into nothingness. Trembling, she backed away, the rushing waves below echoing in her ears.

"What if the security guards show up?" Ian asked Bron. "Is there an escape route?"

"Not to worry—Dragon's Mouth is well hidden. This is no ordinary cavern, this is sacred ground going back centuries. There are ancient powers at work here, spirits and spells, all connected to the Runestone of Arianrhod. The lost enchantments were written in this cavern." Bron lifted her lantern higher. "I've been doing research, see, and I found out the Society of Astercôte held their secret meetings and ceremonies here."

It was the longest speech Zoé had ever heard Bron make. *I knew it*, she thought, gazing around the vast space, suddenly aware of the old symbols and signs, the mazes etched deep into the walls, some receding into the stone. *I knew this place was magic the minute I got here.* Coming into sharp relief were fantastical shapes that seemed to float, dreamlike, across the ceiling and down the sides of the archway.

Zoé slowly walked around, running her hands over the inscriptions. "The Astercôtes held their meetings *here?*" she whispered.

"Aye," said Bron. "Seems this cavern illuminated and strengthened their ancient practices, especially their powers of alchemy and time-and-space travel. I discovered, too, that the glass puzzle was hidden here, protected by spells. What I know for sure is that the runes written on these walls were never intended to go outside this cavern." She pointed to a far wall. "The runestone comes from Wythernsea, and the incantation upon it was written by Arianrhod herself."

Bron set down the oil lamp, sending shadows leaping up the high, sloping walls, illuminating the far side of the cavern. As her eyes adjusted to the gloom, Zoé could see wide, shallow steps leading to a natural stone platform. A mixture of drawings—images of birds and fish—and ancient script covered the wall behind it.

Then the images and writing seemed to fade into the stone, replaced by long, sweeping lines glimmering in gold, creating the outline of a woman with flowing hair. Zoé's breath caught: Arianrhod! Large and imposing, carved deep into the stone, the goddess held a shield in one hand and an oval-shaped stone tablet in the other.

"The runestone!" shouted Pippin, and the three children rushed forward.

"Nay," said Bron, striding over to the image. "Not so fast." She stood before the stone, waving her hands in front of it, and Zoé wondered if she was working some kind of spell. "Right, then. Each of you repeat the gesture."

Zoé was the last to go, and as her hands glided past the runestone, she felt a pure white energy leap into her fingertips. A cool light passed through her limbs, like a current in her blood, and she felt as if she were a high priestess or a queen—or maybe a goddess.

"The stone is yours, Zoé, to watch over and protect," said Bron. "For the moment, that is. When the time is right, you must return it."

Eyeing the runestone with wonder and curiosity, Zoé gently tugged it, surprised at how easily it lifted out of the niche. The stone lay cold in her hands, covered in dust and dirt, thin as slate, just as Dr. Marriott had described. Yet beneath the dirt she could see a dull bluish sheen. There were letters and carvings grooved into the surface—waves and fish and primitive symbols, all with their hidden meanings, if only she could decipher them.

Light began seeping from the edges, flowing from tiny cracks, reminding her of moonlight on snow, so pale it was nearly white, forming a ghostly shroud that clung to the runestone. Then it began to shimmer. Speechless, all Zoé could do was stare into the light, immense and pure, glowing mysteriously.

"Looks like something you'd see in a desert by the Nile," murmured Ian.

"Absolutely wizard," said Pippin.

"No one must know you have this," Bron said quietly. "No one."

Zoé held the runestone, breathing in the smell of it: sweet, like honey, mixed with earth and mold. Each time her eyes fell on the runes, she felt transported, as if she were dreaming her life instead of actually living it. Had this really been written by Arianrhod, handed down through centuries of chaos and wars, pirates and plague—and the sinking of Wythernsea?

"Then this is our weapon against the Scravens," said Ian.

Bron stood for a long moment, smiling that odd smile of hers—as if she knew a thousand secrets but wasn't about to reveal any of them.

"Aye," replied the seeress. "The Runestone of Arianrhod will be their undoing."

Zoé kept the runestone inside her backpack as she wound through the narrow streets with Ian and Pippin. The fog, instead of burning off as the day wore on, had thickened, turning the pale buildings a dreary gray, clinging to the walls of the Old Town. Damp, chilly air swirled around them, and sometimes through the mist she thought she saw someone following at a distance, fading in and out: maybe a ghost from the tunnels, although a ghost would be far preferable to a Scraven.

"Did you see how Bron threw her spell over the guards? Fantastic, eh?" said Pippin, tearing off her raggedy sweater.

She seemed to be gloating—as if, thought Zoé, she'd done the magic herself. "Didn't know what hit them, did they? They'll have aching heads and won't remember a thing. That's the kind of magic Bron works."

"Subtle," said Ian.

"Can I show Granddad the runestone?" asked Zoé. "He won't tell anyone and he loves old things and Arianrhod's his favorite goddess—"

"No!" said Ian and Pippin in unison.

"Granddad's not to know about any of this," said Ian. "We shook hands on it, remember? Our special handshake."

"Bron said not to tell anybody," Pippin reminded her.

"But Granddad's not just *anybody*," argued Zoé.

Then again, she knew it wasn't fair to pull Granddad into a frightening situation involving Scravens and dark magic, not to mention disreputable people like Stokes. They needed to keep him safe.

As they approached the cottage, Zoé saw her grandfather standing in the doorway; she could tell by his uncertain expression that he'd been worrying about them.

"I was up at dawn and your beds were empty," he said. "When you didn't show for breakfast, I got a bit worried, see. Usually when you go out like that you leave me a note saying when you'll be back."

Zoé and Ian exchanged a guilty look.

"Sorry, Granddad," she said. "We didn't think—"

"It's my fault, Mr. Blackwood," Pippin cut in. "I asked

them to meet me at North Beach early this morning to search for puffins and we forgot the time."

"Puffins?" Granddad scratched his head. "Well now."

"Mirielle Tate, who runs the pub, she's seen 'em gathering there at dawn," Pippin went on, and Zoé had to admire her bravado. Pippin was a spectacular liar.

As they entered the antiques shop, Granddad shut the door behind them, hanging a Closed sign over the doorknob. "I daresay you haven't heard the latest, have you?"

Zoé's heart began to thump.

"What's happened, Granddad?" asked Ian, his voice tense.

"There's been another accident off Caldey, the third in the past week. A cruise ship was lost in the fog and broke up on the rocks. Perhaps you saw the rescue boats heading out from North Beach."

"We did, as a matter of fact," said Pippin evenly, and Zoé cringed at the lie. "But we didn't know about the disaster. Everyone okay?"

Granddad shrugged. "I can't answer that, I've only just heard the news. There's been a fair bit of scaremongering going on, and it seems the fog and shipwrecks are driving holidaymakers away from Tenby. The tabloids are calling this area a *dangerous destination*."

"Oooh, that'll be bad for business," said Pippin. "Tourists keep the town ticking over, that's what my Auntie Gwennie says."

"I'm already feeling the pinch," said Granddad, and an

uneasy silence fell over them. "Right, then, think I'll have a lie-down," he said at last. "There's bread and Branston Pickle in the pantry. Help yourselves."

Zoé studied her grandfather's wan face, noticing dark circles beneath his eyes. "Are you okay, Granddad?"

"Fancy I've a cold coming on. Snuffles, congested chest, nothing to worry about. Ta-ta." Granddad strode out of the room in his typical elegant fashion, ducking beneath a beam and vanishing up the stairs.

"Hey, guys, do you think the Scravens are connected to these accidents?" said Ian.

"What if all this is part of the Scraven invasion?" said Zoé, feeling a flash of panic. The thought hadn't occurred to her before.

"C'mon, here's our chance!" whispered Pippin, and Zoé, seeing a wild glint in her eyes, felt suddenly nervous. "Where's the puzzle?"

"Forget it," said Ian. "We can't go to Wythernsea, it's too much of a risk. More Scravens could escape!"

"Scared, are you? Now, there's a pity," said Pippin with a grimace, and Zoé could tell she was acting. "You've got rare mist and a runestone to scare off anything that comes your way, but I guess what you don't have is adventure in your bones. Derring-do, blood-and-guts courage, that's what we Welsh have. We're tough as old boots."

"Huh! I'm just as brave as you," muttered Ian. "Braver, even."

"Just because we're Americans doesn't mean we're wimps," Zoé snapped. "We're rugged and brave, and we've got Welsh blood, too, so there. We're—what was it Bron called us?—*harrowers!*" Suddenly, she felt the pull of the puzzle, drawing her upstairs.

"What's stopping us?" persisted Pippin. "You said time goes really slow in Wythernsea, so we'll be back in a jiff, before your grandfather wakes up, and the Scravens won't even have time to escape! Come on, don't be fuddy-duddies."

"Nope. Too dangerous," said Ian, consulting his watch. "Aren't you late for school?"

"No matter," said Pippin. "I can miss one day."

"Ian's right. Besides, Miss Glyndower said not to come back until we know who The First is," argued Zoé. "I don't want her getting mad at us."

"Give your Miss Glyndower the runestone," said Pippin. "That'll make her happy."

"I just thought of something," said Ian, looking even more worried. "Don't we need the runestone to defeat the Scravens? I mean, why are we supposed to take it to Miss Glyndower after we find The First? Tenby's where all the Scravens are headed! We need the runestone more than she does! I think we should go down there right now and straighten this out."

It was a losing battle, Zoé realized: the puzzle had a hold on all of them. They were dazzled by it, drawn to it, unable to resist its magical force.

"Harrowers we are, then," said Pippin with a grin. "Show me the way to Wythernsea."

CHAPTER NINETEEN
RETURN TO WYTHERNSEA

Clutching the runestone to her chest, Zoé felt herself falling through the glass tunnel, Ian's shouts and Pippin's fierce screams echoing around her. All she could see of them were blurred shadows, and she worried about the stone shattering or turning to dust, it was so ancient and fragile. That fragility was why she'd decided to carry the stone instead of putting it in her backpack, where it might get smashed.

To calm herself, she remembered sitting with her mom on the front stoop of a rented house, red and orange leaves falling around them. Her mom was talking about the past, something she rarely did, describing her life in Tenby when she was Zoé's age—taking shortcuts to school, hiking with her chums along the headland, watching Punch and Judy shows, riding donkeys on the beach—it had all sounded magical.

Spinning down through the blue depths of the puzzle, Zoé rocked and shuddered, a clammy mist enfolding her. She felt as if all the oxygen had gone out of her lungs. After what seemed like an endless fall, she looked down to see a patch of green coming up beneath her.

Moments later her feet grazed brambles, grass and tasseled fronds. She sat up, catching her breath, relieved to see Ian and Pippin nearby—and to see the runestone still in one piece.

Beside her, Pippin lay flat on her back, giggling hysterically. "I'm all befuddled," she said with a hiccup. "Ohhh, me blinking brain, my bones are aching."

Zoé watched Ian struggle through the high grass, like an explorer setting foot on some new planet.

"Where are we?" he murmured. "This doesn't look like Wythernsea."

"Course it is," said Zoé, gazing uneasily at the skeletal branches hung with moss, blocking out the light. "Wythernsea's the only place the puzzle takes you to."

Gray mist drifted around her, and from the moist black earth came a bitter smell. *We're in a forest,* she thought, heart rising to her throat. *A creepy primeval forest.* The flowers were hideous and black, bobbing on thorny stalks, and dead leaves swirled through the air. They seemed to be in the middle of a swampland, with weird creatures slinking through the grass, shaped like squid and jellyfish and eels, and strange reptiles with heads like miniature crocodiles.

Zoé felt a strange prickling all down her spine. This wasn't at all how she remembered Wythernsea.

In the distance beams of sunlight fell through fog-shrouded trees, and she gazed at the mechanical claws snapping and revolving, and the motionless weathervanes high on the turrets. Beyond the city wall rose a jumble of rooftops and chimneys, gleaming beneath a brilliant blue sky.

"Oh no!" she gasped, feeling air rush out of her lungs. "We're on the wrong side! We should've landed over there, in Wythernsea!"

"Are you kidding? We fell short of the wall?" said Ian in a panicky voice. "That means we're in the Harshlands!"

Pippin stopped laughing and bolted upright. "The Harshlands, what's that?" she demanded. "Not where them creatures live . . . is it?"

The others didn't answer.

"It's your fault this happened," Zoé said accusingly to Pippin. "We never should've listened to you! You bugged us to come here and we told you no, but you went on and on about going through the puzzle, calling us fuddy-duddies and stuff, so we caved in." Hot, angry tears splashed down her cheeks. At this very moment she hated Pippin with a passion.

"You're blaming *me?*" said Pippin. "I'm just an innocent bystander!"

"It's nobody's fault, so stop your bickering," growled Ian. "We need to figure out how to scale that wall."

"Okay, okay," said Zoé, still upset but aware that she was being unfair to Pippin.

She sensed a movement in the trees and, turning, saw with a flash of terror a dark shape in the mist. It was a Scraven crouched on a branch, knobbled and hunched, eyes smoldering, leathery wings snarled across its back.

"Scraven!" she yelled.

"Head for the wall!" shouted Ian.

Gripping the runestone, Zoé ran for her life, feet squelching through wet grass and slurry mud, stumbling over thick roots, vines snagging her ankles. She reached the wall first and scanned it hurriedly: the stone was falling apart in places, chunks of it gouged out, but she could see no footholds to climb or cracks to wriggle through.

As Ian and Pippin caught up with her, a shriek rang out. Through a scrum of leaves she saw a Scraven launch itself from a tree the height of a four-story building. She froze in her tracks, watching two gigantic wings snap open. The Scraven catapulted down, heading straight for them.

There was a loud *thwack!* and the creature screamed as a flaming arrow plunged into its chest. Zoé watched the Scraven plummet, crashing through leaves and branches, landing with a sickening thud on the earth.

"Hurry, you dim-witted fools!" shouted a voice, and she saw a Defender waving his crossbow at them. Stern and massive, he'd thrown open a hidden door in the wall; a shaggy, long-snouted dog stood next to him, growling deep in its throat.

Zoé scrambled with the others through the narrow doorway, too frightened to worry about the barker. High-pitched shrieks echoed through the forest, and as the door closed behind them, she saw more Scravens leaping from the trees.

"What were ye doing in the Harshlands?" demanded the Defender, bolting the door with a leather-gloved hand.

Zoé stared at his torn chain mail and scuffed boots, his impassive face and bloodshot eyes. The barker had stopped growling and was gazing up at her, tongue lolling on one side of its mouth. The poor animal was a mess, its white coat filthy and matted, with cuts on its snout and one eye glazed over.

"If my arrow had been a few centimeters off, d'you know what would've become of ye?" The Defender curled his lip in contempt.

"We'd be toast," said Pippin, brushing a huge snail off her sleeve.

"Aye, gruesome toast, and that's a fact." The man rubbed his grizzled chin. Somehow Zoé felt reassured by his large, blunt presence.

"That creature would've taken the three of you at once, it was that big." When he spoke, it sounded as if he had marbles rolling around inside his mouth. "We're waging a war here, can't ye see?"

Throat tickling, Zoé was suddenly aware that the air was heavy with smoke. There were scores of Defenders along the wall, some on ladders, others balanced on the turrets, flinging burning arrows.

"Thanks for helping us out," she heard Ian say in a quaky voice. "We'd be dead if it weren't for you."

The Defender grunted.

"Ach, that Scraven was disgusting, eh?" said Pippin.

"We have to go now," said Zoé, noticing the Defender eyeing the runestone, his expression one of a plundering pirate.

"What's that you've got?" he demanded, looming over her.

Zoé gave him a defiant look, determined not to be browbeaten. "This belongs to Miss Glyndower, and we're here to deliver it."

"That's right," said Pippin in her street-tough voice. "And she'll cut off the head of anyone who tries to take it."

"Get a move on, then," the man said gruffly, waving them away, but not before casting a last glance at the runestone.

Aware of the Defender watching them, they turned and marched off. When Zoé looked back, the barker had vanished into the smoke and fog, along with its master and all the others defending the wall.

❧

Overhead the Wythernsea sky was a rich, searing blue, but the waterfront lay still and silent. Taverns, inns and warehouses were shuttered; shopfronts had been boarded up. There were no people selling goods in the marketplace or hawking baskets of eels, no fishermen on the wharves, no workmen repairing boats. It saddened Zoé to see the bright fishing boats abandoned on the docks.

They came to an arched bridge, the same one Gwyn Griffiths had taken them across, but there was no sign of the furry long-necked animals. *Seems like ages ago*, thought Zoé, thumping over the wooden boards.

Pippin gasped when she saw the great sweeping staircase to the Retreat.

"We're here, we're here!" shouted Zoé, crunching over shells and slipping on wet seaweed as she raced up the steps.

The polished door gleaming in the sunlight, the image of Arianrhod and the whale's jawbone all seemed welcomingly familiar. Zoé stood on her toes and lifted the worn knocker—a silver crab that looked alarmingly real. The knocker fell and there was a brief silence, followed by shufflings and mutterings on the other side. The hinged door at the bottom flapped open and Zoé saw two eyes, set wide apart, blinking behind the grille.

"Tegan?" she ventured.

"Do I look like a girl?" said an indignant voice. "'Tis Jasper here. Jasper Morgan." The boy paused. "And who be you?"

"We're Zoé, Ian and Pippin," announced Zoé.

"I've orders to open this door to no one," said the boy.

Ian bent down, speaking quietly through the grille. "We've got something extremely important to deliver to Miss Glyndower, so please open up," he said in a coaxing tone. "She's been waiting for us."

"Sorry," said the boy. "I've orders, see, and nobody gets in."

"Unlock this door at once!" shouted Pippin, pounding her fist against the wood. "Else we'll break it down!"

Zoé heard the boy say in a tiny whisper, "Hold on."

Minutes passed before the door swung wide, revealing Miss E. Morwenna Glyndower in a luminous beaded gown, her diaphanous hair blowing around her face as she gazed down at them with a stern expression. Behind her stood a moon-faced boy with springy curls and a face like an angry bulldog. *Jasper Morgan*, thought Zoé, glaring fiercely back at him.

"My dear children," said Miss Glyndower. "I was not expecting you this soon."

CHAPTER TWENTY
THE RUNESTONE OF ARIANRHOD

"Here it is," said Zoé, triumphantly holding up the runestone. "We found it!"

"The Runestone of Arianrhod," murmured Miss Glyndower as Zoé placed it into her hands. "Thank you, my dear."

"Weren't easy getting it, mind," said Pippin. "Took some doing. I'm Philippa Jenkyn Thomas, by the way, the one who found the glass puzzle. You can call me Pippin."

Before Miss Glyndower could respond, Ian said excitedly, "First we went to the museum looking for the runestone, then we went down into the tunnels."

"To a place called the Tombs," said Zoé. "A seeress took us."

"The seeress Bron Gilwern of Tenby, a friend of mine,"

explained Pippin. "Bron chanted some cryptic words, see, and knocked the guards down flat. Like a hex, it were."

"And old Stokes the assistant curator chased us down the tunnels," said Zoé. "But he didn't catch us, we were too fast and—"

"I've no doubt you were all extremely brave—and clever as well, to have retrieved the runestone so swiftly," said Miss Glyndower, examining the relic, turning it over in her hands. "Very well then, it is time to plan our strategy." She motioned for the three to follow.

"I'm a little concerned about how this is all going to work," said Ian as Miss Glyndower led them down a corridor. "Because we need the runestone in Tenby to fight the Scravens! It doesn't make sense to leave it here when back home—"

"Everything will happen in its own time," she said, her manner abrupt, "and in the proper order. In these early days, the threat is greatest against Wythernsea, as the Scravens become stronger. The runestone will weaken them, rendering them incapable of attacking us again."

"Any chance you guys could help us in Tenby?" asked Ian.

Miss Glyndower gave a rueful smile. "We would dearly love to help you defeat the Scravens, but I fear it is impossible, as we Wythernfolk cannot travel beyond the boundaries of Wythernsea. None of us would survive going through the puzzle."

"Too bad," said Zoé, thinking how exciting it would be if the Wythernfolk joined forces with the people of Tenby.

As they walked along, she took mental notes on the

richly polished wood and Oriental carpets, the oil lamps in glass bowls, the curtains of watered silk. There were tapestry chairs with velvet cushions and expanses of wall embedded with shells. But where were Gwyn Griffiths and all the other kids? The house struck her as oddly silent.

"Why is the Retreat so empty?" she asked.

"After the last attack I sent the Messengers to the cloister in town," said Miss Glyndower, dashing Zoé's high spirits: she wouldn't be seeing her friends this time. "It lies atop a steep cobbled hill near the harbor: a dark granite structure with numerous chimneys and a Celtic cross. The cloister has thick walls and a deep cellar, and solid doors they can easily bolt. They'll be much safer there."

"You've been *attacked?*" said Ian.

"Since your last visit much has changed. The Scravens grow infinitely more brazen." Miss Glyndower lifted the hem of her gown as they mounted a spiraling staircase. "Despite our precautions, more Scravens are breaching the wall each day. The Retreat has suffered two attacks, with several weathervanes destroyed."

"If it's so dangerous, then why is Jasper here?" Zoé blurted out. "Why isn't he in the cloister with the rest of the kids?"

"Jasper is my nephew," explained Miss Glyndower. "He was distraught at the prospect of being separated from me, so I allowed him to remain here. I am all he has left in this world, you see."

"Oh," said Zoé in a meek voice.

"A difficult journey, was it?" asked Miss Glyndower.

"We landed on the wrong side of the wall," said Ian, and Miss Glyndower's golden eyes widened in alarm.

"One of them horrid creatures came flying right at us," said Pippin. "I thought for sure we was goners."

"A Defender killed it with a burning arrow and saved our lives," added Zoé.

"There were no end of Scravens screeching and flapping," said Pippin with grim relish. "Escaped by a thread, we did."

Zoé watched Miss Glyndower's expression darken.

No one said a word as they climbed four flights to a narrow, circular turret with white walls and a trestle table with high-backed benches carved with seascapes. Zoé studied the rough boards nailed across a row of windows, imagining Scravens clawing their way into the Retreat. *Things are going downhill here fast,* she thought.

Miss Glyndower poured water from an earthen jug and motioned for them all to sit down. "Everyone in Wythernsea is in hiding," she said, handing them each a tumbler. "If the attacks continue much longer, we may not be able to hold out. The town walls are in a dreadful state."

"But you've got those huge mechanical claws, right? They'll make mincemeat out of the Scravens," said Zoé confidently. "And those Defenders are super tough."

"Their crossbow skills are really impressive," said Ian.

"They are brave men, of course, but even the Defenders have their limits," said Miss Glyndower, and Zoé had to admit she was right, thinking how the Defenders had looked pretty battle-weary.

"But everything's tip-top now, isn't it?" said Pippin cheerfully. "We found the runestone!"

"Yeah, and we're ready to do battle," Zoé piped up.

"Have you forgotten something?" Miss Glyndower's piercing eyes flashed angrily. "What about The First? I trust you've brought that information with you. Yes?" Her tone was icy. "If not, you've wasted precious time coming here—and time is something we have very little of."

"The First? The Scraven leader?" Zoé rattled on, her mind racing. "We found The First."

"We did?" Pippin gaped at Zoé over the rim of her tumbler.

"Sure," said Zoé, trusting the others to back her up. "It's Iris Tintern."

"Hmm," said Ian with a ponderous frown.

"Okay, maybe we're not one hundred percent sure," Zoé forged on, "but we saw a humongous eye on Iris's forehead, didn't we? That counts for something."

"They've all got them monstrous eyes," said Pippin.

"Two Scravens escaped when you put the puzzle together, yeah, Pippin?" Zoé reminded her. "That means one of them took over Iris."

"Zoé's got a point," said Ian. "Because it wasn't until *after* we saw Iris Tintern that we put the puzzle together and more Scravens escaped."

"It was *you* who let the first ones out," said Zoé, pointing her finger at Pippin. "All this started when—"

"Stop blamin' me for everything!" Pippin slammed her

tumbler on the table. "Wasn't my fault, never was! And what about your chum Dr. Marriott? I'll wager he let a few of them things get out!"

"He didn't!" shouted Zoé. "He was too scared to put it together!"

The sound of Miss Glyndower's sharp, authoritative voice interrupted them: "Your impetuous natures and reluctance to follow orders may well have landed you on the wrong side of the wall, not to mention that Scravens may be getting through into your world while you're here in Wythernsea. Now you waste my time with silly arguments! This is not a game, my children. You cannot *guess* the identity of The First, you must know it beyond all doubt. If you do not defeat The First, it is certain that Tenby will fall to Scravens. So . . . enough quarreling."

Looking at one another with sheepish expressions—Zoé could see Ian's face turning bright red—the three children fell silent.

"Listen carefully, for this is our strategy, first in Wythernsea, then in your world. The words of the runestone must be memorized, then whispered within sight of the goddess weathervanes," instructed Miss Glyndower. "The incantation is timeless, uniting everything that has happened before and everything that is to come, evoking the ancient powers of Arianrhod. It may take minutes or hours, but the incantation must be recited until the goddesses awaken."

"So the goddesses will destroy the Scravens?" asked Ian.

"They will be defeated but not destroyed," replied Miss

Glyndower. "You see, it is not in the nature of Wythernfolk to take the life of anyone or anything, not even Scravens. After all, Scravens were once human beings such as ourselves."

"But them Defenders are out there killing 'em with flaming arrows," Pippin pointed out.

"In self-defense, yes, but our true intent is to weaken the Scravens, undermining their evil, sapping their strength, rendering them harmless so they are no longer a threat. An imperfect solution, I realize."

"Oh," said Zoé, feeling somewhat deflated. Then it wasn't the end of the Scravens in Wythernsea after all.

"Your world is a different matter," continued Miss Glyndower. "The Scravens have invaded Tenby, and over time The First will grow stronger. We've no choice but to destroy them using the power of the goddess."

"So Arianrhod's still alive?" asked Pippin.

"Goddesses are eternal, and Arianrhod is indeed a celestial being," said Miss Glyndower, hair floating like a cloud around her head. "Her spiral castle Caer Arianrhod moves back and forth between the bottom of the sea in a sunken town off the coast of Wales and her other home, the North Star."

Zoé grew suddenly excited. "Arianrhod's castle is in *Wythernsea?*"

"Nay, her town is near Carmarthen," said Miss Glyndower. Seeing Zoé's face fall, she added, "Yet Wythernsea holds a special place in her heart. Centuries ago, her castle rose up through the waves of Carmarthen Bay on its way to the North Star and was attacked by sea scorpions—treacherous, deadly creatures—and the Wythernfolk went out in their boats and drove them off."

What an extraordinary story, thought Zoé, wondering what a sea scorpion looked like. Not any uglier than a Scraven, she was sure.

"So the goddess gave you the runestone," said Pippin.

"Yes. And she bestowed upon us our shallows."

Zoé felt a thrill of amazement. Their shallows were a gift from the goddess!

"But how do we destroy the Scravens exactly?" Ian asked. "How do we memorize the incantation? Isn't it written in some ancient tongue?"

"It is—and therefore you must seek help. Someone must translate it for you. Your seeress friend, perhaps? Hmm, I wonder," murmured Miss Glyndower, tapping her long fingers against the runestone. Mystical blue light flowed out, making her look more otherworldly than ever. "I fear there is a problem," she said quietly, "one that I could not have anticipated. You see, the incantation is locked: the runes are unreadable. A spell was laid upon the stone, no doubt by the Astercôtes, and there is no way to lift the enchantment."

"You can't *read* it?" croaked Ian. "Oh no, does that mean we're all doomed?"

Zoé's throat felt suddenly dry. The runestone was their mega-weapon against Scravens and—what was it Bron had said?—it was *the Scravens' undoing!*

Miss Glyndower's fierce expression grew more distant. "No one in Wythernsea can lift this spell."

"There has to be a way," said Zoé. "We can't just give up."

Miss Glyndower, looking weary, ran her hand over the surface of the stone.

"My dad says even the most difficult math problems have solutions," added Ian. "But it might take, er, a hundred years or so to figure them out...." His words drifted off.

"I know: we'll ask Bron!" said Pippin, jumping up. "She's an expert on runes and enchantments. If anyone can unlock it, Bron can."

Miss Glyndower looked doubtful, but Zoé could see she was running out of options. "Very well," she said at last, "take the runestone to your seeress, but she must work fast. The weathervanes will not hold out much longer, and we've only three days until Midsummer, when the Scravens are weakest."

"We'll be quick," promised Ian. "Oh, there's something else I was wondering about. Have you ever heard of the Thirteenth Piece?"

Miss Glyndower blinked at him in surprise. "Indeed I have. Made of Wythernsea glass, it is laden with old enchantments. The Astercôtes took it with them when they left Wythernsea, but it was my understanding that the Thirteenth Piece had been lost."

"It's not lost, exactly," said Zoé. "A monk has it."

"Our friend Dr. Marriott told us that one of the missing Astercôtes bequeathed the Thirteenth Piece to his grandson, a monk on Caldey Island," explained Ian.

"This may well be a turning point," said Miss Glyndower. "For as long as the puzzle remains a gateway between our worlds, your lives are in peril. The Thirteenth Piece will seal the puzzle and prevent Scravens from escaping into Tenby."

Zoé felt her chest tighten. "But if we do that, we can't come back to Wythernsea!"

"My dear girl, you have no choice," said Miss Glyndower. "The gateway is flawed, and The First is infinitely clever. If the gateway stays open, The First will travel between worlds, stirring up chaos and terror. Sealing the puzzle is crucial to subduing the Scravens. In fact, I shall make sealing the puzzle part of our plan."

Zoé bit down on her lip, trying not to cry. It wasn't fair: she'd found this mysterious and fantastic universe, and now it was going to be ripped away from her, as if it had never existed at all.

"Make certain this Tintern woman is truly The First," added Miss Glyndower. "To save Tenby, you must have the correct knowledge."

Ian leaned forward. "How will we know for sure?"

"Once you have the Thirteenth Piece, carry it with you at all times. Should the glass dim, you'll know you're in the presence of a Scraven. Should it lose all color and turn black, you are in the presence of The First," explained Miss Glyndower. "When you return to Wythernsea, be sure to arrive when the sun is high: that is when we'll set our plan in motion. Only then will the battle truly begin—if you are willing."

Zoé looked Miss Glyndower squarely in the eye. "Oh,

we're ready for battle, all right," she said, a chill running through her. "We're harrowers and we're Welsh."

"We're brave," said Ian resolutely, "and we'll fight the Scravens to the death."

"To the death," Pippin echoed.

CHAPTER TWENTY-ONE
THE SMUGGLERS' TUNNEL

Zoé stood with Ian and Pippin beside the shuttered ticket booth in Castle Square. The early-morning wind was especially cold for late June, and it was blowing hard on the town from the north. Once or twice she saw shapes in the mist, slipping between the buildings and town walls, but they seemed more like phantoms than flesh-and-blood people.

A notice taped outside the booth read ONLY THESE BOATS LAND ON CALDEY ISLAND. That was before someone had taken a red marker pen and written *All Boats Canceled Until Further Notice* in thick letters over the sign.

"I hope Arthur Angel's around to give us a ride," said Pippin, squinting into the distance. Pippin had turned up at their door while they were eating breakfast with the exciting news that school had been canceled for the week, due to some kind of electrical problem caused by the high winds.

Granddad was back at the cottage, in bed with a cold. Zoé and Ian had asked if they could go to Caldey with Mr. Angel, but after hearing reports of boats lost in the fog, Granddad said definitely not. So, although they hated being deceptive, the two cousins had decided to take matters into their own hands. Finding the Thirteenth Piece was crucial to defeating the Scravens.

"I feel guilty about Granddad," said Ian. "I told him we're going off for the day so I can take pictures, but it's not really true."

"Well, it's partly true," said Pippin. "You've got your camera, yeah? It's just that you'll be taking pictures of Caldey Island instead of Tenby."

Ian sighed. "I suppose."

"I feel really bad, too," said Zoé sympathetically. "I hate telling fibs, and Granddad's the greatest, we all know that, but just think how much he'd worry if he knew Scravens were trying to take over Tenby—"

"Isn't that Mr. Angel's boat down there?" interrupted Pippin.

The three raced down Penniless Cove Hill, gulls screeching overhead. At the far end of the pier, a man in a knit cap and bulky sweater was hauling crates into a bright blue boat. Zoé could just make out the words *Sea Kestrel* in peeling letters on the side.

"Hey, Mr. Angel!" shouted Pippin.

The man turned his ruddy face in their direction. "Hullo there, kids."

"We were wondering if you're going to Caldey Island," said Pippin.

"I'm leaving this very minute, as a matter of fact," he said, loading a crate filled with parcels into the back of the boat. "I make the run to Caldey Island twice a day—thirty minutes each way, weather permitting."

Zoé exchanged excited glances with the other two. Arthur Angel was obviously a friendly sort. She was certain he'd give them a ride.

"What are you taking out to Caldey?" she asked. "There sure are a lot of crates and boxes."

"Well, there are the letters I deliver to the monks, and other things, too: tea and dishwashing soap, paraffin candles, tins of powdered Ovaltine. Live there year-round, the monks do, always in need of something." He straightened up, rubbing his whiskers. "Not from these parts, are you?"

"We're here from America," said Zoé. "But my mom and Ian's dad were born in Tenby. We come here every summer to stay with our granddad."

"We're cousins," said Ian. "You took us out on your boat last summer. Our granddad's John Lloyd Blackwood."

Mr. Angel nodded approvingly. "John Blackwood. A fine man."

Zoé grinned. "He's the best."

"Need any extra hands on board, Mr. Angel?" asked Pippin. "We have to get to Caldey, but we haven't any money. We'll work to pay our fare and we won't be any trouble."

"Sorry, but I can't take the responsibility." Mr. Angel shook out a length of coiled rope. "The voyage is too risky for young folks without someone coming with yer. Squalls, fog, unpredictable tides and now these tourist boats getting caught on the rocks: we're a dangerous destination, according to the tabloids. It's gotten so treacherous out there they've canceled all boats indefinitely. Seems I'm the only one going; the mail has to get through."

"I wouldn't be scared, no matter how high the waves," declared Zoé. "Anyway, Granddad says the tabloids print rubbish."

"Pirates don't scare us, either," said Ian. "And I'm a real whiz at tying knots."

Chuckling softly, Mr. Angel checked his watch. "Another day, perhaps, when things are back to normal. Time to head out, then—the monks are expecting me." He hopped into his boat and started up the engine. "Cheerio!" he called.

Zoé waved, her high spirits deflating as she watched the *Sea Kestrel* vanish into the fog.

"Phooey," she said, turning to Ian and Pippin. They gazed back with glum expressions.

The waves were growing fiercer, whitecapped and steep, and the smell that rose up was strong and cold—as if, thought Zoé, it was bubbling up from the deepest, blackest part of the sea.

"Need a ride to Caldey, do you?" said a voice.

Zoé turned to see a lean, bony figure walking down the pier, hunched inside a yellow raincoat, his broad-brimmed hat flapping in the wind, eyes hidden behind aviator sunglasses.

"It's Ned Larkin. His mum is head postmistress," said Pippin, her voice dropping to a whisper. "Bit of a layabout, Ned, spends his time trawling but never catches anything."

Pippin stepped forward. "We do need a ride, Ned Larkin, and we need to go this very minute."

"Follow me," said Ned, but with the wind howling, Zoé could make out only half of what he was saying. "Boat's over there, see? Black with green trim. A real beauty . . ."

Zoé had seen Ned around town, but today she had a funny feeling about him. As she pulled out the puzzle-glass, the wind tore Ned's hat from his head. She stole a quick look: on his forehead was a whirling black eye.

"Scraven!" she yelled.

They sprinted down the pier, Ned Larkin shouting after them, "You'll have to swim, then—there's no one who'll take you!"

Running up Penniless Cove Lane, the three disappeared into the crooked streets of the Old Town as the fog enclosed them, muffling their footsteps, turning them invisible.

🐉

Bron stood waiting outside the Smugglers' Haunt, one of the older hotels overlooking North Beach, eating a fried egg sandwich. Today her hair was a rich canary yellow. Zoé couldn't decide which of Bron's hair colors she liked best: pink, purple, orange or yellow.

On the hotel doorstep a workman stood leaning on his shovel, smoking a pipe. There was a strong smell of cherry tobacco in the air, and Zoé could see a handwritten sign saying the hotel was closed for repairs.

After their failed attempt to catch a ride with Mr. Angel, Pippin had called Bron, asking about the secret tunnel to Caldey Island, and Bron had offered to take them to the entrance. Zoé found it hard to imagine a tunnel beneath the sea, but Pippin assured her it was real.

"No entry," said the workman as they headed for the front door. "No one's allowed in under any circumstances. Hotel reopens end of July." He puffed on his pipe, sending out fresh waves of cherry tobacco.

"Grumpy old sod," muttered Pippin.

Bron shot the workman a piercing glance. Zoé shared a knowing look with Ian, then watched the man's face go blank and doughy, the shovel clattering to the pavement. He stumbled backward, eyes glazing over, and collapsed into a heap on the sidewalk.

"She's done it again," whispered Ian.

"The bloke won't remember a thing," said Pippin. "There's the beauty of it, see."

They hurried past the prone figure into the Smugglers' Haunt, Bron steering them around sheet-draped furniture, paint cans, ladders and rolled-up carpets. Plaster dust floated through the high, airy rooms.

"I've timed it perfectly," said Bron. "Workers are on break."

They entered a dining hall with mullioned windows and a black marble floor. Bron made straight for an enormous stone fireplace, ducking inside it. Zoé and the others followed, emerging on the other side into a drafty corridor where Bron stood before a set of glazed French doors.

"Tunnel's on the other side," she said, unfolding what looked like a map. "For you, Philippa. Hang on to it."

Pippin nodded solemnly as Bron placed the map in her hands.

"Drawn by French smugglers on a tunnel wall. I copied it," said Bron, and Zoé's ears pricked up. A *pirate map?* How swashbuckling was that? "Moored their ships off Caldey, smuggling brandy and whatnot into Tenby through this tunnel, with no one the wiser."

Zoé studied the map over Pippin's shoulder. A zigzag line ran from Crackwell Street down to Tenby Harbor, then under the ocean to Caldey Island. *What a cool story that would make,* she thought, *a hair-raising tale of pirate maps and spells and tunnels under the sea.*

"Only men are allowed inside the monastery. This gets you through the door." Bron placed a thick envelope in Ian's hand. "Tell the monks it's an urgent message for Father Gwydion Yates from the Mother Superior of the Community of Cistercian Nuns at Holy Cross Abbey in Whitland."

Ian held the envelope up to his face and Zoé could see a wax seal stamped on the outside. "Did you say *nuns?*"

"I copied Sister Agatha's signature exactly. They'll never suspect it's a forgery."

"You forged a *nun's* signature?" croaked Ian.

"Here's where I leave you," said Bron in that clipped tone of hers, ignoring Ian's question. "Who has the runestone, eh? Pippin says there's a spell needs lifting from it."

"Here," said Zoé, opening her pack and pulling it out. "Thanks for helping us, Bron. Miss Glyndower needs it right away."

"Then it comes back to us, so's we can fight off the Scravens," said Pippin. "Miss Glyndower gave us kids instructions to stand near the goddess and whisper the incantation. Think maybe you can help us with that? We need to know it by heart."

"I'll see what I can do," said Bron with a cryptic smile, and before Zoé could say another word, she vanished down the corridor.

Ian adjusted his headlamp, double-checking that everyone had a puzzle-glass in his or her pocket, along with the vials of mist, chocolate bars and water. He pushed open the French doors and the three linked arms, striding confidently over the threshold, across the soft, sandy floor toward the sea. Zoé felt alternately euphoric and terrified, her mind filled with images of ghosts, pirates, wreckers and plague victims. Rats, too: there were bound to be rats down there. But she could handle all those—what she tried hard not to think about were Scravens.

"Nothing to be scared of," Ian reassured her. "The Scravens aren't down here, Zoé, they're aboveground taking over people like Iris Tintern and Catherine Beedle and that ghoulish kid Ned Larkin."

But that didn't do it for her—and she knew he didn't believe it either.

The tunnel reeked of fish and seaweed, although the floor was surprisingly dry, and Zoé could hear a wailing wind echoing around them. The walls were the same rock as the shoreline, only smoother. Ian explained how the tunnel had been cut from sandstone using pickaxes, and every time the diggers hit granite they had to change direction, which accounted for the tunnel's zigzag nature.

Ian checked his compass, the one Zoé admired because it was made of real silver and embossed with his father's initials. How cool would it be to own something with her mom's initials, she thought, like her mom's iPod or maybe one of her sparkly bracelets.

"We're entering Tenby Harbor, all is well," announced Ian.

The three started to run, and Zoé had trouble seeing too far ahead because of the tunnel's jags and turns. Whenever she looked back, it seemed as if shadows were following them.

"Look!" cried Pippin, pointing to the wall. "Brilliant, that is!"

They stopped, shining their lights on the tall letters cut deep into the stone: CALDEY → 1.5 KM.

CHAPTER TWENTY-TWO
THE THIRTEENTH PIECE

Zoé dragged her feet along the tunnel's sandy floor, exhausted from running, yearning for a bite of her chocolate bar. It seemed as if she'd been following the crooked passageway for ages, listening to the wind moaning, fearful that any minute a Scraven would jump out and wrap its leathery wings around her. Fortunately, all she'd seen so far were bats, huddled in tight knots, high up in the cracks of the tunnel.

"Remember Caldey Ghost Pirates?" said Ian, referring to a game he and Zoé had invented a few summers ago. "Remember how scared I used to get because I thought ghost pirates were going to make me walk the gangplank?"

"You used to get, like, catatonic," said Zoé. "You're a whole lot braver now."

She thought she saw him smile through the darkness. When Ian was younger, her murderous tales of pirates and ghosts had terrified him. She remembered his bad dreams and the way he'd wake up screaming in the nights. But things had slowly changed, and every summer he seemed a little bolder, slightly more daring than the year before. Was it because of her? she wondered. Had she inspired him to be braver? She liked to think so.

"Maybe you could teach me how to play Caldey Ghost Pirates," said Pippin, hair floating stormily about her face. "I'll teach you a game called Zombie in the Cellar."

"Deal," said Ian.

"I'd love to play a game with zombies in it," said Zoé. "Sorry I was mean and yelled at you, Pippin. You know, when I said you let in the Scravens and everything?"

"That's okay," said Pippin, and Zoé felt a weight lift from her heart. "Even harrowers get rattled sometimes."

"Hey, you guys," said Ian, "look up there!"

In the half-light of his beam, Zoé could see tiers of arches hewn from rough stone, unfolding one after another. The three began to run, racing pell-mell through the archways, to a massive wooden door with a scrolled handle and thick iron hinges. Leaning their shoulders against the rotted wood, they pushed with all their strength.

This is the kind of thing explorers and archaeologists do, thought

Zoé as the door creaked inward, opening into a vaulted hall with a floor of cobbled stone, its gold ceiling faded and cracked, yet beautiful still. She looked around dreamily at the primitive wooden statues lining the walls, wondering who on earth had made them and why they were there.

"Look how thick these walls are, and those statues, totally ancient!" said Ian, bristling with excitement. "Hey, guys, I think we're under St. David's Church. It's medieval, but originally it was a Celtic chapel, sixth century. Wow, this is like a page torn from the past."

Zoé smiled to herself. She'd read that phrase, "a page torn from the past," in a history pamphlet Ian had picked up at the Tenby tourist office. Was he trying to impress Pippin? On the other hand, tidbits of history always tended to wind him up.

"The monks hid down here when pirates and Vikings raided Caldey." Zoé watched the flash from his camera bounce off the walls. "Then there's the story of the Black Monk of Caldey, who was walled up in the monastery along with his gold, back in the fifteen hundreds. I'd give anything to have been around in those days."

She shuddered. Ian was beginning to sound like Stokes.

"Hair-raising times," said Pippin. "Must seem tame nowadays for them monks. What do they do all day?"

"I know there's a little chocolate factory here where the monks make fudge," said Zoé. "Granddad took us there last summer. And they make perfume from wildflowers on the island."

At the mention of the word *chocolate*, all three pulled out their chocolate bars and finished them off as they climbed a stone stairway up to the nave of a tiny church. Lozenges of colored light fell through the stained-glass windows, and Zoé felt her heart expand. She especially loved the window with a red fish swimming through turquoise waves. It felt peaceful here, peaceful and safe.

Outside the church, they stepped into a flat, stark land-scape wreathed in mist, while dark clouds scudded overhead, threatening rain. The small village was silent, and Zoé imagined the monks hard at work making fudge and perfume.

They traipsed past a cemetery, Ian taking photos of the wooden cross markers, down a dusty narrow road to the monastery, a white building of grand proportions looming up through the mist. Gazing at the red-tiled roof, the immense colonnade and spires and arched windows, Zoé felt suddenly nervous to actually be meeting a real monk—at least, she hoped Father Gwydion would come out and talk with them, since girls weren't allowed inside. What was he like? she wondered. And more importantly, would he be willing to give them the Thirteenth Piece?

A path of terra-cotta stones led to the monastery's wide stairway. At the top they stood before a large wooden door flanked by red and white squares.

"Go ahead, Ian, you've got the letter," said Pippin. "Try to smile, eh?"

Ian hesitated, clenching the envelope tightly in one hand. *He's probably worrying about Bron forging the nun's signature,* thought Zoé. For someone planning to be a secret agent, Ian was awfully squeamish about telling lies. *Maybe he should be a park ranger instead, or a math professor, like his dad.*

"It's okay," she whispered in his ear. "Just act like your normal friendly self. Father Gwydion will think you're a cool kid."

She stood on one side of him and Pippin on the other, staring up at the door as Ian reluctantly shuffled forward and knocked.

"Louder," said Pippin. "A church mouse couldn't hear that."

Zoé choked back a nervous giggle and Ian rapped harder. Her heart beat fast as the door swung open and a bearded monk wearing sandals and a white robe gazed down at them.

"Good morning. Er, my name is Ian Blackwood and I'm here to deliver a letter for Father Gwydion Yates—an *urgent* letter," said Ian, sounding stiff and formal. Zoé felt Pippin nudge her in the ribs and she tried not to laugh. "The letter is from the Mother Superior of the Community of Cistercian Nuns at Holy Cross Abbey in Whitland. Whitland, Wales, that is. And I—I really must speak with Father Gwydion."

Seeing the expression on the monk's face, Zoé grew uneasy. He looked as if he'd seen a ghost. Well, maybe a whole flock of ghosts. Or . . . had he seen something else? She swallowed hard, not wanting to think about the alternative.

"Father Gwydion Yates?" repeated the monk, tugging his beard. "But Father Gwydion is no longer with us." His eyes darted from Zoé to Pippin and back to Ian again.

How can Father Gwydion not be here? thought Zoé. Monks were supposed to stay put in their monasteries, not go lolly-gagging about.

"He's not?" said Ian. "Then where can we find him, Father—sorry, what's your name?"

"Father Bertrand. Our departed Gwydion was laid to rest, oh, it's been a good five years now. You'll find his grave-stone in the cemetery next to St. David's Church."

The monk with the Thirteenth Piece was *dead*? Zoé wondered if the old monk had made a mistake, or maybe he was confused because something had scared him.

"How did you find your way to Caldey?" asked Father Bertrand, narrowing his eyes at them. "These days only the *Sea Kestrel* comes from the mainland, and I know for a fact that passengers are no longer allowed on Arthur Angel's mail boat."

"Um, well, we—" stammered Ian.

Zoé said the first thing that flew into her head. "The coast guard brought us and—" She stopped, worried about what might happen if she got caught telling a fib to a monk.

"That's right," said Pippin, picking up the thread, though Zoé could see Father Bertrand wasn't buying any of it. "We told the coast guard this was a super-important mission and they said, 'Right, then,' and we rode here in one of them big rescue boats."

"You really should leave now!" hissed Father Bertrand in a shaky voice. He bent down until he was at eye level with them. Zoé could see his eyes widening with fright. "A great darkness has fallen upon us here on the island. I cannot explain what is happening, but it seems a strange illness has overtaken the monastery." He glanced back over his shoulder, and Zoé wondered what exactly was going on inside.

"You are in grave danger, my children," he continued. "The island is no longer safe. Please, go home. Go back to the mainland."

Zoé felt the hairs on top of her head lift up. She was certain Father Bertrand was talking about Scravens, and the thought of them invading this tranquil island filled her with a sick dread.

"Sure, okay, that's fine with us," said Ian, stuffing the unopened letter into his messenger bag. "Thanks for letting us know, Father Bertrand."

The monastery door slammed shut.

"What did he mean, 'a great darkness'?" asked Pippin. "Sounds like the plague."

"Don't you get it?" said Zoé. "The Scravens are here on Caldey! They're turning the monks into the Afflicted!"

"I think we should go home—now," said Ian, hoisting the messenger bag over his shoulder. "This place is freaking me out."

"Can we make a quick stop at the cemetery?" asked Zoé. "I want to see Father Gwydion's grave."

"Okay," said Ian. "But let's keep close together so we don't lose each other."

Suddenly they all realized how anxious they were to

leave the abbey, and they ran helter-skelter down the steps and through the trees, along the road to the church.

Walking through the knee-high weeds, Zoé was shocked by the neglected state of the cemetery, where everything had been left to grow wild. She wondered if the Scravens had anything to do with its decrepit state.

"Those plain wooden crosses mark the older graves," said Ian. "We won't need to bother with those."

Zoé walked up and down the rows of tilting headstones eroded by time and wind and the salt air, peering closely at each one, checking for Father Gwydion's name. Sadly, everything was slowly being strangled by vegetation. Tendrils of ivy and leafy plants wound around the headstones, causing some to crack and others to fall over, while drifting fog gave the place an even more surreal atmosphere.

At last she found the gravestone, half buried in moss and lichen, set slightly apart from the others. The monk's name was shrouded in vines, but as she pulled a strand away she saw *Yates* carved into the stone.

"Over here!" she shouted. "I found him!"

Kneeling before the gravestone, she began uprooting weeds, creepers and nettles. Ian and Pippin joined her, tearing away long streamers of ivy.

"Go on, read it out loud, Zoé," said Ian once they'd finished.

The letters engraved on the tombstone were solid and upright, just the way Zoé imagined the monk to have been. "'Father Gwydion R. Yates,'" she read, "'beloved brother of the Order of Reformed Cistericans, Caldey Abbey, Caldey Island, Wales. May He Rest in Peace.'" She ran her hand over his name. "Poor monk."

"Poor us, you mean," said Pippin. "Without that Thirteenth Piece, we're in a right fix."

"You don't think someone murdered him for the puzzle piece, do you?" said Ian.

"That's a bit over the top," said Zoé, though the thought had crossed her mind as well. Pulling more weeds away from the stone, she noticed a figure carved into the bottom of the gravestone; using her fingernails, she began scraping off the lichen.

"Is that a bird?" asked Pippin.

"Bound to be a dove," said Ian. "See, it's directly under the word *Peace*. Doves are recurring motifs."

The lichen fell away, and on closer inspection, Zoé saw that the engraving was a small elegant Welsh dragon.

"Smashing," said Pippin. "It sort of sparkles, doesn't it? Hey, I've just remembered something. *Yates* means 'gatekeeper' in Welsh! Gwydion Yates: Gwydion Gatekeeper."

"Very appropriate," said Ian, aiming his camera at the dragon. "It all fits."

The dragon seemed to exude a faint light the more Zoé scraped away. Too bad she didn't have Granddad's magnifying glass.

"Can I take a look?" asked Ian, crouching down to inspect the carving. "Something's embedded in the dragon's wing, a decoration of some sort."

"Yeah, but monks don't go for fancy decorations," said Zoé. "They like things plain and simple." She bent closer, running her fingers over the dragon, entranced by the glimmering light of its wing. A thought struck her. "What if Gwydion Yates had a premonition?"

"You mean a vision?" said Ian. "I think those are restricted to saints."

"No, what I mean is, what if he knew somebody would come looking for the Thirteenth Piece—and what if he *wanted* them to find it?"

"You're sounding like Bron now," said Pippin, elbowing past Zoé for a closer inspection. "What's that, eh? Looks like a piece of blue glass!"

"What are we waiting for?" said Zoé, her excitement mounting. "We need something sharp to get it out."

"You're going to *desecrate a gravestone?*" cried Ian. "I don't believe this! First we go to the abbey with a nun's forged signature, and now we're robbing the grave of a dead monk!"

"It's okay, Ian, Father Gwydion would totally understand," said Zoé. "We didn't ask to get involved in this, but we're in it now. He inherited the Thirteenth Piece, and he meant for us to find it."

Using a sharp-edged stone, Pippin began chipping away around the glass. "Miss Glyndower said we had to be clever. It's all about outwitting the Scravens."

To her surprise, Ian didn't argue. He just stood there, looking thoughtful.

"It sure seems like magic, doesn't it?" said Zoé, captivated by the blue light. *It's probably really old magic,* she thought dreamily, *as old as the stones and the sea.*

"Stop yer daydreamin' and get on with it," said Pippin.

"Go ahead, Zoé, take it!" said Ian excitedly. "Take the Thirteenth Piece!"

⁂

Across the water, through the mists of Caldey Island, Zoé could just make out the pastel-colored buildings of Tenby in the distance, lined up along the waterfront. And if she looked closely at Castle Hill, she could even see the black maw of Dragon's Mouth cut into its steep cliff. *Strange to be seeing Tenby from so far away,* she thought.

After removing the Thirteenth Piece from Father Gwydion's gravestone, they decided it would be too dangerous to return through the tunnel. Zoé was sure that Scravens were following them or else poised in the tunnels, waiting to attack. So now they were sitting on the wooden jetty waiting for the *Sea Kestrel* because Arthur Angel, they were sure, wouldn't refuse them a ride this time.

At last the mail boat arrived, steering through choppy waves to the far end of the jetty, where two monks stood waiting. Zoé, clenching the Thirteenth Piece inside her fist, watched them unloading boxes off the boat, piling them into a wheelbarrow. Despite Father Bertrand's warning, the monks were not wearing glasses of any kind and seemed harmless enough. The Thirteenth Piece continued to glow in her hand, so she knew there was no danger of them being Scravens.

Even so, Zoé felt a deep unease. Caldey was a solitary island cut off from the rest of Wales: if the Scravens invaded, no one would ever know!

As the monks wheeled the barrow away, the three kids raced across the jetty shouting, "Hey, Mr. Angel!" Zoé saw Arthur Angel's jaw drop in surprise as they crowded around him, telling him how they'd walked through a tunnel under the sea to get to the island.

He stood looking down at them with a puzzled expression. "I can't get over it—you lot walked to Caldey? Through a *tunnel?*"

"We wouldn't lie to you," said Pippin.

"The tunnel starts under the Smugglers' Haunt in Tenby," Ian explained, "and ends up under St. David's Church here on Caldey."

"It took forever," said Zoé. "The tunnel's real zigzaggy." *Plus there are Scravens down there,* she added silently.

"It's one of them smuggler tunnels," said Pippin. "Don't you know about them?"

"When I was a boy, there was talk of a tunnel going out to Caldey, built by pirates and the like," said Arthur Angel. "But the secret tunnel to Caldey was more a folktale than anything else. I'm bowled over that it's actually there and you kids walked all that way."

"It's real," said Zoé. "But I wouldn't recommend that anyone go down there. It's kind of dangerous," she added quickly. Arthur Angel gave her a funny look, but fortunately he didn't ask for details.

"Mr. Angel," said Ian, "could we catch a ride with you to Tenby?"

"I'm not supposed to be ferrying passengers, but—" For a moment the mail boat captain gazed out at the whitecapped waves. Then, with an air of decision, he said, "Well, be quick and get in if you're coming. I'm heading back now."

The boat ride to Tenby Harbor was rough, with heavy swells and screaming winds. The *Sea Kestrel* rocked from side to side as Zoé clung to the gunwale next to Ian and made a supreme effort not to be seasick even though her stomach was lurching. All the while she kept an eye out for the rooftops and turrets of sunken Wythernsea, straining her ears to hear bells clanging, but everything was gray and silent, wreathed in a ghostly mist. It seemed so odd that Wythernsea could be on the other side of the puzzle, yet at the same time it existed right here as ruins beneath the waves.

Then she saw the outline of another small boat and felt the hairs on her neck go up. Standing at the prow was a tall figure, coat flapping like dark wings; whoever it was seemed far too large for such a small vessel. With him she could see a smaller figure who did the rowing. But all too soon they were swallowed by fog, and she wasn't sure exactly what she'd seen, or if she had seen anything at all.

At last the *Sea Kestrel* chugged into the harbor, seagulls wheeling overhead. Zoé noticed that Ian and Pippin were a bit green, too, by the time they finally reached the town landing and Mr. Angel helped them out of the boat. *This must be how sailors and fishermen feel when they return home from the sea,* she thought, relieved to finally set foot on land.

Once they had all *disembarked* (Mr. Angel's official-sounding word), everyone helped secure the boat to the pier, with Ian tying some fancy knots in the ropes. Zoé tilted to one side as she walked down the pier, her legs feeling as if they were made of jelly.

"Takes a few times before you get yer sea legs," said Mr. Angel.

"A real treat, this was," said Pippin, and Zoé noticed she was walking funny, too. "My first time ever on a boat."

Pippin had never been on a boat before? Zoé could hardly believe it. That kid sure had missed out on a lot of things in her life.

"I'm off for a bit of dinner now. Take care, you lot. Looks like there's a storm brewing," said Mr. Angel, shaking hands all around. "Next time you go to Caldey Island by tunnel, be sure to let me know. I might just come along with you."

CHAPTER TWENTY-THREE
MIDNIGHT AT THE KING'S RANSOM

B ack in Tenby, Zoé sensed that things were quickly going downhill there, too. The town was mired in fog and it had started raining cats and dogs, as her grandfather would say. Granddad had spent the day sitting by the fire, a blanket around his shoulders, drinking tea and listening to Radio 4 on the BBC. He'd heard mostly news stories about tourists canceling reservations at Tenby hotels and the inexplicable accidents in the fog off Caldey Island, including the disappearance of a tour boat, its captain, crew and passengers.

"There are strange goings-on in Tenby of late," he wheezed as Zoé handed him a mug of hot milk with honey. "I'd like to know what in Saint Bedlam's kitchen is going on here. Thank you, Magpie, and good night to you both. I'm off to bed."

Later that night, after Granddad was asleep, Zoé and Ian met on the stair landing, wearing patchwork capes fashioned from old quilts (Zoé's idea), and tiptoed silently downstairs. Zoé carried a flashlight and an extra cape for Pippin; the Thirteenth Piece was tucked inside her back pocket, and they both carried vials of mist. With the headlamp attached to his head, Ian looked like a giant insect.

Their mission tonight was simple: now that they had the Thirteenth Piece, they'd determine whether Iris Tintern was The First, the mastermind behind the Scravens. Their plan was to sneak inside the King's Ransom Café using a key borrowed from Bron and scour the place for clues.

A sea wind brushed Zoé's face as they slipped out the back door of the cottage, ducking through the tall grass. They crouched close to the garden wall, just in case Granddad woke up and looked out the window. The rain was just drizzling now, cold wet drops sliding beneath her cape and down her spine, causing her to break out in goose bumps.

They clambered on top of the stone wall, walking along it in the dark. Granddad's old wall always made Zoé feel timeless, as if she'd belonged to this place for centuries. Glancing back, she pictured the cottage floating like a night ship under a square-rigged sail, gallant and sturdy. She imagined it soaring higher, up to the starless moonless sky, taking her dozing grandfather, the goddess weathervane and the glass puzzle to safety.

The two cousins jumped off the wall, cloaks flapping. As they hurried down a sloping lane, Zoé could hear waves crashing against the rocks, the ocean an immense black emptiness, stretching as far as she could see. At the end of the lane, she glimpsed a skinny figure standing beneath a streetlamp, by the old wall. Pippin!

"You brought the key, right?" Ian whispered, and Zoé thought she saw Pippin nod. In the murky light their faces were ghostly. It was so dark. Zoé handed Pippin the cape, fastening it around her neck.

Bron claimed the key would open anything with a lock, except maybe a bank vault or the door to a crypt. Zoé remembered one summer Ian turned up in Tenby with a skeleton key that he'd bought online. For days Zoé had pestered him to borrow it (she wanted to unlock the door to Maisie's Sweet Shop after hours), but Ian had ended up losing the key on the Viper roller coaster at Barry Island, so that was the end of that.

"I haven't a torch, sorry," said Pippin. (*Torch,* Zoé knew, was the British word for "flashlight.") "I thought about taking one from Dai's toolbox, but if he found out he'd hit the roof. No problem, my night vision's excellent."

Poor Pippin, thought Zoé as the three set off.

"Bron says we should search every corner of the café but stay away from Iris's flat," Pippin told them. "Too risky."

"It would be really scary if she woke up and came running after us," said Zoé with a shiver. "But what if we don't find any clues in the café?"

"Miss Glyndower said we need to be in the vicinity of

The First, remember?" said Ian. "If there are no clues, we'll stand at the bottom of the stairs to her flat with the Thirteenth Piece. It'll tell us what we need to know."

I hope he's right, thought Zoé as the narrow streets closed in around them. She noticed that the windows of all the houses were dark, and it gave her a hollow feeling.

"Hmm, maybe this wasn't such a great idea," muttered Ian. "What if an alarm goes off and we get caught? The cops could charge us with breaking and entering! I'm too young to go to jail."

"They don't send kids to prison in Wales," said Zoé. "Right, Pippin?"

"You'd better believe they do," answered Pippin. "I've a cousin in jail over Swansea way and he's not yet sixteen."

"No one's going to catch us. We're like ghosts in the night," said Zoé. "Think of us as superheroes—our capes make us invisible—and Bron said we're harrowers, remember? Anyway, too late, we've passed the point of no return." *Point of no return.* A razor-edged phrase.

Empty of people and steeped in darkness, St. Julian's Street struck her as oddly transformed, its stone shops huddled together like props in a 1950s British movie, the kind her mom liked to watch. They crept down an alley, the wind at their backs. There was hardly time to think. Zoé beamed a flashlight along the row of shops, confused by the rain and fog, the absolute quiet. In the shadows of the alley, the rear doors of the shops all looked the same, grooved and weather-beaten, adding to her confusion. Some doors had graffiti scrawled on them, probably the work of bored teenagers on a Saturday night.

Hardly daring to breathe, Zoé paused before a door and held up her flashlight. CALEB O. TINTERN, APOTHECARY appeared at the top in faded scrolled letters.

"This is it!" she whispered. "Caleb Tintern must be one of Iris's quirky ancestors."

"Maybe Iris is the last in a long line of Tinterns, going back to the pirate days," mused Ian. "Obviously it was a pharmacy at one time."

With a dramatic flourish, Pippin waved the key. "I feel like Sherlock Holmes," she said with a nervous giggle.

"Nothing shabby about that key," observed Ian.

"It looks like a key a mad prince would carry through the crypt of his castle," said Zoé. "I wrote a story like that once."

But Pippin wasn't listening: she was intent on opening the door. "If we're caught," she said, twisting the key in the lock, "we'll say we're looking for my cat and she got locked inside the café by accident. Okay?"

"I didn't know you had a cat," said Zoé.

"Doesn't matter if I do or don't." Pippin turned the key the other way, but it still didn't work. "When you're dealing with the authorities, you just have to *sound* convincing, know what I mean?" She rattled the knob.

"Let me try." Ian gripped the doorknob, jimmying the key with his other hand. "Sorry, Pippin, this is majorly stuck."

"Blimey, what was Bron thinking?" moaned Pippin. "This key's a fake. It's totally useless!"

Using a technique she'd seen in an anime film, Zoé swung her foot, aiming it at the door and kicking as hard as she could. With a loud creak, the door opened and she jumped back, startled.

"What the heck?" said Ian. "I thought everybody in Britain was fanatical about locking their doors."

"That Iris Tintern is totally brainless," said Zoé, peering into a storage room stacked with crates of soda bottles. "Doesn't she know anybody could walk into her café and rob her blind?"

She inched her way inside, inhaling a mix of heady vapors. Ian's headlamp lit up another door and he flicked the latch, pulling it open with a soft *snick*. Standing side by side, the three peered into the darkness of the King's Ransom Café.

Zoé swept her beam along the counter, lighting up rows of dusty bottles and jars, followed by Iris's Electro Freeze soft-serve machine. Images swam before her eyes: daffodil wallpaper, brass spigots, curved mirrors, a metal cash register, words on a chalkboard. The curtains drooped over the café's front window like half-closed eyelids.

Ian scooped something off the floor. "Wow, look at this totally weird snail. I wonder where this came from?"

"Yuck, it's *alive*," said Zoé, seeing its long antennae twitch. It was three times the size of an ordinary snail.

"Totally disgusting, that," said Pippin, holding out her hand. "Hey, look here, what's this, then?"

"That's a trilobite," said Zoé knowledgably. "I've got a collection of those at Granddad's cottage."

"Yeah, but it's movin' around, like."

"No way," said Ian. "Trilobites disappeared two hundred and fifty million years ago."

The three exchanged nervous glances.

Zoé aimed her flashlight at the floor, illuminating a line of stark, primitive creatures that seemed to have no bones—a mélange of slumped crabs, writhing eels and squidlike creatures with heads like tiny crocodiles. Smelling the wet tang of their shells, she felt an instant urge to run.

"What's going on here?" said Ian. "Those things look like biological throwbacks."

"They're not normal, that's for sure," whispered Pippin.

"What if they're from the Harshlands?" said Zoé, remembering. "What if the Scravens brought them here?"

A tense silence fell over them.

"Crikey, look behind the counter! Iris left a door open," said Pippin. "Better check it out, eh?"

They tiptoed across the café, bumping into tables and chairs, Zoé nearly upsetting a tea trolley. Pippin threw open the door and they looked down a stairwell: somewhere far below, Zoé could see a diffused green light, and she felt her stomach start to churn.

"You're not getting me down there," she said, remembering *Invasion of the Body Snatchers* and all the other scary movies she'd seen. Going down to the basement, she knew, was never a good idea.

"It's just Iris's cellar," said Pippin. "We might find clues! I mean, what if Iris is The First and she's holding a big Scraven get-together down there? We can't chicken out now."

"Get ready," Ian whispered to Zoé, his voice wavering. "If Iris is down there, look quick at the Thirteenth Piece to see if it turns black—then we'll make a run for it."

Slowly, they made their way, moving as a unit down the steep staircase. Zoé stepped on something squishy and her heart knocked against her ribs: those creepy-crawlies seemed to be everywhere. At the bottom of the stairs, they entered a freezing-cold room and Zoé pulled her cape tighter over her shoulders.

"A pantry," said Ian, beaming his headlamp across bottles of sauces, jellies, chutneys and relishes, all labeled in Iris's shaky handwriting. *Everything looks ordinary,* thought Zoé, reaching through a sticky cobweb and plucking a jar marked *Gooseberry Jam* off the shelf.

"What's that?" whispered Ian, pointing to where the room stretched back into the shadows. Across the earthen walls rippled waves of luminous green light. "Stay here, I'll check it out. Back in a flash."

"Wait, Ian—" Zoé started, but he was already disappearing into the shadows.

Watching his headlamp bobbing up and down, she thought how brave her cousin was—and suddenly she was frightened for him. She'd never forgive herself if anything happened to Ian. He was irreplaceable.

"It's an old wooden cabinet with water in it," Zoé heard

him say in a loud, excited whisper. She could just make out his outline in the eerie green light. "Something's moving around! Looks like—"

"What's wrong?" shouted Zoé, starting to run.

"Er, stay where you are," said Ian, his voice thick with fear. "Don't come any closer, guys."

Sliding on a wet patch, Zoé skidded into a big old wooden cabinet, the kind Iris might use for displaying wax vampire teeth and tacky souvenirs. Water splashed over the sides, along with clumps of seaweed and black snails. As Ian grabbed her arm, pulling her away, she felt a deep and sudden terror.

"What's in there?" she gasped.

Judging by the look on Ian's face, she knew it was something really scary, like a twelve-legged octopus or a giant sea worm. She broke away from her cousin's grasp, peering into the bubbling water, feeling her breath clog in her throat. It was something else. Some*one* else.

Transfixed, Zoé stared through the glass as a figure rose dreamily through the water. Tendrils of hair floated beneath a spangled hairnet, flowing in eerie slow motion around a face devoid of expression—green gashes for eyes, a lamprey mouth, needle-sharp teeth—and gills along the neck. Leathery wings rippled out and talons sprouted from the ends of its fingers.

She felt as if her brain cells were all stuck together, making it impossible to form a coherent thought.

"That's *Iris Tintern*?" she said in a stunned voice.

Ian nodded dully.

"Ugh, look at her feet." Pippin pointed to a knot of eels, curled around Iris's mossy talons.

"This is proof, isn't it?" said Zoé, feeling as if she'd swallowed a lump of ice. "Scravens are real—and Iris is one of them." Her words sounded oddly detached, as if they were coming from somewhere outside of her.

"I keeping thinking about that movie *Brides of Dracula*," said Ian. "Remember Granddad took us to see it last summer?"

Zoé tapped on the glass. "Yeah, but Iris isn't a vampire."

"She's something worse," said Pippin.

"Worse than the pods left by the body snatchers," murmured Ian. "Iris is a Scraven."

"Yeah, but is she The First?" said Zoé, watching the Thirteenth Piece fade to a dull blue in her hand.

"Maybe we're supposed to look at Iris *through* the glass," said Ian. "Try it, okay? We have to be absolutely sure."

Hand trembling, Zoé put the glass to her eye and saw Iris grinning at her with long sharp teeth. She staggered back, nearly dropping it.

"It's still blue," she croaked.

"Maybe the water's protecting Iris," suggested Pippin.

"Good point," said Ian. "It's possible we can't get an accurate read because she's floating in water and it acts as a barrier." He studied the cabinet, making quick calculations. "Miss Glyndower said the Scravens sleep in the bottomless swamps of the Harshlands. I bet Iris comes here every night to rejuvenate—she's used to a swampy habitat. Okay, we need to get the water out so we can get a reading."

Zoé nodded, reassured by the quiet authority in his voice. Gripping the edge of the cabinet, the three of them pushed, tipping it up on two legs. Stomach heaving, Zoé watched Iris float to the top, water bubbling out of her froglike nostrils.

"Steady," said Ian.

Gritting her teeth, Zoé pushed again, giving a stifled scream as Iris's eyes flew open.

"She's waking up!" cried Pippin.

"Don't look into her eyes!" shouted Zoé, remembering all the late-night horror movies she'd ever seen.

"Almost there," puffed Ian.

The cabinet weighed a ton. Water sloshed over the sides, giving off a hypnotic light; then suddenly they let go all at once and the cabinet righted itself, the lid flying open.

The Thirteenth Piece was glowing faintly. *So I guessed wrong*, thought Zoé. *Iris is just an ordinary Scraven.*

Two talons shot out of the water and into the air as a strange archaic shape rose out of the glass cabinet. Clutching one another, Zoé and Ian and Pippin recoiled in fright. Dripping black snails and seaweed, Iris Tintern swayed in the glimmering darkness, her shadow filling the room.

Zoé threw the vial as Iris lurched forward. It smashed against the floor, sending waves of mist swirling around them. Screaming in unison, the three children bolted, Zoé tripping over her cape, running up the stairs as fast as their legs could take them.

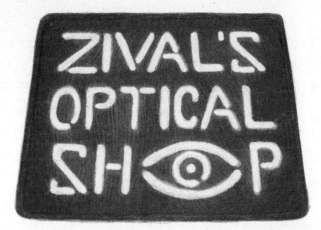

CHAPTER TWENTY-FOUR
THE SEARCH FOR ZIVAL

Through torrential rain, Zoé and Ian made their way to meet Pippin outside the apothecary the next morning, leaving Granddad by the fire reading *The Count of Monte Cristo*.

"Bron will have my head, she will," moaned Pippin as they crowded under Granddad's big umbrella. "There'll be blood on the moon when she finds out her key's stuck in the back door of Iris Tintern's café."

"Wasn't your fault," said Zoé. She found it hard to imagine a cool character like Bron losing her temper. "The key was a dud."

"I wonder if all the Afflicted are sleeping in watery places," said Ian. "Iris Tintern can't be the only one. Makes sense, right?"

"Gives me the collywobbles just thinkin' of it," said Pippin with a shiver.

"I've never seen anything so awful in my life," agreed Zoé, haunted by the image of Iris rising out of the murky water.

Soaked to the skin, they marched up to Dr. Marriott's house, where Zoé lifted the knocker, letting it fall against the lacquered door.

"Ye-eees?" warbled Mrs. Prosser, blinking her watery eyes. Zoé was relieved to see she wasn't wearing glasses, tinted or otherwise.

"We'd like to speak with Dr. Marriott," said Ian. "It's urgent."

Mrs. Prosser shook her head. "I'm afraid the professor isn't seeing visitors at the moment. He has a dreadful head cold."

"We have to see him, he's expecting us," insisted Zoé, infuriated by the way Mrs. Prosser was so overly protective of Dr. Marriott.

"We'll keep our distance if he sneezes," said Pippin, but Mrs. Prosser was already closing the door.

"Who's out there, Mrs. Prosser?" wheezed a voice, and Ian grabbed the door before it shut.

"Dr. Marriott, Dr. Marriott!" shouted Zoé, peering around Mrs. Prosser to see their friend ambling down the hallway in sheepskin slippers and flannel robe, a watch cap pulled over his bald head. She thought she could smell lemon cough drops.

Tugging at the scarf wrapped around his neck, the professor broke into a smile and welcomed them in. Moments later they were sitting inside a second-floor room overlooking Tenby Harbor—the *upstairs front room*, Dr. Marriott called it—with a coal fire crackling in the hearth.

"Now then, bring me up to date," he said in a throaty voice, prodding the coals with a wrought-iron poker. "Have you found the runestone?"

Before anyone could say a word, Mrs. Prosser charged through the doorway with a tray of tea and cakes. Zoé could tell by her stilted movements and sharp tone that she was annoyed.

"I'm not one to pass judgment, Professor," said the housekeeper with a stern look, "but you're in no state to entertain visitors."

"Yes, Mrs. Prosser, I quite understand, but I've my reasons for allowing these young guests in, so let's leave it at that, shall we?" Dr. Marriott eased himself into an oversized leather chair, reminding Zoé of Granddad. "Would you mind pouring the tea, Mrs. Prosser?"

Mrs. Prosser doled out four cups of tea with an indignant sniff, then stormed out. Seeing Dr. Marriott wince, Zoé wondered if the professor might be a little afraid of his housekeeper.

"Help yourselves, my friends," he said. "Mrs. Prosser makes a mean Welsh cake, I guarantee."

Ian and Pippin grinned at Zoé and she knew they were all thinking the same thing: *That's because she is mean!*

The tea was stewed and had a bitter taste, but Zoé

thought the Welsh cakes were superb. Munching away, the three took turns telling Dr. Marriott about the runestone, landing on the wrong side of the wall in Wythernsea (which sent him into a coughing fit), their mission to locate The First, finding the Thirteenth Piece on Caldey Island and, most dramatic of all, their horrific encounter with Iris.

Zoé watched Dr. Marriott's face turn a sickly white. "Iris Tintern, floating inside a glass cabinet? Positively chilling. However, given the fact that Scravens dwell in the deep waters of the Harshlands, I am not surprised. I've no doubt that all the other Afflicted in Tenby have also found dark, swampy places to sleep."

"I knew it," said Zoé, biting into another cake. "Didn't I tell you guys a hundred times? Scravens are down in the tunnels where it's real clammy and wet, and in the underground streams, too. I bet the Afflicted are sleeping down there."

"But that's not our main worry, is it?" said Ian. "We need to identify The First! We've eliminated Iris, so . . . who could it be?" He stared into his tea as if it might hold the answer.

The cakes were nearly gone and Zoé, noticing that Pippin had piled up four on her saucer, grabbed two more. Dr. Marriott sat gazing into the fire, his thoughts far away, until at last he appeared to remember the three children were there.

"The First will be someone out of the ordinary," he told them. "The First will choose to inhabit someone aloof and distant, perhaps a bit enigmatic, who doesn't mingle on a daily basis with the average citizen."

"I'm racking me brains," mused Pippin, "but I can't think who it could be."

"Stokes chased us down the tunnel and swore at us," said Zoé. "Then there's Zival. They're both strange characters. And I don't trust Stokes," she added darkly.

"But Zival works with the public," said Ian, "and so does Stokes."

"Yeah, but Stokes keeps a low profile," argued Zoé. "And nobody even knows what Zival looks like, which is pretty weird."

Opening a box of cough drops, Dr. Marriott popped one into his mouth. "Sounds as if both these chaps are viable candidates for The First. I know Stokes by sight—bit of a slippery sort—and there've been disturbing rumors about Zival the optometrist."

"I think Zival's The First," said Zoé, swallowing her last bit of Welsh cake. "Remember the prophetic writings in the tunnels that Bron told us about? 'Beware the Measurer of Sight . . . moving unseen through Tenby.'" Goose bumps went up and down her arms as she recited the words.

"I vote for Zival," said Ian. "It fits. Optometrists measure sight." He threw Zoé a grim smile. "Maybe it's time to go for an eye exam."

Zoé shivered, despite the warm fire.

The door cracked open and Mrs. Prosser angled her head into the room. "Time for your medicine, Professor. And time for you children to go home. Dr. Marriott is not a well man."

"Yes, of course, Mrs. Prosser," said Dr. Marriott. "A few minutes and they'll be on their way."

Mrs. Prosser tapped her watch. "I'll be timing you."

"The Runestone of Arianrhod," said Dr. Marriott as the door clicked shut. "You're saying the Astercôtes put a spell on the stone?"

"Miss Glyndower said they needed to protect it," explained Ian. "They didn't want anyone reading the incantation."

"Bron Gilwern has it now," said Pippin. "If anyone can fix it, she can."

"As I mentioned at our last meeting, there's a chapter in *The Book of Astercôte* about the runestone," said Dr. Marriott, drumming his fingers on the arm of his chair. "Perhaps the book would be of use to your friend Bron."

"You mean . . . we can borrow your special book?" said Pippin.

"That would really be helpful," said Ian.

"Certainly you may take it. Just look after it, that's all I ask. The book is, as you know, irreplaceable."

"We won't let it out of our sight," promised Zoé.

Looking more rumpled and ill than ever, Dr. Marriott stood up, dabbing his swollen nose with a handkerchief. "Take care, whatever happens, and good luck with your endeavors to find this blackguard Zival. And should you fall into trouble, don't hesitate to knock on my door. I'll be here for you."

That is, if Mrs. Prosser lets us in, thought Zoé, trying not to giggle. Yet she knew he meant every word of it: Dr. George Marriott was a true friend.

🐉

Zoé, Ian and Pippin stood in line for nearly an hour outside Zival's Optical Shop before they were allowed inside. Since Pippin lived in Wales and was on the National Health Insurance, she was the logical choice to request an eye exam.

The three sat in a dark, airless waiting room overflowing with people of all ages, and Pippin was told to take a number. Zoé was tempted to whip out the Thirteenth Piece and sneak looks at everyone, but she knew it was too risky. Instead she held the glass inside her fist. *I wonder if it knows things*, she thought, remembering Granddad saying there was old memory in glass.

At last Pippin's number was called and they rushed to the front desk, where a pinch-faced man with rectangular blue-tinted glasses stood holding a clipboard. "Philippa Jenkyn Thomas?"

"Aye, that's me. Are you Dr. Zival?"

"I'm Dr. Brown," he replied, staring at them as if they were insects he wanted to squash.

Zoé experienced a sudden burst of nervous energy as the glass seemed to beat like a tiny heart inside her fist. Staring down at the floor, she thought, *Watch out, we're in enemy territory.*

"Dr. Zival has gone to Caldey Island at the behest of the monks," Dr. Brown continued, "so Dr. Davies and I are doing eye examinations today. We're both highly qualified optometrists."

"I'd like Dr. Zival to do the exam, if that's okay," insisted Pippin.

"Then you'll have to come another day," said Dr. Brown, pushing aside a strand of lank hair.

"When is he coming back?" asked Pippin.

"I really can't say. Dr. Zival comes and goes when he pleases, so there's no telling when that will be."

Zoé threw a fierce look at Dr. Brown—she was sure he was lying—but he ignored her. *Zival's the one*, she thought, *and these guys are covering for him.*

Zival, she knew with absolute certainty, was The First.

CHAPTER TWENTY-FIVE
THE CLOISTER

Sitting cross-legged on the attic floor, Zoé and Ian sorted through the puzzle pieces as morning light flooded through the window. Without warning, the door flew open and they both jumped.

"Good news!" announced Pippin, standing in the doorway, arms clasped around the runestone. "Bron used *The Book of Astercôte* to unlock the spell! Took her half the night, but she says we can read the incantation now."

"Superlative," said Ian. "Bron's a genius."

"I wish Bron could come with us," said Zoé wistfully. "Are you ready for this, Pippin? The Harrowers' Expedition is about to roll." She loved the label *harrower* that Bron had given them. It had a medieval ring, spiced with a hint of adventure.

"Your granddad said I'd find you up here," said Pippin, handing the runestone to Zoé. "I said, 'We're playing a board game and we'll be a rather long time,' and he was fine with that. He was talking away with a posh lady in a fur coat, then this gothic twosome showed up wanting directions to the train station."

"Granddad loves talking with people," said Zoé, "even when he's not feeling well. He's a real conversationalist."

"Granddad has the gift of the gab," added Ian, handing a flashlight to Pippin.

Zoé noticed that Pippin's hand looked a bit grubby and her shirt had stains and the sleeve was torn. She wondered what Pippin's life was like on a day-to-day basis, because there were times when Pippin seemed sad and secretive.

"Based on our past two visits, I've calculated that three hours in Wythernsea equals fifteen minutes of our time here," said Ian. "If we leave at ten o'clock this morning and stay there six hours, we'll be back in Tenby by ten-thirty. Then we'll seal the puzzle."

Zoé felt her heart crumple: she couldn't bear the thought of losing her friends and never seeing Wythernsea again.

"What about the Tenby Scravens, eh?" asked Pippin.

"We'll deal with them when we get back," said Zoé, though secretly she wondered if Miss Glyndower's magic was a bit antiquated. "First let's deliver the runestone."

"Our timing's perfect," said Ian as they began assembling the puzzle. "We were last in Wythernsea three days ago and today's June twenty-first, the longest day of the year, when

Miss Glyndower said the Scravens would be most vulnerable."

As the last piece slotted in, Zoé wrapped her arms around the runestone, feeling the invisible power of the puzzle drawing her into its shimmering depths. Her breath caught, the way it always did, as her gaze fell on the circle of blue glass swirling with mystical light, an image of a dragon rising from the center.

The first thing Zoé saw, through swathes of dark smoke, was the Wythernsea wall. Relief flooded through her: this time they'd managed to land on the right side. The wall was still standing, although more sections had fallen; drab-coated workers were shoveling rubble and sods of earth into the gaps.

The mechanized claws spun crazily, threatening to crush whatever got in their way. It was heartening to see the goddess weathervanes still standing on the turrets, although they seemed to Zoé more fragile than ever.

Dark ragged shapes swept in circles over the Harshlands, shrieking madly. Scravens! She could see the Defenders patroling the wall, their faces bleak and weary, the barkers looking even scrawnier and hungrier than last time.

"Let's get the heck out of here," said Ian, pulling Zoé and Pippin to their feet.

Dusting themselves off, the three tramped off into the smoke-filled gloom, passing uprooted trees and charred vegetation. Through scorched leaves Zoé glimpsed the Wythernsea Retreat for the Rescued, the Lost and the Ship-wrecked. Feeling strangely nervous, she raced ahead, heart thumping.

The arched windows were now gaping holes, with most of the roof torn away and the goddess weathervanes nowhere to be seen. At the top of the staircase, Zoé found Miss Glyn-dower's black and gold sign lying in pieces on the ground. The front door was splintered and cracked, with deep gouges in the wood, most likely from claws and teeth. The image of the goddess had been totally obliterated.

"We're wasting our time," said Pippin. "The Retreat's dead empty."

"Let's try the cloister," said Ian.

Blinking back tears, Zoé set off, her anxiety mounting, hearing shouts and screams and explosions coming from the direction of the town wall, where smoke seemed to be thick-est. She tried to keep alert, scouting around corners, listening for footfalls or the flapping of wings overhead, checking be-hind them at every turn. It seemed as if overnight her idyllic Wythernsea had turned into a place of treachery.

Down by the wharves, they passed empty market stalls, boarded-up warehouses and ramshackle dwellings. Zoé breathed in the clammy air, inhaling the reek of mackerel and eels. Aside from the Defenders, she saw no one. The townspeople must still be hiding, she thought, waiting for the next attack. She longed for the old Wythernsea, a bus-tling seaport in another world, where people had webs between their fingers and toes—and, oh yeah, magical eyes on their foreheads.

"Over there!" shouted Ian, pointing. "That looks like it!"

They climbed a steep cobbled hill toward a multi-chimneyed building of dark granite, with narrow windows spaced wide apart and a Celtic cross on the roof. As Zoé drew closer she saw letters carved into the lintel over two red timber doors: SOLITARIES OF WYTHERNSEA.

"What do you think *Solitaries of Wythernsea* means?" she puffed, hoping this was the cloister, because she suddenly felt exhausted.

"Hermits," said Pippin. "They never come out, like."

"Oh great," said Ian. "Does that mean they won't answer the door?"

But, without warning, the doors swung slowly open on brass hinges. Instead of a silent nun in white robes, whom Zoé half expected to see, there stood Miss Glyndower in the entranceway, as if she'd known the exact moment of their arrival.

"Hurry, children, come inside," she said, towering over them like some elegant rare tree, her eyes a vibrant gold. Zoé sensed an anxiety in her voice.

"Are nuns living here?" asked Pippin as they filed into a dark hall.

"Oh no, they died out centuries ago," replied Miss Glyndower. "The Solitaries were a contemplative sect who worked with the orphaned and homeless. The Retreat took over their work and only the building remains—austere, yet strong and stalwart. As you will soon see, however, the cloister lacks the ambiance of our Retreat."

Zoé could hear the longing in her voice. *Hiraeth*, she thought, recalling the Welsh word for nostalgia, and wondering if Miss Glyndower knew that her beloved Retreat had been ravaged by the Scravens. She was tempted to say something, then decided that now might not be the best time. They needed to focus their energy on the positive, and not be sad or lose heart.

"I trust your journey here was less eventful than the last," Miss Glyndower continued.

"We landed on the right side of the wall, if that's what you mean," said Ian.

"No one was at the Retreat, so we came here," said Zoé, ceremoniously handing the runestone to Miss Glyndower. "Here you go. The stone is fixed!"

"Bron's done a brilliant job," added Pippin. "Took her all night to lift the spell. You should be able to read the incantation now."

Miss Glyndower pressed the runestone to her heart. Odd, but she seemed even taller than Zoé remembered.

"You've no idea what this means for Wythernsea. The incantation is our last hope," she said quietly. "Come, they wait for us in the great hall."

Zoé followed, noting the brick walls and slate floors, and the way everything in the cloister was clean yet unadorned, without distractions—the way nuns preferred their surroundings, she supposed.

"When the sun is at its zenith, the Messengers will make their way to the Wythernsea wall," explained Miss Glyndower. "There are dangers, but the Messengers are brave and quick-witted, and they know every corner of Wythernsea: the shortcuts, the underground passages, the gaps in the fortifications. They'll move through the town undetected, eluding any Scravens that might find their way over the wall."

"The Messengers are going to fight the *Scravens?*" said Zoé, sharing a look of bewilderment with Ian and Pippin.

Why wasn't Miss Glyndower using her ancient magic instead of sending the Retreat kids to defeat the Scravens? Sure, the orphans were tough and scrappy, even the little ones, and they had plenty of survival skills—but how could they defeat such a ferocious enemy?

"Never underestimate the strength of sacred words, my child: the incantation is extremely powerful," said Miss Glyndower. "I cannot win this battle alone; I can only strategize. The Messengers will not fail, for they have the goddess on their side."

Her words set Zoé's bones tingling. She had a hundred questions to ask, but Miss Glyndower was rushing down a narrow flight of steps.

"I bet in the old days they shot arrows through those windows," whispered Ian as they entered a gloomy hall with a high domed ceiling. "This cloister's built like a fortress."

The great hall looked to Zoé like a vast cathedral. Watery light fell through windows of leaded glass, each no more than a hand's width, but most of the hall was lost in shadow. She could see rows of rough wooden benches and tables, and primitive statues—Celtic goddesses, she guessed, or maybe famous Solitaries—set into niches along the walls, candles burning next to them.

She suddenly realized that the room was filled with children, their shallows giving off a soft ethereal light. The orphans!

"Where's Gwyn Griffiths?" she asked, looking wildly around. "Do you see Tegan?"

"Too shadowy," said Ian, shaking his head. "I can't make out any faces."

A hush fell over the room as Miss Glyndower stepped forward, her quartz-colored shallow glowing. Zoé could see this imposing woman had earned the Messengers' undying loyalty: they were like old-time knights, ready to do battle for their queen.

"All this year you've learned the ancient poems and enchantments, in readiness for this day," began Miss Glyndower. "Our friends Zoé, Ian and Pippin have delivered the Runestone of Arianrhod. The incantation will set us on a new path and free Wythernsea from the scourge of Scravens." She lifted the runestone into the air. "Now, Messengers, close your eyes, keeping only your shallows open. Let the words of the goddess melt into your hearts and into the farthest reaches of your souls. And remember. Remember."

Entranced by the scene before her, Zoé watched as the

children held hands and huddled together, their shallows glowing. Miss Glyndower began reading from the stone, hesitatingly at first, her lyrical voice deepening with each word.

The archaic sounds whirled through Zoé's head like smoke, like firelight, like the spells of mystics, without beginning or end, flowing ceaselessly like the sea.

And, with eyes closed, the children listened.

CHAPTER TWENTY-SIX
MESSENGERS AND GODDESSES

After Miss Glyndower had finished, Zoé could see the Messengers' shallows burning with intense light.

"Amazing," whispered Ian. "That's how they absorb knowledge: through their third eyes!"

Silence fell, followed by a bustling at the back of the hall. Kids in aprons appeared, putting tureens of vegetable soup on the tables and plates of boiled eggs, potatoes and lentils, bowls of endive-and-radish salad, small rounds of cheese and loaves of brown bread, all looking quite delicious, in Zoé's opinion.

She sat at a table with Ian and Pippin, the leonine-haired Miss Glyndower explaining what would happen next: "When the sun is highest, the Messengers will spread out through town, into the fields and farmlands, heading for the

Wythernsea wall, taking turns reciting the incantation beneath the weathervanes. Remember all that you see here, and the order in which things happen, for when you return to Tenby you must make the incantation work for you."

Unsure of what Miss Glyndower was saying, Zoé threw a sidelong glance at Ian. He looked confused, too.

"But we don't have goddess weathervanes on the walls of Tenby," said Ian. "So how can we—"

"Ah," Miss Glyndower cut in, "but there is one such goddess, is there not? On the roof of your grandfather's cottage. This will be your vantage point. And the seeress will help you, of that I've no doubt."

Their conversation ended abruptly as Miss Glyndower gave a signal and all the children stood up, filing down a passageway that opened onto a cobbled courtyard. Grouped in small clusters, the Messengers milled about, heads bent as they quietly conversed. Zoé wondered if they were frightened, though their expressions gave away little emotion.

Overhead the sun was a golden disc in the sky, and her heart skipped a beat as she realized that the moment of attack was quickly coming. Hearing Ian shout Gwyn's name, she whirled around to see the shaggy-haired boy come barging out of the cloister, followed by a girl whose pale dress seemed to float around her.

Zoé raced over, a lump in her throat, hugging both Gwyn and Tegan. "I was afraid I wouldn't see you again!" she said, trying not to burst into tears. She hadn't realized until now how much she'd missed them.

"Tegan and I, we've been readying for today," said Gwyn. She noticed he was blushing, he was so pleased to see her.

Ian shook hands with Gwyn while Zoé introduced Pippin and Tegan shyly offered handfuls of boiled sweets. Ordinarily they'd be joking around, Zoé realized, or playing Caldey Ghost Pirates, but the mood here was too somber, the future too uncertain.

"It's right good to see ye again," said Gwyn, his voice quaking the tiniest bit. Zoé suspected he was more nervous than he was letting on. "Hard times here in Wythernsea, eh? Truth be told, we need friends like you at a time like this, to beat back the Scravens once and for all."

"We will, Gwyn. We'll crush them," said Zoé fiercely. The words tumbled out: "We're going with you to the wall, to fight the Scravens. Right, Ian? We'll go, yeah, Pippin?"

Seeing their startled expressions and panicky eyes, she realized that Ian and Pippin hadn't expected her to offer them up as warriors.

"We're coming," said Pippin, and Zoé smiled with relief.

"We'll make sure Scravens never attack Wythernsea again," said Ian. "Take no prisoners! Solidarity handshake, yeah?"

They grasped each other's hands, webbed and non-webbed, in a five-way shake. As her friends' fingers entwined with hers, Zoé felt a rush of affection, followed by a burst of courage. *Guess I'll be needing all the courage I can get*, she thought, gazing at the sun high above the cloister roof.

Zoé, Ian and Pippin stood at the gateway watching the Messengers prepare to head out.

"If we had more weathervanes in Tenby, we could put them on the Old Town wall," said Zoé. "Then we'd defeat the Scravens the way you're doing."

"You've just the one goddess, so your strategy for Tenby will be of a different nature. Once you've sealed the puzzle, remain in the cottage, where the goddess will protect you," Miss Glyndower instructed. "Inevitably The First will appear, seeking the puzzle—and with intentions to destroy you. This is why you must hold fast to the runestone. The moment you see The First, begin the incantation."

"But we don't know how to read runes!" argued Ian.

"Have faith in the seeress," said Miss Glyndower with a cryptic smile. "She will see you through this. And have faith in yourselves."

"I guess," murmured Ian, exchanging a worried look with Zoé.

"And the Afflicted?" said Pippin. "What happens to them?"

"She means the people taken over by Scravens," said Zoé. "Oh, but you don't know about the Afflicted, do you?"

"As a matter of fact, I do," said Miss Glyndower. "It was I who warned the Astercôtes what would happen if Scravens escaped into their world."

"But . . . why didn't you tell *us*?" said Ian.

"We're getting fed up with adults not telling us things," seethed Pippin. "It's really annoying."

Zoé nodded in agreement, recalling how Dr. Marriott had neglected to inform them that Scravens might fly out of the puzzle.

"Please forgive me, children. You have every right to be angry. I withheld the information because I didn't wish to frighten you too much."

"We don't frighten easily," said Zoé. "You really should've told us."

"I see now that I was wrong. You are all very brave." Miss Glyndower looked almost humble. "If the goddess awakens and you succeed, the Afflicted will become human again, transforming back to their true selves. The incantation will cast out the Scravens and, like parasites without a host, they will become hollow shells, spinning off into the ether, until they vanish completely."

"Sounds like a kind of exorcism," murmured Ian.

Zoé frowned, trying to imagine the Scravens coming apart, unraveling like the neck of Stokes's wool sweater.

"Are ye coming, then?" asked Gwyn, tapping her on the shoulder. "Me and Tegan, we's heading out now. It's up to you kids, like."

"I'm with you," said Zoé. No way was she staying behind.

"Count me in," said Ian.

Pippin nodded.

"Me too," said a scratchy voice. "I'm coming with you to the wall."

Zoé whirled around, startled to see Miss Glyndower's nephew step forward. Wide-eyed and round-faced, Jasper Morgan looked every bit as angry as the first time she'd seen him.

"Very well," said Gwyn. "The six of us it is."

They said farewell, Miss Glyndower tearing up when she saw her nephew among them, and the six ran through the open gate and into the town. Zoé, Ian and Pippin stuck close to Gwyn, creeping through gardens and along cobbled streets, weaving between factories, market stalls and warehouses. Once Gwyn swung back in alarm at the sound of frantic barking, and they all dove behind a ring of hawthorn bushes, concealing themselves.

Zoé held her breath, listening to the Defenders' boots as they marched over the rocky path. Through the branches she could see three of them, crossbows hitched over their shoulders, leading three wolfhounds.

"Er, I have a question," said Ian once the Defenders were out of sight. "Why are we hiding? Aren't those guys supposed to be on our side?"

"Aye, the Defenders are here to protect us," said Gwyn. "It's the barkers I worry about."

"Sharp teeth," whispered Tegan in a small, frightened voice. "I'm scared of the barkers."

"We're all wary and that's a fact. Most barkers are okay, but a few of 'em are erratic, being so high-strung and all," continued Gwyn as they started running again. "I don't take chances."

Lungs bursting, Zoé did her best to keep up with the

others, all the while thinking about the barkers, starving and unkempt. It didn't surprise her that some of the dogs had gone a little barmy, as Granddad would say. At times she noticed Ian and Jasper lagging behind, while Pippin seemed to exude boundless energy. As she ran, Zoé's thoughts turned to the warrior goddess Arianrhod and she sent out silent pleas: short snappy requests like *Keep me brave!* and *Make this happen fast!*

By the time they reached the wall, she was breathless and disoriented. Gwyn and Tegan stood beneath a turret, gazing up at a goddess weathervane that was in complete shambles; leaning to one side, it threatened to snap off at a moment's notice and crash into one of the mechanical claws.

Standing before the ancient wall, breathing in smoke and the acrid smells of the Harshlands, Zoé thought with despair, *This is crazy, kids can't fight Scravens!* Her gaze traveled to the utter darkness on the other side, and she felt a nameless fear twisting deep inside her.

She imagined this was all a dream and she'd wake up to find sun streaming into her room at Granddad's cottage, with its lace curtains and iron bed, the bureau with brass handles tucked under the eaves. She longed more than anything to be back there sorting through her trilobite collection or having tea by the fire with Granddad.

"Don't stand there, you're fair game for Scravens!" shouted Jasper, pulling her toward a niche in the wall, and they both began to run.

"Thanks, Jasper," she said once they were safe, and a smile flickered across the boy's face.

Huddled with the others, eyes bright with anticipation, Zoé thought, *These Messengers aren't afraid; they're kids, but guess what—they're warriors, they're brave.*

"Right, then," said Gwyn, "we've no time to lose."

"What about us?" asked Pippin. "What should we do?"

"We didn't memorize the incantation," said Ian.

Gwyn thought a moment. "Keep an eye out for Scravens, chase 'em off if you have to."

"We'll stand guard," promised Zoé.

"No interrupting, mind," added Gwyn. "Ending an incantation before it's finished could be fatal."

Zoé nodded, wondering uneasily what Gwyn meant by *fatal.*

The three Messengers closed their eyes and began reciting the incantation, their shallows glowing eerily. Zoé let the poetry flow over her, like shadows on water, sunlight against stone: timeworn words shaped like stars, like shells, like the ruins of lost temples, soft as the breaths of mystics.

She heard a great terrible whirring as a shadow passed overhead, blotting out the sun. Was Arianrhod coming to life? Wildly excited, she leapt out of the niche, Ian and Pippin crowding close behind her. Craning her neck, Zoé stared up at the wall, expecting to see the warrior goddess waving her shield in a gesture of triumph.

She felt her body go numb as her breath stopped inside her throat. An immense winged shape hung suspended above the turret, wings crackling, only inches from the goddess.

Pippin clutched Zoé's arm. "It's one of them Scravens!"

"Oh cripes," croaked Ian. "We have to get out of here, like, *now!*"

Zoé could see that the Messengers were too immersed in their incantation to realize what was going on.

"Gwyn told us to chase off the Scravens," she said to Ian. "We're not supposed to stop the incantation."

"Can't you see?" Ian's eyes were enormous. "The incantation's not working!"

Zoé looked up at the Scraven's face, shrunken back around its long, sharp teeth. It seemed to be grinning at her.

Ian shouted, "Hey, Gwyn, there's a Scraven up there and it's about to come down!"

Eyes closed, the three Messengers droned on, lost inside their secret mythology, oblivious to their friends' frantic warnings.

"Oh no!" screamed Ian. "It's coming!"

Something came hurtling toward them: openmouthed, the Scraven swooped down. Ian staggered back, Pippin clutched her head to her knees, and Zoé gave a sob of terror, feeling the strength rush out of her. *It's over,* she thought. *The Scravens are too powerful, we can't destroy them.*

As the Scraven flew closer, bringing with it a terrifying darkness, Zoé heard a rumbling sound, like a giant awakening, and she realized the ground was shaking, the earth trembling beneath her feet as the noise grew stronger and more insistent. Chunks of rock fell from the wall, plummeting down around them, dust billowing up into their faces.

There was an enormous crack as, far up on the turret, the

goddess weathervane shimmered with unearthly light, filling the sky with a profusion of colors. The next instant Zoé saw the goddess begin to move—slowly, imperceptibly—picking up speed, eyes shining fiercely, growing larger, brighter, more luminous.

The Scraven, hovering so near that Zoé could smell its swampy breath, gave a startled cry as flames charred the tips of its wings. She watched the goddess continue to whirl faster, throwing off waves of light—gold, silver, emerald, crimson—raining sparks down on the Scraven. The creature howled, flinging itself backward and fleeing over the wall, back into the Harshlands.

More Scravens swooped down, flapping and snarling, talons slashing at the air. Zoé watched in amazement as, one by one, they flew into the dazzling light, wings catching fire, their bodies weakened and shriveling. With terrified shrieks they retreated into the forest, their powers quelled, just as Miss Glyndower had predicted: defeated but not destroyed.

❧

Traipsing back to Wythernsea, her heart lighter, Zoé listened to Gwyn explain how the Messengers would take turns beneath the goddess weathervanes, reciting the incantation.

Miss Glyndower, anxiously waiting at the cloister gate, threw her arms around them, murmuring, "What brave children!" She gave them each a thick white candle, scrounged from the nuns' cupboards, to light their way up a windowless staircase to what Jasper called the Round Tower.

Before heading up, Zoé turned to Miss Glyndower. "If we seal the puzzle, is there any way we can contact you? What if we put on scuba suits and dive down to sunken Wythernsea— would we find you then?"

"I've often wondered whether Wythernsea was of the earth, attached to your world by some mystical thread." Miss Glyndower gave a wry, sad smile. "But over time I've come to realize that our world is totally apart from yours. Wythernsea exists in the *beyond*. I am afraid that our Wythernsea and your world will always be separate."

Tears running down her face, Zoé emerged at the top of the tower into bright sunlight, thinking how she'd soon be leaving and wondering how to keep herself from falling apart. More Messengers appeared, congratulating one another and exchanging stories about their experiences, all in a state of high excitement.

"Never seen anything like it," said Gwyn. "Like the Aurora Borealis, it was—brilliant light coming off the goddess and them monsters making a mad dash for the forest."

"Frightened to death, they was," added Tegan in her fairylike voice.

"Same with us," said a girl with hair falling in spirals. "The Scravens flew off, their wings all afire." She leaned so far over the tower rail that Zoé was afraid she'd fall off.

"Will ye look at the town wall now!" said Jasper in an awestruck voice. "Never seen anything like it!"

One by one, the goddesses flared—the weathervanes on the east wall, the south wall, even the worst-damaged ones on the far wall to the north—throwing off glimmering waves of color, ringing the city in a necklace of light, far brighter than the rays of the sun. Zoé heard shouts all around her as the Messengers wrestled and cheered and laughed, thumping each other on the back. Even Jasper Morgan was smiling.

In the Harshlands, the forest was turning an ominous shade of blue, and it was clear that beyond the town walls something extraordinary was happening: countless Scravens were on the run. Zoé imagined them fleeing into the swamps, taking refuge in the dank dreary shadows, exhausted and weakened, their dark powers thwarted, the evil scorched right out of them.

Hurtling through the tunnel of glass, clutching the runestone to her chest, Zoé was overwhelmed by sadness.

Miss Glyndower had given them the runestone, along with instructions on defeating the Scravens, and Zoé had embraced her, knowing that Wythernsea was lost to them forever and their paths would never cross again. When at last she hugged Gwyn and Tegan, she broke down sobbing as they said farewell.

Will I ever see them again? she wondered. Her common sense told her no, yet another part of her said something else. After all, who really knew what the future might hold, especially when magic was involved?

CHAPTER TWENTY-SEVEN
THE FALL OF ARIANRHOD

Zoé, Ian and Pippin spread out on the attic floor around the glass puzzle. Zoé was in her favorite position, legs folded, arms wrapped around her knees; Pippin sat cross-legged, cradling the runestone; Ian lay flat on his back, arms propped under his head.

"Ten-thirty a.m. exactly," he said, checking his watch. "Am I brilliant or what? I guessed we'd be away six hours and I was right."

"It seemed longer than that to me," said Pippin. "It seemed like forever when that wretched monster was comin' at us."

"I hate that we have to seal it," said Zoé, leaning over the puzzle.

"Yeah, but we don't have a choice," said Ian. "It's like chess, when you sacrifice a pawn or a knight. *For the higher good*, that sort of thing."

Zoé rolled her eyes, thinking that Ian had been reading too many historical novels. "We're not talking about chess pieces. Those are real people down there!"

"But the puzzle's flawed! We can't leave the gateway open for The First to come and go as he pleases," said Pippin. "End of story, as Bron would say."

Zoé held the Thirteenth Piece between her thumb and forefinger, watching the glass reflect light from the window. It felt oddly heavy, as if weighed down with spells and old memories, and she could see the others staring at it with dreamy expressions.

She heard the wind pick up outside, wailing past the corners of the cottage as dark clouds rolled past the window.

"Storm's brewing," said Ian, snapping back to attention. "C'mon, guys, let's do this."

Yet there was no clue at all where an extra piece might go. *If this puzzle's really magical*, Zoé reasoned, *it's not about using my brain the way Ian does*. As her mom would say, Zoé would have to go with her gut.

Before she could make a move, her grandfather's voice boomed up the attic stairs. "Ian! Zoé! Are you kids up there?"

Oh no! she thought, alarmed by his shrill tone. *What's happened now?*

"I need your help! It's the weathervane!"

"Be right down!" Ian shouted.

"Quick, take it apart!" hissed Zoé.

Moments later they were thundering downstairs, the puzzle safe inside the sea chest. Granddad was standing at the front door with a cup of tea, looking weary and overwhelmed.

"I was up in the kitchen and I heard a clattering on the roof," he wheezed. "I think the blinkin' weathervane's come loose. Sounds like the bolt holding it up has popped out."

"Don't worry, Granddad," said Zoé. "Stay here and finish your tea, we'll see to it."

They rushed outside into the cobbled street, rain falling in torrents, soaking through their clothes. Hair hanging in limp strings, Zoé breathed in the smell of the wet stones, watching tiles clatter off the cottage roof. Thunder rumbled, the wind shaking streetlamps, whipping the awning off the fish-and-chips shop across the way and flinging a child's tricycle clear across the road.

Then her heart gave a little flip at the sight of Granddad's goddess weathervane turning in reckless circles on the roof.

"The wind's got hold of it!" shouted Ian. "It's moving too fast!"

The weathervane spun wildly, completely out of control. Hearing a loud *crack!* as lightning glanced off the shield, Zoé gasped as the goddess lurched to one side. The wind howled, gusting around them, tearing the weathervane from the roof and lifting the goddess into the air. Arms outstretched, Arianrhod soared skyward in a graceful arc.

"She's being spirited away!" cried Pippin.

Zoé stood beneath the ragged clouds, watching Arianrhod sail off into the thickening fog. "She's going home," she said excitedly, and for a moment she believed it was true. "Arianrhod's going back to the North Star!"

The goddess seemed to float on air, weightless and transparent, a mist of light around her head like a halo, distancing herself from the ordinary world. Then with a shudder she came to a halt in midair and Zoé gasped as she plunged earthward, falling at breakneck speed, plummeting down, down, down, vanishing behind the cottage.

"I knew that was going to happen," Ian groaned.

High on the roof where the goddess had stood, a wisp of smoke hung in the air, shimmering like ghostly runes.

"Looks like a signal from another world," said Pippin, her voice muffled by the wind.

Zoé didn't have time to speculate. "You know what this means, don't you?" she yelled. "The cottage isn't protected anymore!"

"Granddad, Granddad!" shouted Zoé as she rushed inside the shop, the goddess hoisted across her shoulders, dripping water and wet clods of earth, the wind howling at their backs.

"The goddess fell off the roof and we're bringing her inside!" yelled Ian. "We found her in the back garden!"

"Arianrhod's pretty banged up, but at least she's still in one piece," puffed Zoé, setting the metal figure on the floor. All around she could hear beams creaking and walls rattling, as if the cottage was ready to fly apart at any moment.

"You were right, a bolt came loose," said Ian. "The weathervane fell behind the cottage and the pole snapped off. The metal was rusted."

"I knew it," said Granddad. "Lovely, though, ain't she? A right beauty. Always brings me luck, the goddess does."

Zoé had never seen Arianrhod up close before: roughly two feet high, she was made of copper, her features finely detailed, and beautiful in a dreamy medieval sort of way. Zoé was drawn to her solemn eyes and starburst hair—and she adored the unsmiling mouth that hinted at dark secrets. One wing was twisted from the fall and the shield was mangled, making the dragon appear a bit squashed.

When Zoé touched Arianrhod's face, flakes of copper came off in her hand. She pressed her lips to the goddess's ear, which resembled a delicate shell, whispering, "Please keep us safe. And don't let the Scravens get inside the cottage!"

"Zoé, Ian!" shouted Pippin from the front door. "Come look!"

Zoé rushed over, her knees going weak as she gazed into the street. Adults and children were walking over the cobblestones, moving steadily through the fog toward the cottage, all of them silent, none of them smiling. Many were faces she recognized: Catherine Beedle, Fritha Pooke, Ned Larkin, Dr. Thistle, Iris Tintern, Mirielle Tate, Dr. Brown the optometrist. And although they looked like humans, she knew they were nothing of the sort. They were . . . *Scravens*!

"They've all got blue-tinted glasses," said Ian. "No surprise there."

"They're coming this way," hissed Pippin. "Catherine Beedle's leading them! And look, there's old Bascomb!"

"We have to go—*now!*" gasped Zoé, slamming the door and bolting it. So much for the cottage being a vantage point for fighting off Scravens, she thought. Miss Glyndower's strategy was now in total disarray.

"The puzzle!" said Ian, heading for the staircase.

"Don't forget the runestone!" Zoé shouted after him.

"*The Book of Astercôte's* up there, too!" yelled Pippin.

Zoé grabbed her granddad's raincoat and scarf, along with his galoshes. Pippin ran to the kitchen, emerging with cans of soup and corned beef and packets of tea, which they loaded into their backpacks.

"I don't understand. . . . Did I miss something?" said Granddad while Zoé helped him put on his coat, trying not to appear too panicky. "Where are we going in such a rush? And what's that girl doing with my Glengettie tea?"

"It's all right, Mr. Blackwood," said Pippin, hooking her arm through his. "The house isn't safe because of the storm: we've had to call a plumber because the pipes are overflowing, and, oh yeah, rain from your gutters disturbed the moles in your garden, and, well, frankly, it's just one big mess, so we have to leave for a short while."

"Moles, you say?" Zoé could see Granddad looking more befuddled than ever. "That's funny, I've never seen moles near my cottage before."

"We won't be gone long, Mr. Blackwood," said Pippin in a convincing tone. "Just be sure to bundle up warmly."

Zoé tossed *The Count of Monte Cristo* into her backpack as Ian came charging downstairs with the silver box, Dr. Marriott's book and the runestone.

"They're almost to the front door," he said, his eyes wide with fear. "We'll have to go out the other way. Here, you carry this stuff in Zoé's backpack, okay, 'cause she has to see to the goddess." He handed the runestone and *The Book of Astercôte* to Pippin. "We'll go through the neighbors' back gardens to Upper Frog Street. I've got the puzzle in my messenger bag. And the vial's in my pocket."

Zoé lifted the goddess, cradling the metal figure in her arms, trying to straighten out her bent wing. The sight of Arianrhod's serene face made her feel a little bit braver.

Pippin guided Granddad out of his shop, murmuring reassurances.

"Are we in some sort of danger?" Zoé heard her grandfather say.

"Not at all, Mr. Blackwood, but with all these water problems, we might get our feet wet!" Pippin giggled. Zoé had to hand it to her: Pippin was a fabulous trickster. "Let's say we're playing a kind of game, Mr. Blackwood, and we need to move very quickly. This way."

As they hurried through the parlor and out the back door, Zoé winced, hearing loud noises coming from the antiques shop.

Scravens had made it to the cottage—and they were *inside!*

CHAPTER TWENTY-EIGHT
RISE OF THE SCRAVENS

Zoé felt like a standard bearer from medieval times, carrying the warrior goddess in a procession through the fog-laden streets of Tenby, the sea wind howling in her ears. It was only eleven o'clock in the morning, yet the skies were black with clouds and the streetlamps had flickered on.

The fall of the weathervane had turned their game plan on its head: Granddad's cottage was obviously no longer a danger-free zone. They'd decided to enlist Dr. Marriott's help in their battle against The First. He'd offered to help if there was trouble, and they were in trouble, all right. They also needed to get Granddad somewhere safe.

"Why are you carrying the weathervane goddess,

Magpie?" asked their grandfather, looking mystified. "I don't understand—"

"We rescued her, Granddad, remember? She's too valuable to leave lying around." Zoé knew she didn't sound very convincing, maybe because she lacked Pippin's dramatic talents.

"She's right, y'know," said Pippin. "Some little urchin might come around and spirit Arianrhod away. Then you'd be in a right pickle."

"Hmm, perhaps my hearing aid needs adjusting," murmured Granddad, and Zoé could see all this was too much for him. Everything was happening so fast.

Her grandfather looked fragile and confused; his skin had taken on a sallow tint. As she looked at his trim mustache and silvery hair, Zoé's heart ached. For a moment she contemplated telling him everything, beginning with Iris's demented behavior and the events of the past few days. On the other hand, a crash course in Scravens might be too much of a leap for him; Granddad was too old for this kind of struggle.

But how on earth were they going to keep Granddad safe from the Scravens? How were they going to keep themselves safe and at the same time defeat The First?

"If I was to add up the total volume of all the tea I've drunk in my day, I could float a blooming battleship," Zoé heard her grandfather say to Pippin. Smiling to herself, she thought how lucky she was to have such an interesting and joke-cracking granddad.

A few more turns and they stood before the tall pink house with bay windows and a black lacquered door. Zoé could hear waves rising and falling at the bottom of the cliff, the sea obscured behind a thick, soupy fog. The sign by the front door that read GEORGE R. MARRIOTT, ANTIQUARIAN BOOKSELLER looked reassuringly normal—but was everything normal inside? There was only one way to find out.

"Why, I was here not long ago," said Granddad. "George Marriott sold me a second edition of *The Count of Monte Cristo*. Fabulous illustrations. After all these years, that story is still my favorite."

Pleased to have remembered to bring his favorite book, Zoé pictured her Granddad reading it in a comfy chair next to the fire in Dr. Marriott's upstairs front room.

"Dr. Marriott says we can stay here with him. Brilliant, eh?" said Pippin with a wide smile. "Just until the pipes and gutters get sorted out at your cottage," she added quickly.

At first Zoé had wondered if all these fabrications might be wearing Pippin down, but she'd soon realized that wasn't the case at all: Pippin seemed to be enjoying herself immensely.

Ian clanged the knocker and the door swung open. Mrs. Prosser stuck her head out and Zoé tensed, seeing blue-tinted half-moon glasses perched halfway down her nose. "You'll be wanting to see the professor again, is it?" said the housekeeper, not looking at them directly. "*Four* of you this time? Well, I never. Come in out of the rain, then." She pointed to the goddess with a look of distaste. "*That* stays outside."

"No way, I'm not leaving her out in the street," said Zoé, refusing to be intimidated by Mrs. Prosser. "She's too valuable." She marched into the hallway, noticing the housekeeper eyeing the goddess warily, keeping a safe distance from it.

"Put that thing in the umbrella stand," ordered Mrs. Prosser. "I won't have you dripping water over the professor's good carpets."

Setting the goddess next to the umbrellas, Zoé felt her anxiety ratchet up a few notches. With a sigh she followed Mrs. Prosser into the room piled high with timeworn books and furnished with a threadbare rug.

"The professor will be with you momentarily," said Mrs. Prosser, the door clicking firmly shut behind her.

"She didn't have glasses before, did she?" Zoé whispered to Ian.

He shook his head. "I don't think so."

"A fine collection of old books, George has," said Granddad, wandering over to inspect the shelves. "Some of them extremely old, and most are in excellent condition."

The three children huddled by the window, whispering to one another and gazing out at the fog.

"I never saw Mrs. Prosser wearing glasses," said Zoé, feeling chills down her arms.

"She didn't look us in the eye, either," said Ian, gripping his messenger bag. "And you know what that means."

"Well, it *could* mean she's a Scraven," said Pippin, "but

maybe she's had them glasses forever, for knitting or whatever. Or maybe she's turned and Dr. Marriott doesn't know. He's afraid of Mrs. Prosser, if you ask me."

"People don't wear *tinted* glasses to knit," argued Zoé.

Ian nodded grimly. "She's one of the Afflicted."

Just then the door flew open and Zoé's heart fell to her feet. There stood Dr. Marriott—*like one of those pod people* was all she could think—wearing a pair of black horn-rimmed glasses with blue lenses.

"Hello, George," said Granddad. "Nice to see you, old man."

Dr. Marriott gave John Blackwood a curt nod, then turned to the others, not making eye contact with any of them. "I trust you've brought *The Book of Astercôte*," he said. It almost sounded like his normal voice, but Zoé detected a slight change. "And the runestone, have you that as well, Philippa Jenkyn Thomas?"

Pippin seemed to wither for a moment, then quickly pulled herself together. "The book's in your hallway." She threw a sidelong glance at Zoé and Ian. "The runestone as well. Bron did a cracking job."

Pippin guided Granddad out into the hallway, the two cousins following as Dr. Marriott breathed down Zoé's neck.

"We can't stay," Zoé said as she rushed to the goddess, knocking over the umbrella stand. *I'll never let you out of my sight again*, she promised Arianrhod.

"Oh no, I'm afraid I can't let you leave—not yet," said Dr. Marriott, briskly sidestepping the goddess. He flashed a cold smile that chilled Zoé to the core, and she felt a sudden ache of loss. She could hardly believe their trustworthy friend George Marriott had been taken over by Scravens— now *he* was the enemy!

"And do you know what happens next?" he said in a cracked whisper. "You will become one of *us*!"

"Run, guys!" shouted Ian, and they fled down the hall, Zoé brandishing the goddess at a snarling Dr. Marriott. His front teeth seemed to have grown and looked frighteningly sharp. Ian kicked the front door open as Pippin, snatching up her backpack, bundled their grandfather outside.

Oh no! thought Zoé. *Granddad can't run fast enough!*

There was a high-pitched scream and Zoé froze as Mrs. Prosser leapt from the staircase, wings unfurling from her bony shoulders. Ian wheeled around with the vial and Mrs. Prosser's taloned hand lashed out, sending it flying. Glass shattered against the wall, with waves of silvery mist engulfing them.

Sprinting out the front door with Ian, Zoé could hear Mrs. Prosser's furious shrieks.

"Hurry!" cried Pippin, and the four stumbled into the fog.

Granddad had trouble moving quickly, so they were forced to slow down. Zoé hoisted the goddess into the air, ready to wield her against anything that threatened them.

"Do you think the mist worked?" whispered Ian. "Like maybe it paralyzed or confused them so they couldn't come after us?"

Zoé glanced back. There was no sign of Dr. Marriott or Mrs. Prosser running down the street. "Yeah, something like that. The mist gave us time to get away! Good work, Ian."

"Let's head over to Bron's cottage," said Pippin. "Cob Lane's not far, and Bron's our last hope, really."

They wound their way up the narrow cobbled path of Quay Hill, past the Tudor Merchant's House. But as they crossed St. Julian's Street, Zoé noticed shadows milling about on Cob Lane—and what seemed to be the glint of blue lenses.

"Scravens!" she warned.

The four of them hurried away, Ian and Pippin holding Granddad on either side. He had a look of confusion that nearly broke Zoé's heart.

They made their way through Castle Square, following the old walls of the castle. As they neared the archway Zoé screeched to a halt, seeing a shadow step out of the mist, a gaunt shape not much taller than she was.

"There are unearthly creatures afoot in the fog," said a splintery voice, and Zoé tightened her grip on the goddess. "You one of 'em, eh? What've you done with the runestone, I'd like to know? And where's my key to the Tombs?"

Stokes! Heart pounding, Zoé stared at the man's pitted face and oily hair, his scowling expression. Stokes wasn't wearing glasses: a good sign. Even so, she didn't trust him. *If Stokes really is The First,* she thought, *we're done for.*

"Ah, Mr. Stokes," said her grandfather. "A treat to see you, old chap."

Stokes squinted at them. "That thing yer holdin' looks a relic," he rasped, pointing to the goddess. "Been plundering the tunnels again, have you?"

Zoé had no idea whether Stokes was joking or not, but before she could reply, Granddad cut in: "We've had a devil of a time today, Stokes, what with the storm blowing my weathervane off the roof and water problems at the cottage and people acting rather, well, *strangely*, to put it mildly."

Stokes rubbed his grizzled chin. "Aye, and that's not the half of it. The whole town's gone mad. Another boat's gone missing off Caldey and people I've knowed fer years are going off their heads. Dr. Thistle, he's gone odd all of a sudden, lost all interest in the Black Barty exhibit."

Zoé felt relief wash over her. If Stokes was The First, he wouldn't be saying these things.

"What do you know about the Scravens?" she asked. Stokes struck her as the secretive type, which meant he probably knew more than he was letting on.

"I knows more than most." Stokes gave a loud sniff. "You're the ones, ain't you? The word is out that you kids took a smugglers' tunnel to Caldey looking for a monk who's been years dead, and you left the island with an ancient treasure. Is that so?" Not waiting for an answer, he continued, "You're in serious danger, mates. I heard that your sorceress friend nicked a stone from the tunnels. Very old, it is, and worth a few bob. And something else you have that them Scravens are after." There was a dry whistling intake of breath. "A puzzle, is it?"

Zoé felt her stomach drop. How on earth did Stokes know about all those things?

"Rumor has it the Scravens have orders to find you and"—Stokes hesitated, eyes darting between Zoé and the others—"well, *dispose* of you. Same as in the old days, when pirates and wreckers got rid of their enemies. *Dead men tell no tales*, as they say."

Dispose of sounded like the kind of term the CIA would use, thought Zoé.

"Just where are you getting your information, Stokes?" demanded Pippin angrily. "Or are you making it up?"

"And don't lie to us!" said Zoé.

"Whose side are you really on?" asked Ian.

"It's Gawd's truth, I swear," said Stokes. "Dr. Thistle's been holding secret meetings in his office. I put my ear to the keyhole and find out all sorts of int'resting things. He says you kids and Bron Gilwern are trouble, and he's sent his minions to follow yer. Calls them Scravens, he does."

"And who exactly goes to these secret meetings?" asked Ian, sounding dubious.

"Iris Tintern, for one. Mirielle Tate and Ned Larkin. I saw them through the keyhole," said Stokes, counting on his fingers. "Then there's Mrs. Owen from the bakery, Dr. Brown the optometrist, and a slew of others from Zival's. Kids your age, too: a pie-faced girl with rhinestone glasses."

"Catherine Beedle!" said Ian, and the three children gaped at one another.

"It's Zival, isn't it?" Zoé burst out. "Zival's the one giving orders!"

"Are you discussing Dr. Zival, the new optometrist in town?" asked Granddad. "Folks say he's got a whopper of a sign outside his shop."

"Sounds to me like Dr. Thistle is second-in-command," said Ian. "I bet it was Zival who told him to smash the rune-stone!"

Stokes rubbed his bristly jaw. "Zival weren't at the meetings, but come to think of it, they did keep mentioning his name. . . ."

"I knew it!" said Zoé. "Zival's The First!"

Pippin's eyes flashed angrily. "All this time he's been spying on us! I'll wager he knows where we are this very minute."

"We're trying to get to Bron Gilwern's flat on Cob Lane," Ian told Stokes. "It's really important that we find her, but the Scravens are all over the place and there's no way to get there."

"Why not ring her up?" said Stokes.

"There's a thought," said Pippin. "Can I borrow your cell?"

Stokes stared at her as if she had two heads. "I don't have no cell."

"Neither do we," said Zoé.

"Our American cell phones don't work here," explained Ian. "And Granddad prefers his landline."

"Then we need to find a telephone kiosk," said Pippin. "One that's not been vandalized."

"Follow me," said Stokes. "There's a kiosk outside Tenby Museum—if the vandals haven't got to that one, too."

As they headed toward the museum, Zoé hoped Stokes wasn't planning to charge them for finding a telephone. Remembering how he wanted to trade secrets for gold, saying everything comes at a price, she knew it was definitely the kind of thing that Stokes would do.

CHAPTER TWENTY-NINE
RETURN TO DRAGON'S MOUTH

Minutes later, Zoé was crunched inside a red telephone kiosk between Pippin and Granddad, hugging the goddess to her chest and feeding the telephone with coins she'd collected from everyone.

At last there came the *brrr-brrr, brrr-brrr* of the phone on Bron's end, and Zoé heard someone pick up.

"Bron?" said Pippin. "It's us, Bron; Cob Lane's cut off by Scravens and we can't get to you! What? Oh aye, the incantation worked: the goddess weathervanes were absolutely crackin'. Scravens were all in a kerfluffle—"

As the two talked, Zoé peered through the kiosk windows at Ian and Stokes, standing as lookouts in a thick fog.

"Right, then, ten minutes." Pippin hung up the phone and they all piled out. "We're to meet Bron at Dragon's Mouth. She's certain The First will be there."

"But Dragon's Mouth is a sacred space!" argued Zoé. "Why would The First go to a cavern full of spells and enchantments?"

"Hold on, think of all the power and energy inside that cavern," said Ian. "The First is probably thinking he can just go there and grab it all for himself. I bet he knows we're going there with the puzzle, because he's sent out his spies and they're watching our every move."

"No way can The First get the puzzle," said Zoé through clenched teeth.

"Then it's war," said Pippin. "The battle begins."

Ian nodded. "We fight to the death."

"Can you take us to Dragon's Mouth, Stokes?" asked Pippin.

"I knows the way," he growled, "if you're not afeard of goin' down into the tunnels."

"The tunnels don't scare us," said Ian.

Through swirling fog, Zoé glimpsed a wraithlike figure sneaking around the back of the telephone kiosk. For a fleeting moment a face appeared, blurred by the mist; then it melted away.

"It's Catherine Beedle!" she yelled, but the girl dashed into the fog and vanished.

"Oh no," groaned Pippin. "What if she heard us talking

about Dragon's Mouth? She'll warn Zival and he'll have the jump on us." She threw up her hands. "There's nothing for it, is there? We'll have to take our chances."

※

"I thought the town council closed the tunnel entrances," said Granddad, looking more baffled than ever as Stokes guided them around Tenby Museum to a sturdy oak door half buried inside the building's stone exterior.

"Aye, they have," said Stokes in a gravelly voice. "But some of us were never much fer obeying rules, if you get my meaning." Extracting a key ring from his pocket, he chose a medium-sized key and turned it in the lock. "Got yer torches?"

Zoé handed her flashlight to her grandfather. "Here, Granddad, I can't carry this and the goddess, too."

"Why on earth are we going down into the tunnels?" asked Granddad. "Shouldn't we get a bite to eat first?"

"No need to worry, Mr. Blackwood. We won't get into trouble," said Pippin. "Stokes is taking us on a special tour."

As the three children exchanged nervous looks, it was clear to Zoé that they were all thinking the same thing: this was the final battle. In Dragon's Mouth they would confront The First and, whatever the outcome, the fate of Tenby would be determined.

"But it's gone noon," said Granddad, squinting at his heirloom pocket watch. "I've missed my elevenses."

"Sorry, Granddad," said Ian. "All I have is soup, but there's no way to heat it."

"It's quite all right. Back during the war we went days without eating, so I expect I'll survive."

"Hey, I forgot about this," said Pippin, pulling a chocolate-and-nut bar from her backpack. "Here, Mr. Blackwood, this should tide you over."

Zoé shot Pippin a grateful smile.

"Mind how you go," warned Stokes, opening the door. "There's moss and weed all over them steps, and Gawd knows what else." He laughed deep in his throat, and Zoé thought it sounded like someone gargling.

Carrying the goddess under her arm, she descended a metal ladder, freezing to the touch, straight down into what looked like an impenetrable darkness. Ian switched on his headlamp and she could see a faint glaze of moss on the walls around them.

"You okay, Granddad?" Zoé called out. "Are you warm enough?"

"Everything's tip-top, Magpie, don't worry about me." Her grandfather's words echoed back up to her. True to his nature, Granddad seemed to be keeping his spirits high.

Stokes led them down a much more disquieting tunnel than the one they'd taken to Caldey Island, and Zoé grew increasingly uneasy, noticing how it branched out into numerous smaller tunnels. *Smells all salty and seaweedy*, she thought, sniffing. *It's like we're walking under the sea again.*

The juddering beam of Stokes's flashlight cast uneven shadows on the stone walls as they moved through a labyrinth of echoing passages, each colder than the last. Zoé moved warily, afraid that at any minute a Scraven would come leaping out. Her teeth rattled noisily inside her head—at least, it seemed that way to her—as she shivered with the damp.

"The minute we get to Dragon's Mouth, we seal the puzzle," said Ian quietly, patting his messenger bag. "Then it's done."

This time Zoé didn't object.

The passageway grew increasingly narrow, and after what seemed like endless turns and twists, Zoé thought they'd reached the end. Then she realized the tunnel was shrinking to an even smaller passage, barely wide enough for them to pass through one at a time. The ceiling was so low that Granddad had to duck his head. *You'd better not be tricking us, Stokes,* she thought, watching him squeeze himself through, *because if you are, you'll be sorry.*

Zoé hesitated for a moment, heart thumping, staring at the dark entrance. It looked so small and constricted. *Gives me the shivers,* she thought. *I can't go in there.* Then, holding the goddess to her chest and imagining what the Messengers would do, she stormed ahead, her thin wiry frame slipping right through. Far ahead she could see the others' heads bobbing up and down.

She stepped into the cavern and, for a moment, felt the weight of her fears fall away. The goddess in her arms began glowing faintly. Breathless, Zoé stared at the glimmering symbols and shapes—elegant, incomprehensible—spiraling across the walls and the archway of Dragon's Mouth.

"Extraordinary," said Granddad. "Most folks in Tenby say

Dragon's Mouth has no entrance—unless you scale the cliff, hah! A real eye-opener, this is, a special tour indeed. Well done, Stokes."

"Bron!" Pippin shouted. "Hey, Bron!" There was no reply, so she shouted again.

Zoé, more nervous than ever, began chewing on her lower lip. What if the Scravens had taken over Bron?

"Is that you lot?" came a disembodied voice.

Hearing Bron, Zoé felt a rush of relief—she was a little less frightened now. A light flickered from inside a low entrance, and Bron emerged holding a storm lantern.

"I was afraid you— Hold on." Bron doubled over, taking deep gulps of air. "Got to catch my breath. Took a steep shortcut."

Bron straightened up, her jaw tightening as she caught sight of Stokes. Zoé saw him cringe as he shambled a few steps back, arms hanging at his sides.

"What are *you* doing here?" demanded Bron, scowling.

"Stokes helped us find a phone kiosk to call you," said Ian. "He brought us here through the tunnels."

"We'd never have found Dragon's Mouth otherwise," said Pippin. "Stokes is on our side, Bron."

"I knows about the Scravens, I knows what they're up to," said Stokes, keeping his distance from Bron. "Zival's spies are on the move, hunting down these kids. Zival wants them got rid of."

"Zival's The First!" cried Zoé. "The Scraven mastermind!"

"Zival, eh?" said Bron, still throwing toxic looks at

Stokes. "Good to know who we're up against." For a moment she stood silent and intent, and Zoé thought how fearsome she looked. "And the runestone?"

"We took ever such good care of it," said Pippin, unzipping Zoé's backpack. "Here you go."

"The Runestone of Arianrhod must be returned to its rightful place in Dragon's Mouth. We took a risk, removing it from the cavern." Bron set down her lantern.

"What d'you mean?" asked Pippin. "Spirits will haunt us?"

"No telling what the theft of a runestone might stir up." Bron turned to Zoé. "Remember me telling you it was yours until the time came to return it? Go on then, put the stone back."

Mounting the wide steps, Zoé stood before the carving of Arianrhod, watching the runestone's unearthly symbols begin to glow. With a gesture of deep reverence, she set the runestone inside the shallow gap, feeling a tug at her heart, knowing a part of her didn't want to let it go. She watched as the markings deepened into bold colors, the stone looking as if it had been part of the rock for centuries.

Bron unclasped a leather bag slung over one shoulder. "The incantation," she said, handing them papers. "Printouts."

Ian's face fell. "Er, we can't read runic Ogham, Bron."

"No problem," said Bron. "I've printed the words out phonetically."

Ian grinned. "Stellar."

"You're brilliant, Bron," said Pippin.

"I know," said Bron, snapping the bag shut.

"All we have to do now is find Zival," said Zoé. "Otherwise known as . . . The First." Ironic that her name and their enemy's name both began with a Z. *Too creepy*, she thought, remembering Ian telling her that there was no letter Z in the Welsh alphabet.

"The game plan's changed now," said Ian. "We were supposed to stay at the cottage and fight Zival, but now everything's in a mess because the goddess fell off the roof and Dr. Marriott's turned into a Scraven and—"

"And Zival's probably down here already," Pippin cut in.

"We can't just sit here twiddling our thumbs," said Ian. "We've got to hunt him down."

"Yeah, but it ain't just you looking fer Zival, don't forget," said Stokes, his thin upper lip curling as he spoke. "Zival himself is out there, not far off I reckon, and *he's* looking fer *you.*"

CHAPTER THIRTY
BEWARE THE MEASURER OF SIGHT

"He's right, Stokes is. We needn't go looking for Zival," said Bron with a disquieting smile. "Zival will come to us."

Zoé felt her skin go clammy. This was what she'd been dreading: a head-on clash with Zival, the Scraven mastermind.

"Right, then," said Bron. "We stand near the goddess and whisper the incantation."

"And we don't stop until the goddess wakes up," added Zoé. "Then the fireworks begin."

"Oh no, the puzzle—we forgot to seal it!" said Ian, digging the silver box out of his messenger bag. "We have to do this first!"

"Isn't that the box I gave you, the one with the antique glass inside?" asked their grandfather. "Why on earth have you brought that?"

"It's a puzzle, Granddad," said Zoé.

"What's that, Magpie? What did you say?"

Maybe it hadn't been a good idea after all, keeping things secret to protect their grandfather. But how could they have known Granddad would be with them in Dragon's Mouth as they prepared to face Zival? That hadn't been part of the plan. Ian was right, everything was in a mess. And now there was zero time to explain anything.

"Those pieces of glass fit together to make a puzzle," she went on, but her grandfather's gentle blue eyes, so similar in color to her own, gazed back at her in confusion.

"We'll explain later," promised Ian. "Okay, Granddad?"

Their grandfather gave a weak smile and Zoé thought, *Poor Granddad. He probably thinks we've all gone crazy.*

"Bring the puzzle over here!" shouted Pippin from the mouth of the cavern. "The light's better!"

Handing the goddess to Bron, Zoé joined Ian and Pippin beneath the archway overlooking the sea. She could hear the distant crash of waves, and when she looked down to the water below, a drop of hundreds of feet, she felt queasy. Ian, sitting across from her, was acting jittery, and his face looked ashen. Not surprising, she thought, since he was terrified of heights. But there was no time to worry about that now.

Zoé watched, almost hypnotized, as the puzzle took on its ancient round shape, and she gasped at the beauty of it: a circle of blue glass, eerie and enchanted, glowing with a fierce inner light. It was, she thought, the most mysterious thing she'd ever seen. She had a sudden fantastic feeling, as if the spirit and essence of the puzzle were taking hold of her.

"Do you have it?" whispered Ian. "The Thirteenth Piece?"

Zoé rummaged through her pockets, faint with fear, worried that Zival might appear before they could seal the puzzle.

"Hurry!" said Bron from the depths of the cavern.

"Got it," said Zoé, dropping the glass piece into Ian's hand.

She watched light glance off the Thirteenth Piece as he held it between his shaking fingers. "Okay," he said, leaning over the puzzle, "we need to apply some logic here. . . ."

Zoé could tell that Ian had no idea where the Thirteenth Piece should go—nor did she.

"Just get on with it," said Pippin, sounding anxious.

Hearing a noise behind them, Zoé felt her skin crawl. A fearful silence closed in. She sensed a presence—something malevolent, savage, *unspeakable*—and she stared wildly into the cavern, seeing Bron's lantern swing, making shadows jump.

She saw a figure moving toward them.

All at once something shot past with alarming speed, knocking her aside: a gnarled hand, talons silted with dirt, snatching the Thirteenth Piece from Ian's grasp.

"I'll take that, if you don't mind," said a voice as cold as death.

Rigid with fright, she gazed up at Zival's spare, illusory

shape: hands fused into claws, a reptilian face, and a body that was light-years away from human. The Thirteenth Piece, pincered between Zival's talons, went black; all of its light had gone out.

"Hey!" shouted Ian. "Give it back!"

"Ah yes, I'll take this as well." Zival went for the puzzle.

"No!" screamed Zoé, throwing herself on top of it, kicking wildly as he tried to claw his way to grab it.

Dripping seaweed and foul-smelling water, Zival appeared to be part reptile and part monstrous bird, his neck marked by gills, with a glistening sheen on his skin, like a newt or a salamander. Black scales fell from his leathery wings, scattering across the cavern floor.

Sprawled over the puzzle, staring up at him, Zoé realized that Zival the optometrist was simply a myth: Zival the person had never existed. *Zival's not an optometrist,* she thought, *he's just a Scraven!* He'd obviously come straight from Wythernsea, the first Scraven through the puzzle, and he'd remained a Scraven, taking charge of all the others, masterminding the invasion of Tenby.

"He took the Thirteenth Piece!" yelled Ian. "Get it!"

Everything seemed to happen at once. Ian and Pippin threw themselves at Zival, scratching, biting and kicking, trying desperately to wrench the Thirteenth Piece from his claws. Shouting in Welsh, Bron thundered across the cavern, and from a dark corner Zoé heard Stokes hurling out pirate curses.

In a fury Bron leapt at Zival. Brushing aside Ian and

Pippin, Zival lunged forward, lashing out with his wing, flinging Bron backward onto the ground. Zoé watched him pivot on clawed feet and slither off, clutching the Thirteenth Piece, moving eel-like across the cavern. He looked like an amphibious vampire as he vanished into the wall.

"That's Zival's hiding place!" she cried, pulling Bron to her feet. "He's been spying on us from inside the wall!"

Bron winced as she rubbed her elbow, but otherwise she seemed unhurt.

"We've got a problem," said Ian. "The puzzle's not sealed!"

"Leave it, we've no time," said Bron. "When Zival returns, we'll weaken him by reciting the incantation. We'll take back the Thirteenth Piece and seal the puzzle then. End of story."

"I guess so," said Ian, throwing worried glances at Zoé and Pippin.

"We must act fast—he'll be here any moment," said Bron in a take-charge voice, gathering the three children around her. "This is serious stuff, so pay attention. Philippa and Ian, you'll whisper the incantation using the printouts as I read off the stone."

Ian's resolute expression reminded Zoé of a knight preparing for battle. He was a combination of all the heroes she'd ever read about, both modern and old-time. *Wow*, she thought, *Ian's come a long way.*

"Get Stokes and Mr. Blackwood well away from the fracas," Bron continued, shoving her leather jacket at Pippin. "Give this to Mr. Blackwood; he needs to rest, and it'll ward off the cold. Keep a close eye on them both, in case."

Before Zoé could ask *In case of what?* Bron pointed to an alcove on the other side of the cavern, directly opposite the carving of Arianrhod. "See that hollowed-out niche? A powerful space, riddled with lost enchantments. Go up there and I'll pass the goddess to you. Believe me, Arianrhod will respond as she did in Wythernsea. But you'll have to focus."

"I can do that," said Zoé, trying to sound confident.

Bron makes everything sound so easy, thought Zoé, running to the alcove, wondering how they were going to take the Thirteenth Piece from Zival. Ian and Pippin caught up with her and, linking hands, secured a foothold, hoisting her up.

"Your grandfather fell asleep," said Pippin, and Zoé felt a rush of relief.

"That's the best we can do, right? Hope that Granddad sleeps through this," said Ian, looking up with a solemn expression. He seemed so small and vulnerable, yet she could see on his face an expression of hope, which seemed to lift her spirits. "Don't worry, Zoé, we can beat Zival. We'll drive out the Scravens! Think of the Messengers and what happened in Wythernsea. Don't be afraid."

"Yeah, remember Wythernsea," said Pippin encouragingly.

"Remember Wythernsea, remember Wythernsea," Zoé whispered to herself as they ran off. But in Wythernsea there hadn't been any Zival.

Gazing at the symbols in the walls, some she'd never seen

before, Zoé sensed the lost enchantments beginning to stir, and she felt a little braver. The stone was wet underfoot and for a moment she nearly slid off the edge; regaining her balance, she tried to keep focused.

"When Zival appears, raise her high into the air. Believe in what will happen," said Bron, handing the goddess to her. "*It is the goddess that matters.* Take care of her."

Alarmed, Zoé noticed that Bron was trying to keep her quaking body still. *Oh no,* she thought, *Bron's scared, too!* She'd always admired Bron's remoteness, her cool self-control. Yet nobody was immune from fear, she realized, not even a seeress. Was Bron tough enough? Zoé wasn't sure—especially now that Zival had the Thirteenth Piece.

The air grew colder, as if the sacred spirits were being sucked right out of the cavern. Zoé watched Bron step up to the runestone. The flame inside her lamp guttered. Blinking through the gloom, Zoé felt suddenly all alone, watching the stone walls fade into shadow.

A dark flailing shape dropped down, landing on the floor, and a numbing fear cut through her. Breathless, she watched the hideous entity that was Zival slither across the cavern, dragging leathery wings, its shallow a whirling pit rimmed in green fire.

Flattening herself against the wall, not daring to move, Zoé watched Zival loom over the puzzle. "Mine," he whispered in a gloating voice, sounding powerful, triumphant. "All this is mine."

"No! It's not yours!" Ian shouted, startling Zoé with his

bravery. "Forget it, you don't own the puzzle. It doesn't belong to anyone."

What was he trying to do, reason with Zival? She silently willed him to be quiet, yet at the same time she was proud of her cousin's courage.

Zival gave a harsh laugh. "Stupid child, of course it is mine. Have you never heard of the spoils of war?"

Despite the hopelessness of the situation, Ian held his ground. "It's nothing to do with war. The puzzle's not something anyone can own!"

Zoé felt a glimmer of understanding pass through her. The puzzle was a gateway and, as with certain kinds of magic, no one person could lay claim to it: it belonged to everyone and no one.

Without warning, a clot of darkness shot up through the puzzle, flapping into the air. Her stomach churned as more Scravens appeared in a flurry of claws and teeth, wings unfurling as they hung suspended above the puzzle in a hushed, menacing cloud.

Zoé slumped against the wall, consumed by a black dread. *We can't defeat Zival, he's too strong and so are the Scravens,* she thought. *This is the end of everything.*

A single note rang out: Bron's deep, husky voice, precise and clear, not quite chanting yet not singing either, joined by the whispery voices of Ian and Pippin. Zoé heard fragments of oddly familiar sounds echoing through the cavern, the same words and phrases whispered by the Messengers when they'd stood beside the Wythernsea wall.

She felt the goddess grow warmer in her hands. The symbols inside the niche flared luminescent gold, as if they'd caught fire, filling the cavern with a soft brilliance.

The Scravens hung motionless above the puzzle and Zoé could almost see them shrinking inside themselves, their malefic strength leaking out of them. Zival, licking his fishlike lips, assumed an arrogant stance. The incantation seemed not to have touched him.

Then everything happened fast: Zival turned to Bron, Ian and Pippin with a predatory smile, the sharp points of his teeth glistening. Zoé gasped in horror as his leathery wings wrapped around her beloved cousin.

CHAPTER THIRTY-ONE
THE POWER OF UNEARTHLY CREATURES

Zoé's heart stopped beating as the air went out of her
lungs. She felt the inside of her body go hollow. With a
crazed, terrified wail, she jumped from the ledge, still holding
the goddess, managing somehow to land on her feet.

"No!" she roared. "Get away from him!"

Half blinded by tears, she launched herself at Zival, gripping the weathervane with one hand and pounding her free
fist against his slimy skin, while Ian struggled to break away.

"What were you saying about the puzzle? Who does it belong to, eh?" shrilled Zival. "The puzzle is mine, and you cannot drive me away. None of you can defeat me. I am The First!"

Zoé could see Ian trapped inside two massive wings.
Spreading beneath his skin was an eerie green light: his

fingers looked translucent. It was as if the pattern of his bones had changed, shifting from human into something else. *Ian was turning into a Scraven!*

"Let him go!" she screamed, seeing the ring of green fire dancing at the edges of Zival's shallow. "Get your disgusting claws off my cousin!"

She looked up to see an enormous black wing sweeping toward her, then felt it slam her onto the floor, knocking the breath from her and sending the goddess flying. Disoriented, she tried to stand, but her legs gave out and she sank to the ground.

"You are nothing. Nothing!" said Zival with a sneer. "You cannot defeat the Scravens. We are far too powerful." He held the Thirteenth Piece in his hooked claw, taunting her. "The end has come at last; our battle is over. Tenby belongs to the Scravens."

Staggering to her feet, Zoé was too devastated to say a word. Ian had stopped moving beneath Zival's wings, his body gone limp and lifeless. She felt her heart clench like a stone inside her chest. *I'll fight to the death for Ian. Nobody, not even Zival, is going to turn my cousin into a Scraven!*

High whispers filled the cavern; this time it was Bron, Pippin and Stokes. Zoé's heart pounded wildly as she remembered the quest Miss Glyndower had sent them on, the Messengers scattering across Wythernsea, the goddess weathervanes creaking to life. Her strength nearly gone, she dove for the goddess, hugging the luminous figure to her chest, recalling Bron's words: *It is the goddess that matters.*

Zoé could see waves of silver, gold and crimson rising off Arianrhod, shifting and changing before her eyes, mixing with light from the puzzle, infusing the cavern with an unearthly glow.

An expansive feeling came over her, giving her fresh courage. Whatever it took, she would save Ian. *If we defeated the Scravens in Wythernsea,* she told herself, *we can defeat them in Tenby.*

Lifting the goddess with both hands, she hurled herself at Zival, The First, the pure evil Scraven mastermind. Summoning the last of her strength, she brought Arianrhod down hard against his wing.

Zival swayed from the force of it, loosening his grip on Ian. The Scravens hissed through their teeth, looming over her, but as light flared from the goddess they shrank back, their eyes fearful, and Zoé was sure the incantation had weakened them.

Baring his teeth in fury, Zival swung around and lunged at her. At the same moment she felt her feet leave the ground. The goddess was lifting her up into the air! Zoé was stunned to find herself in Arianrhod's grasp, floating high above the cavern floor.

Blue flames streamed from the goddess's eyes, striking one of Zival's wings, and a sharp burning smell filled the cavern. Screaming, he lurched to one side, talons flying up, wings opening, releasing Ian. Zoé saw her cousin fall to the ground.

Zival gave a shrill cry of rage as one wing caught fire.

Smoke and ash swirled through the cavern as the flames leapt higher, throwing wild shadows against the walls. Zoé watched the Scravens circle desperately overhead, beating the air with their wings and flying out through Dragon's Mouth, abandoning their master.

Zival stumbled to the archway, flapping his good wing and shrieking in frustration as the charred wing failed to move. Losing his balance, he lurched sideways, claws sliding across the surface of the puzzle, his grotesque form skidding uncontrollably to the edge of the cliff, talons grasping at the air. Zoé watched, astounded, as he slipped over the side and plummeted down, down, down into the crashing waves below.

The next thing Zoé knew, her feet were on the ground. She sprinted to Ian, placed one hand on his arm and shook him gently: "Wake up, Ian, wake up!"

He looked brittle and delicate, his eyelids fluttering open and shut, his complexion a sallow green. Yet she was certain he was alive, because she felt his heart beating beneath her hand.

Swallowing back a sob, she lifted her cousin into her arms, willing his breath to grow stronger. "You were so brave, Ian," she whispered into his ear. "I can't believe it—you stood up to Zival!" The thought of losing her best friend in the entire world was suddenly too much to bear; tears began streaming down her cheeks.

At the sound of her voice, his eyes blinked open for a moment, and on his face was the ghost of a smile. She felt her heart turn over.

"Is Ian okay?" cried Pippin, running over. "Is he a . . . *Scraven*? Say no, Zoé—tell me he's not!" she pleaded tearfully.

"He's alive, but—" Zoé began.

Seeing Ian's fists unclench and his face relax, she felt her spirits lift. Then his eyes slowly opened.

"He's coming round, looks like," whispered Pippin.

To Zoé's relief, the color came rushing back into his face. He stared blankly at Zoé and Pippin, looking confused, then recoiled in terror.

"It's all right, Ian, it's us, me and Pippin," she said. "Zival's gone, he fell through Dragon's Mouth into the sea!"

"You're not a Scraven, are you?" asked Pippin.

"N-no," murmured Ian, rubbing the side of his face. Zoé could see the faint imprint of scales on his skin. "I don't think so." He looked around, slowly adjusting to his surroundings. "Did you just say Zival fell into the sea?"

"Food for the fish," said Pippin, grinning.

"But how . . . ?"

Suddenly Bron appeared with a puzzle piece. Handing it to Zoé, she said in a solemn tone, "We need to know if he's one or not."

Hand trembling, Zoé held the glass to her eye, gazing down at Ian. At first she saw a swirling blue light; then Ian's face swam into view. There was no third eye.

She held her breath, thinking she might faint.

"He's not a Scraven, he's Ian! Bron's incantation saved him!" Zoé shouted. "Arianrhod's magic worked, too!"

Shaking and weeping, she gave Ian an enormous hug, then all at once the three kids were hugging one another.

"Come see what happened," she said, helping Ian to his feet.

They stepped to the edge of Dragon's Mouth and peered over the cliff—Zoé growing dizzy as she looked down and Ian's face going pale—searching for traces of Zival. There were gulls and waves and rocks, and the *Sea Kestrel* chuttering toward Caldey Island—but there was no sign that a Scraven had fallen into the sea off the cliffs of Tenby.

"Zoé whacked Zival's wing with the goddess," Pippin told Ian, "and then the goddess lifted Zoé right into the air! His wing caught fire, all dramatic like, and he slipped on the glass puzzle. Then over the edge he went."

"You're braver than any smuggler or ship's captain!" said Ian, looking at his cousin with admiration. "You'll go down in the history books. 'Braver than any pirate who ever set foot in Tenby,' that's what they'll say."

"I'm tough, all right," joked Zoé, her face going red. "Not really, it was Arianrhod. And Bron, too . . . and Pippin and, well, all of us really."

"A pity the Thirteenth Piece went down with Zival, but there you are," said Bron, and Zoé felt her heart sink. "We'll have to destroy the puzzle. Do we smash it or throw it into the sea?"

"Neither," said Pippin with a lopsided grin. Reaching into

her pocket, she whipped out a chunk of blue glass. "When Zival let go of Ian, this fell from his claw and I chased it across the cavern." She handed the puzzle-glass to Zoé.

"The Thirteenth Piece!" said Ian in an awestruck voice.

Zoé gazed at the glass, the reality of the past few days suddenly hitting her. Knowing she could never go back to Wythernsea, she felt herself spinning away from Miss Glyndower, and Gwyn and Tegan, cut off from their sunlit world, their joy and beauty. With the puzzle sealed, all that she had been, all that she had experienced, would disappear.

But she had no choice: she had to let them go.

First she put back the piece Bron had given her. Then, taking a deep breath, she emptied her mind and, holding the Thirteenth Piece inches above the puzzle, let it fall. The glass rolled, landing on the image of the dragon, at the center of its wing. A moment later it snapped into place with a delicate *clink!* Zoé watched, as if in a dream, as the dragon seemed to stir, turning around and around, its wings seeming to move ever so slightly, talons opening and closing, stony eyes gazing up at her.

The Thirteenth Piece, glowing like a blue gem, was now embedded deep inside the dragon's wing. The dragon went still, as if nothing extraordinary had happened, and Zoé rubbed her eyes, unsure of what she'd just seen.

"The gateway's sealed," she said with an air of finality.

Pippin glanced up and Zoé saw a funny look on her face. "Um, did I just see that dragon move?"

"I think it did," whispered Ian. "But maybe we should keep it to ourselves. What do you think?"

The others nodded.

"No one would believe us anyway," said Zoé.

"Ian? Magpie?" Granddad, looking somewhat distressed, came stumbling toward them, Bron's jacket thrown over his shoulders, and Zoé felt a lump at the back of her throat. "Are you kids all right?"

"They're golden, Mr. Blackwood," said Bron, and Zoé saw the lines in Granddad's face relax.

"I fell asleep back there, see," said their grandfather, shaking his head. "I dreamed of this terrifying beast coming out of the shadows. It seemed frightfully real."

"Don't worry," said Zoé, hugging her granddad. "The scary beasts are gone."

"Everything's shipshape, Granddad," said Ian, giving their grandfather a bear hug.

"How about if I bring a ladder round to your cottage, John?" said Stokes. "I'll put the weathervane back on yer roof."

"Thank you, Stokes, I'd like that," said Granddad. "The roof is where she belongs."

"Look at the Thirteenth Piece," Pippin whispered to Zoé and Ian. "Like a jewel, it is, like it's always been there."

"Er, I know this defies the rules of logic," Ian whispered back, "but look how the pieces fused themselves together into a solid circle of glass."

"Oh my gosh," said Zoé. "It's not a puzzle anymore!"

A wind smelling like the sea blew in, pushing away the fog, and thick beams of afternoon sunlight fell through the mouth of the cavern. High over the water they glimpsed the winged outlines of Scravens, soaring over the town as little more than empty husks, fragmenting and splitting apart, crumbling into the sea, carried off past Caldey Island, moving inexorably toward the horizon, until at last they were gone from sight.

"It's the end of the Scravens!" yelled Zoé, and everyone cheered, voices echoing off the walls of Dragon's Mouth cavern. "Tenby's free at last!"

CHAPTER THIRTY-TWO
TENBY REVISITED

They emerged from the tunnels into the warm, sunlit afternoon. The air was crisp, charged with light from the sea. Zoé was already planning a story that would include all the strange and terrifying details of the past few days. The title would be "The Scravens of Dragon's Mouth."

"Zoé and I won't be long," Ian was telling Granddad. "We just want to check on our friends in town."

"See you back at the cottage then," said their grandfather, his tone growing lighthearted once again.

"See you, Granddad," said Zoé, lifting her face to the sun. At last it felt like summer. "But before we go—" She was about to launch into the explanation they'd promised Granddad, but she realized suddenly that it was all far too complex to explain in a few sentences. "Can we tell you everything when we get back, Granddad?"

"Sure thing, kids. Cheerio, then." Leaning down, he embraced them both. "I'm looking forward to a cracking good yarn when you return, don't forget."

"It'll knock your socks off," said Zoé.

"Deal, Granddad. Oh, and thanks, Mr. Stokes," said Ian, startling Stokes by shaking his hand. "For everything."

Zoé shook his hand, too, knowing she'd totally misjudged Stokes: he'd turned out to be their friend after all. Stokes had helped them get past the Scravens and guided them through the tunnels to Dragon's Mouth. Not bad for a crusty old museum curator.

"Ach, nothing to it," said Stokes, smiling. It was the first time Zoé had ever seen him smile in a normal sort of way. "Watch your backs, eh? That's my advice." He knitted his brows together, looking more like his old self. "Always treachery afoot in pirate towns like Tenby."

"We'll be careful," said Zoé cheerfully.

Zoé, Ian, Pippin and Bron set off, making their way through the streets of the Old Town.

"So, are the Afflicted okay now?" Pippin asked. "They're human beings again, right?"

"Miss Glyndower said the Scravens would be cast out, remember?" said Ian. "And the humans would turn back into their true selves."

"With Zival gone, the Scravens are history," said Zoé.

Everywhere she walked, she found herself crunching

over glass lenses, plastic and metal frames, and fancy eyeglass holders. Hundreds of pairs of tinted glasses were scattered all over the cobbled streets, dropped into the gutters, and thrown into dustbins.

"What's with all these glasses?" asked Ian.

"Folks've got rid of their specs," said Bron. "No need anymore. A good sign, when all's said and done. They've been, well, de-Scravenized."

De-Scravenized, *what a cool word*, thought Zoé, deciding to use it in her story.

From time to time she held up the fused puzzle, curious whether it still had the power to show her things, and looked with trepidation through the blue glass—slightly awkward, yet no one seemed to notice. None of the people she looked at had a third eye.

They passed several townspeople Zoé remembered as being the Afflicted—Mirielle Tate, Dr. Thistle, Dr. Brown and all the optometrists from Zival's Optical, Ned Larkin, Philip Fox, the baker Mrs. Owen and her son Derek. Everyone seemed to be, understandably, confused, staring at one another in disbelief, as if they'd just awoken from a nightmare, and she noticed the dark lines of their faces were already beginning to soften. Many of them were talking excitedly about sightings of gigantic winged creatures.

"I know what I saw," Mirielle Tate said to Mrs. Owen, walking arm in arm along Upper Frog Street, "and what I saw was the dragon of Dragon's Mouth, the very same one my granny told me stories about. It was every bit as real as you or I."

"Aye, was the legendary dragon, to be sure," agreed Mrs. Owen, looking thoughtful, "and no one will ever convince me otherwise."

Every so often Zoé would catch Ian's eyes and smile, knowing he was thinking the same thing she was. *We're so lucky to have each other, can you believe it? No one in the world would be daring enough to go on an adventure like this one.* He was like a brother—better, even. And her heart would flip over, recalling how she'd almost lost him to Zival.

And Pippin! How could she ever forget Philippa Jenkyn Thomas? Fiery and brave, Pippin had proven to be the truest of friends.

Wandering the familiar streets of old Tenby, Zoé could feel the presence of the past gathering around her: spirits, friends, relatives, ghosts, all connecting her to what came before—and what was yet to come—whispering long-lost secrets, embracing her, welcoming her.

Okay, magic was about spells and enchantments, but magic was about other things, too, like knowing who you were and where you belonged. It was the history handed down from generation to generation, passed from grandfather to granddaughter, cousin to cousin, friend to friend. Magic was in the cobbled streets, the timbered houses and crumbling castle walls, the shifting patterns of the sea. Magic was everywhere, if you opened your eyes and looked.

When they reached St. Julian's Street, Zoé was surprised

to see townspeople gathered outside Zival's Optical Shop with hammers and nails and two-by-fours, boarding up the front door and windows.

"Hey, what's occurrin'?" Bron shouted to Mrs. Prosser. Zoé gazed up to see Dr. Marriott's housekeeper at the top of a ladder, whacking at Zival's neon sign with a rolling pin.

"A disgrace, this," Mrs. Prosser shouted back. "If the Board of Health won't shut it down, then we citizens of Tenby will!"

"Mrs. Prosser," Ian yelled, "can you tell us where Dr. Marriott is?"

"You'll find the professor at the King's Ransom, said he fancied some soft ice cream."

"Here's where I leave you," said Bron. Uncharacteristically, she opened her arms, and all three children hugged her at once.

"Thank you, thank you," they whispered.

With a mysterious smile the silent seeress threw back her shoulders and strode off into the sunlight.

Zoé pushed open the door to the King's Ransom Café and a familiar smell of smoked bacon wafted through the air. Sitting at one of the vinyl-covered tables were Fritha Pooke, Philip Fox and Catherine and Trevor Beedle. Zoé held up the puzzle and looked through it, relieved to see that none of them had third eyes.

"Hey, hiya," said Pippin. "How's everything going?"

"Great," said Catherine, smiling in a friendly way.

"Maybe we can get together for a game of Caldey Ghost Pirates later?" said Zoé. "It's more fun with lots of kids playing."

"Cool idea," said Philip.

Trevor threw her a big grin.

The old wall fixtures emitted a dim light, giving the café a grainy, out-of-focus appearance. *It's like coming home,* thought Zoé, admiring the daffodil wallpaper and the chalkboard advertising *Special today~pork pie & chips* and *Fresh strawberries & clotted cream.*

Sitting in the corner, George Marriott was dipping his spoon into a dish of ice cream.

"Dr. Marriott!" Zoé shouted.

He looked up with a puzzled frown, then smiled and raised a hand to greet them, and Zoé knew right away he was back.

"I had a funny turn this morning, wasn't myself at all," he said, and the three kids exchanged knowing looks. "I certainly needed this ice cream, though. Try some, it's delicious."

"We're returning *The Book of Astercôte,*" said Pippin, pulling it from her backpack. "Thanks for the loan."

"You're very welcome," said their old friend, leaning back in his chair. "Well now, I'm eager to hear the latest. Have you accomplished your mission?"

Everyone started talking at once, telling Dr. Marriott what had happened—leaving out the part where he'd been turned into a Scraven, of course. As Granddad was fond of saying, *Let sleeping dogs lie.*

"Oh my gosh," said Ian, opening the flap of his messenger bag. "I completely forgot about this!"

Zoé leaned forward, curious.

"Whatever's that?" asked Pippin.

Ian dropped a small object into the palm of Zoé's hand—it fitted perfectly—and she looked down to see a small dragon carved of blue glass.

"Right before we left Wythernsea, when we were saying goodbye, Gwyn Griffiths gave me this," Ian explained. "Years ago his grandmother shared her ancient medical knowledge with the Astercôtes, and in turn they gave her this dragon made from Wythernsea glass. They said it could lead to an escape route in times of danger, a secret way between Wythernsea and Tenby—I'll explain the details later. Gwyn wanted us to have it."

"A gateway, in other words," said Dr. Marriott, straightening up. "You know, this may sound totally outlandish, but I'm wondering. Perhaps it's high time we begin again, to organize a completely *new* Society of Astercôte. What do you say?"

"You mean . . . we'd be members?" said Ian. "We kids would be the new Astercôtes?"

"Is it even possible?" whispered Pippin.

"We can travel back to *Wythernsea?*" Zoé could hardly believe what Dr. Marriott was saying.

"Yes to all your questions!" said the professor, smiling broadly. "There's a chapter in *The Book of Astercôte* which contains all the information we'll need. If we make a go of it this time, ensuring that this portal is without flaws, then why not give it a try?"

A ripple of excitement passed among the three children and Zoé couldn't stop smiling. *Am I really going back to Wyth-*

ernsea? That means I'll see Gwyn and Tegan and Miss Glyndower again!

She suddenly jumped, hearing a dry, papery voice behind her: Iris Tintern with her crisply waved hair, oatmeal sweater and drab apron (minus the yellow plastic-rimmed tinted glasses), waving a pencil stub.

"Right, then, what will it be today?" asked Iris, staring at each of them with a laserlike intensity. "How about trying some Mister Whippy–style ice cream from my brand-new Electro Freeze machine?"

"I'll have the ice cream, Miss Tintern," said Ian. "Chocolate, please."

"The same for me," echoed Zoé and Pippin.

"We're having a special on wax dragon teeth," said Iris. Zoé felt herself shrinking beneath her intense gaze, yet at the same time she was relieved to see the old, familiar Iris again. "Cut-rate prices, today only. Any takers?"

"I think we'll skip the teeth," said Ian.

"Yeah, they look kind of melted," added Pippin.

"They are *all* melted, dearies, which is why I've marked them down," snapped Iris. "If I charged any less, I'd be giving them away."

With a scornful glance, Iris shuffled off in her crepe-soled shoes.

"Hey, guys," whispered Zoé, "isn't it great to be back?"

ACKNOWLEDGMENTS

My sincere thanks to:

Stephen Fraser, literary agent extraordinaire, for his vision, expertise, friendship and guidance along the way.

My marvelous editor, Krista Vitola, for her keen editorial eye, her creative suggestions and her boundless enthusiasm.

Beverly Horowitz and the Delacorte Press team, especially copy editor Colleen Fellingham and crew. Also the artists who transformed this book: designer Jinna Shin, illustrator Charles Santoso, cartographer Fred van Deelen and above all, Fernando Juarez, whose beautiful artwork graces the covers of *The Owl Keeper* and *The Glass Puzzle*.

My critique group members, who offered sage advice, brainstormed ideas and read endless versions of this book—Laurie Jacobs, Donna McArdle, Christopher Doyle, Lenice Strohmeier, Valerie McCaffrey, Patricia Bridgman, Linda Teitel—and Pat Lowery Collins, longtime champion of *The Glass Puzzle*. Many thanks also to Lila Olson, the book's first young reader!

My sons, Ian and Derek, and my daughter-in-law, Heather, who all took the time to read early drafts and cheered me on. An enormous hug for my husband, Peter, my Welsh consultant, who shared his thoughts and ideas, read and edited countless pages and helped me in a thousand ways. If not for him, I'd never have discovered Tenby.

Finally, a tip of the hat to the real Tenby. I hope the people of Tenby will overlook any liberties I've taken in my descriptions of their one-of-a-kind seaside town.